The Handbook of
GOLF
Alex Hay

Foreword by
Peter Alliss

Pelham Books
STEPHEN GREENE PRESS

The Handbook of Golf was designed
and produced by
The Rainbird Publishing Group Ltd

Editor Julian Worthington
Designed by Hayward Art Group

PELHAM BOOKS/Stephen Greene Press

Published by the Penguin Group
27 Wrights Lane, London W8 5TZ, England
Viking Penguin Inc., 40 West 23rd Street,
New York, New York 10010, USA
The Stephen Greene Press Inc., 15 Muzzey Street,
Lexington, Massachusetts 02173, USA
Penguin Books Australia Ltd, Ringwood,
Victoria, Australia
Penguin Books Canada Ltd, 2801 John Street,
Markham, Ontario, Canada L3R 1B4
Penguin Books (NZ) Ltd, 182-190 Wairau Road,
Auckland 10, New Zealand

Penguin Books Ltd, Registered Offices:
Harmondsworth, Middlesex, England

First published 1985
Reprinted 1986, 1988 and 1989

Text Copyright © Pelham Books Ltd, 1984
Artwork © The Rainbird Publishing Group Ltd,
1984

Text set by SX Composing Ltd, Rayleigh, Essex
Illustrations originated by RCS (Graphics) Ltd,
Pudsey, West Yorkshire
Printed and bound by
Printer Portuguesa Indústria Gráfica

British Library Cataloguing in Publication Data

Hay, Alex
The handbook of golf.
1. Golf
I. Title
796.352'3   GV965

ISBN 0-7207-1540-7

Contents

The Handbook of
GOLF

Foreword   by Peter Alliss

Alex Hay is a remarkable person in many ways. I have watched his development in the world of golf since the early 1960s with great interest.

Born in 1933 in Musselburgh, a few miles east of the grand city of Edinburgh, he started his working life in the Scottish Stock Exchange. But his heart was really in the game of golf and he left the Stock Exchange to become apprentice clubmaker with the old established firm of Ben Sayers at North Berwick.

After completing his National Service, he joined Bill Shankland at the Potters Bar Golf Club, North London. Shankland was a hard taskmaster who stood no nonsense from his young assistants. But if they managed to stay the course, they learned their profession well.

His first full professional job was at the East Herts Golf Club, and it was there that his reputation as a teacher began to grow. Guy Hunt, who went on to win the Masters Tournament and Ryder Cup honours, was one of his schoolboy pupils.

In 1961 he was offered the post as professional to the Dunham Forest Golf Club south of Manchester. It was a brand new club with only 25 members. With Alex teaching up to 11 hours a day, the playing membership grew rapidly to 250 – and Alex taught them all.

Such was the demand for lessons from within the club that he found it impossible to accommodate many of the people from other parts of the country who, on hearing of his teaching skills, wanted tuition. So when the professional's job at Ashridge became available in 1965, he applied for it. Ashridge had for some years been the home of the legendary Henry Cotton and the opportunities and facilities there for a teaching professional were first-class. Alex got the job and was on his way.

Golf Illustrated magazine offered him a three-week trial as writer/artist and he is still there today, some 10 years later, providing a full page, sometimes two, every week fresh with new views in the entertaining style that had secured him the job all those years ago.

From Ashridge, the Summer School for young golfers at Stowe School began, and it was here that Alex met the young Paul Way, then 13 years old, who went on to attain such fine honours in the amateur ranks and who latterly became the most promising young British professional to emerge for several years.

One might have thought that Ashridge would have remained Alex's home, for he was extremely happy at the club. But a new challenge appeared on the horizon; Woburn Golf and Country Club was a superb opportunity and Alex always enjoyed a challenge.

Rather like Dunham Forest there was no club house, no warm professional's shop, just temporary accommodation and a vision. To Alex there was no risk at all in this magnificent setting with its great family background. Being part of the Duke of Bedford's estate, it was surely destined for success.

The pupils came to Woburn from far and wide, professional and amateur, men and women, many of them household names. Young club professionals arrived from the four corners of Britain, travelling in groups as much to learn about teaching the game as about analysing their own swing problems.

Alex's key to teaching is simplicity. He does not believe in too much theory, claiming that he does not understand what some of the theorists are talking about, anyway. Perhaps that's being ultra-modest, but those of us within the game would heartily agree with him.

To him there are three areas of the golf swing. The first is the set-up, where the club head is placed against the ball, accord-

Foreword

ing to the type of shot to be played, and the body positioned for that purpose. Each type of shot is made possible or not, depending on the correct posture at the address. Ninety per cent of swing faults are caused at this stage.

The back swing, where the muscles are set up on a direct swing plane, is the second phase. From a correct set-up it is possible to move to the top of the swing in one movement, very different to the two movements or two directions in the old days, when the back swing stretched to hip high in its first move and then, with a complete change of direction, moved vertically upwards. Today, with a stronger emphasis on swing plane, the back swing is a direct preparation.

The third and final stage is the through swing, which although started by hips and legs is thought of as one complete journey to a stylish finish. Holding the follow-through is the only way to maintain a consistent angle in the swing plane and all pupils must keep this position well into the ball's flight.

Alex feels that a disciplined training in these three areas of swing is the necessary platform for beginner and expert alike, from which flair and talent, if available, may launch themselves. Anyone who thinks he can survive on feel alone is mistaken, says Alex. Well, perhaps

Severiano Ballesteros might argue on that score, but he is a lone genius.

Alex's knowledge has been gained from talking to and studying closely the best players in the world. He watches what they all do the same – not differently, which is the excuse given by the uninformed who think instruction is a waste of time.

One of the major points in the book, which fascinates me, is Alex's idea on the spinning ball. A spinning trick shot when played by an expert is a form of intentional mishit. By understanding how the ball is flighted differently, the reader may diagnose from the flight of his own shots what he is doing wrong and so take the necessary steps to cure the fault.

Alex has already produced four books and one, *The Mechanics of Golf*, is acknowledged and used at the United States PGA School in Florida for the training of their young professionals. He joined the BBC commentary team in 1978 at the British Open championship and has remained with our crew ever since. What a valuable contribution he makes. I hope you enjoy this book, for it has indeed been put together by a master craftsman in the simplest of terms.

Alex Hay (behind) joined Peter Alliss on the BBC commentary team in 1978 and his contribution has been highly valued by colleagues and viewers alike.

Introduction

For more than 400 years golf was a British game, only being spread about the world by enthusiasts who took it with them during the expansion of the British Empire. It was not until the 1920s that the game made any real headway in the United States – largely due to the performances of Bobby Jones – but before long American players were to dominate the sport.

With typical enthusiasm the Americans made great advances in the golf swing and other techniques of the game. Most of the young professionals were brought up with steel-shafted clubs, which required a technique different from the traditional hickory shaft, familiar with most British players. When the Americans' novel ideas reached Britain, they were frowned upon by the golfing establishment. The attitude of the older professionals who refused to change their lifetime habits was to set Britain back many years.

After the Second World War, players from the younger golfing countries, like Australia's Peter Thomson and South Africa's Gary Player, ignored such traditional ideas in their eagerness to reach the top. The younger British golfers, too, began to switch techniques and players like Bernard Hunt, David Thomas and Neil Coles came in for a fair amount of criticism when they altered the style of their play.

The change was a basic one. As these players swung the club up from the ball into the back swing, they arched the left wrist joint instead of cupping it, the technique required when using the hickory or, even earlier, the flatter-lying long-headed clubs. When using the new technique they were described as 'shut-face merchants'.

The break-through on the European side of the Atlantic came in around 1960, after Arnold Palmer had made his first appearance in the British Open, subsequently persuading his colleagues to do the same, when it was obvious that the American

Graham Marsh puts great emphasis on his set-up procedure, which he explains here to Alex. The Australian has won in more countries than any other professional.

teaching methods were producing a much higher standard of play. Today many of the young European players, as well as those from the golfing countries to the East, are being weaned on the modern style of swinging and the larger size of ball – another factor that demands a more accurate and consistent technique. So the gap between American players and those from the rest of the world is narrowing, although sheer weight of numbers and the availability of good facilities will keep the United States ahead. But its golfers will no longer have things all their own way.

As a coach I am very much involved with helping young players, both amateur and professional, and those at club level, to develop their swing. How different it is teaching the mechanics of today's swing, with its simpler and more direct

9

Introduction

movements, compared with those I learned as a youngster in Scotland. The most noticeable aspect is how few big slicers there are nowadays. When the old technique was being used, at least 25 per cent of club members were plagued with slicing, and only those with considerable natural talent – people who were good at all ball games – seemed capable of timing the complex changes of direction in the swing. Today, however, there need be only two balanced movements: one to prepare and the other to achieve. These can be performed in just two directions – both clearly described in this book.

In recent years I have been fortunate enough, because of my contributions to magazines, books and television, to have had the opportunity to spend many hours with players of the calibre of Peter Thomson, Gary Player, Johnny Miller, Jerry Pate, Severiano Ballesteros and Graham Marsh, listening to and carefully noting their views on the swing. They know a great deal about the swing, and over the years have made deliberate adjustments and alterations to it and are more than capable of discussing it.

Many of the best players, particularly the younger ones, know only a limited amount about the golf swing, quite rightly concentrating on the senses of feel that determine individual movements. For some of them, to delve into the mechanics of the swing would only lead to confusion and upset their natural rhythm.

It is far better for these players to have

Alex on the forest-lined course at Woburn, his home club in England.

someone helping who is an authority and whose job it is to understand most of what golfers do. These people can quickly spot any flaw in a player's game that is having an effect on the swing, then make the necessary adjustments within that person's natural swing shape.

I make no excuse for the detailed way in which I have dealt with the swing. Although the players I have mentioned, and many others, make a fairly complex chain of movements flow so smoothly, the average players need to study each part of the swing separately so that they can understand their faults at any one stage and rectify them.

During the close study I have made of professionals in their competitive play, on the practice grounds at major championships and, most importantly, by talking to them, it has become clear to me that they have a strict routine from the moment they select a club through to the completion of the follow-through. Although there are slight variations, by following the pattern described, players of any standard can enjoy better and more consistent golf.

What is becoming more and more apparent is that good young players are capable of winning at a much earlier age – and very quickly after turning professional. The most important contributory factor is the swing.

My instructions are all based on what the best players in the world are doing. They, of course, have spent hours – and in many cases years – of dedicated practice to perfect what they do, thus it would be too much to expect the novice to absorb everything in this book at the first attempt. I have therefore aimed the book at both beginners and more accomplished players, so that when confidence is gained, natural flair and talent may flow. The book can also be used for reference, particularly when problems arise.

Wise students will carefully study the disciplines of golf, for without this continuous progress cannot be made. This

Severiano Ballesteros demonstrates an aspect of his set-up to Alex. Much of the valuable information in this book has come from such discussion with the top players on the world's golf circuits.

applies even to those who may have played for a considerable period without the advantage of sound tuition. In other words, it is never too late to learn. Golf is a game of a lifetime, so all the effort made and the comparatively short time required to acquire the techniques that form the basis of the professional's game will soon be forgotten when improvement in play becomes noticeable.

Too many poor players look at those parts of the game – particularly the swing – that many great players do differently. But, in fact, it makes more sense to concentrate on those they do the same.

Finally, I must apologize to all left-handed golfers. For the sake of simplicity I have written this book with continual reference to right-handed players. So if you are left-handed, please reverse left and right in each instruction.

The history of golf

Arguments on just when and where golf started have raged for generations and perhaps the whole truth will never be known. Among the many theories advanced is one that it was derived from *paganica*, a game played in Roman times using a feather-stuffed ball. Going back even further, claims have been made that 'golf' was played in China in about 200BC.

A more likely explanation is that golf originated from a game called *Ket Kolven* played on the ice in the Low Countries (Belgium and Holland) some 500 years ago. The implement used by the players to hit the ball was known as a *kolf*, a word derived from the German *Kolbe*, which simply means 'club'. However, the Scots contend that the ball used by the people of the Low Countries was about the size of a tennis ball and that since it was hit towards

markers hammered into the ice the game could not possibly have been what they call golf. The common element, of course, is that a ball was struck by a 'stick'.

Because there were strong trading ties between the Scots and the people of the Low Countries, there is also a strong argument in favour of the reverse situation – that is to say, the latter took it over and adapted the Scottish game for the ice. As early as the 12th century, coal mined by Scottish monks was exported to the Low Countries from the harbour of Cockenzie, a small fishing village situated midway along the Firth of Forth. Along this estuary existed what must then have been one of the finest strips of golfing terrain.

It was here that Scottish golf was born. The area between the sea and the mainland was sandy, common ground – a 'link' between the two – which was used by the players and so gave rise to the term 'golf links'. Although often used for any course, the term should more strictly be applied to

Left: Golfers in 1790 playing at Blackheath, the first club to be formed in England.
Below: Dutch 'golfers' on ice in the 17th century.

13

The history of golf

those constructed in sand dune country.

By the 15th century golf had entered the annals of history, for in 1457 the Scottish Parliament recorded a ban on the game because it was seriously interfering with archery practice. To this day, a regiment of archers marches on to the links at Musselburgh and holds a tournament there. Musselburgh, the oldest remaining golf course in the world, is just a few miles from Edinburgh and, incidentally, claims to have been the first club to have a competition for women.

In Edinburgh itself, the historic Leith links have long since given way to docks and industry. But Leith, too, played an important part in golfing history. Charles I was playing there in 1641 when a messenger delivered news of the Irish Rebellion. Charles immediately summoned his charger and galloped off to resolve the problem. It is said that he was happy to ride off, being six down with eight holes to play at the time. Also, historians claim it was at Leith that caddies got their name – from the young French naval cadets who, in order to earn extra money while their ships were loading, carried the golfers' clubs round the course.

One distinctive British characteristic was the formation of clubs. In 1744 the Honourable Company of Edinburgh Golfers had its first meeting and within 100

Mary Queen of Scots enjoying a round of golf at St Andrews in Scotland in 1563.

Willie Park and Tom Morris junior watch as Tom Morris senior plays his shot on Leith Links in Scotland, during a professional players' tournament on May 17, 1867. Park was the first British Open winner.

years there were 30 other clubs in Scotland alone. The Royal and Ancient Golf Club (the R & A) was formed in 1754 as the St Andrews Club and in 1897 the same club agreed to become the governing body on the rules of golf, which it still is. Other countries affiliated to its rules committee, while across the Atlantic the United States Golf Association (USGA) had been formed in 1894 and became the governing authority there.

Like all rules and regulations, those of golf evolved over a long period; at one time each club had its own. As far as Britain was concerned, this situation was resolved in 1897. However, because traditions, conditions and attitudes were somewhat different in the United States, the USGA rules were also different. To avoid complications and arguments, a joint committee of the R & A, the USGA and Commonwealth representatives met in 1951 and produced a unified code, which took effect in 1952. The British and American bodies continue to have joint committee meetings, where changes to the rules are proposed.

Growth worldwide

By the turn of the century, the game was spreading across the world. South Africa had its first course, courtesy of a Scottish regiment that built six holes near Cape Town just before the Boer War. At about the same time some other Scots were designing and building the first course in the USA – at Yonkers, New York.

Many well-known Scottish professionals were employed to travel abroad to design courses, among them Willie Park of Musselburgh, the first winner of the British Open championship, and Willie Dunn. Dunn had been designing courses in France when he was spotted by the Vanderbilt family and taken to the United States to build the first major golf club there – at Shinnecock Hills, Long Island.

Traditionally there was a reluctance in Britain to build golf courses inland. In winter the ground was soggy and in the summer it was baked hard. Because Britain was a comparatively small island and golfers few in number, it was generally felt that the strips of linksland surrounding the coast were both ideal and sufficient.

With the increased demand for the game, particularly in the London area, Willie Park came south to design the Old Course at Sunningdale, possibly still the

The history of golf

finest inland course in the country. He was probably only persuaded to do so because the sandy subsoil and heathland character of Sunningdale were so similar to the links courses he had grown up with. This was one of the first courses where hazards had to be created artificially. Incidentally, the water hazard at the fifth hole must surely have been the predecessor of those large expanses of water that are a feature of courses in the United States.

As people travelled and took their golf clubs with them, it became clear that the seaside links courses were inadequate and often not convenient. So more and more inland courses were built – and no more so than in the United States. Many magnificent courses were opened, one of the most beautiful being the Augusta National in Georgia, designed by the legendary Bobby Jones in partnership with a Scottish doctor called Alister Mackenzie. Jones had retired prematurely as a player and Mackenzie had given up his job in the medical profession. Shortly after that, Jones was confined to a wheelchair for the rest of his life, while Mackenzie went on to design great courses all over the world.

Europe was slow to break from the linksland tradition. In Holland a fine course was built at Zandvoort, while in Sweden what is regarded by many as the best of that country's courses was created at Falsterbo on a peninsula. In France, magnificent links were used at Le Touquet, which is unique in that it has one championship course – the famous Sea Course – and on the same area of land the Forest Course, set entirely in the trees.

It was at the Spa towns that golf in Germany began; Baden Baden was one of the first, and best, courses. Rome became the major centre for golf in Italy, although one of the finest courses is at Ville d'Este, close to the Swiss border.

The boom in golf is most obvious, however, in the southern parts of Europe, particularly in Southern Spain and Portugal, where it has been instrumental in creating a new prosperity for those regions. Spain has taken greatest advantage of the game's popularity and golf courses have sprung up in abundance, especially along the Costa del Sol. Here the courses have been designed in such a way that properties can be built alongside the fairways, much to the delight of property developers and time-share agencies.

This is an American idea, which operates successfully all over that country, particularly in Florida. Many of these courses have been designed by Robert Trent Jones, whose best work can probably be seen in Spain – at Sotogrande and Nueva Andalucia, the latter now called Las Brisas, where the 1983 Spanish Open was played. In Portugal he built the superb Vilamoura course. Born in England, Jones is, with his American design, influencing courses all over the world. Just as in the early days Scottish courses were copied in the United States, now American-styled Spanish courses are influencing British designers.

With the influence of the British Empire throughout the world, it was inevitable that golf would go east as well as west – and in fact it was being played in Calcutta more than 150 years ago. The Royal Calcutta Club still flourishes, as does the Royal Hong Kong, while the Singapore Club has more than 2000 playing members and four courses for them to play on.

There are many fine courses to be found in Australia and New Zealand, particularly in Australia where the Royal Melbourne, partly designed incidentally by Dr Mackenzie, is probably the best. It is no real coincidence, therefore, that many great players have come from that area.

British designers were invited to Japan in the 1920s to plan golf courses there. Unfortunately not enough were built and now, with the biggest golf explosion in the history of the game, Japan simply has not the space to cope with the huge demand.

New courses are springing up all the time, especially now with the help of

The proposed site for the tee of the 12th – a 620yd hole – at the course designed by Jack Nicklaus at St Mellion in Cornwall, England.

modern machinery and new watering techniques, which make it possible for good quality grass to be maintained all the year round.

The current trend is towards top professionals taking on the designer's role. Jack Nicklaus is busy designing, one of his masterpieces being at Ohio where the course has been called Muirfield after the famous Scottish links where he won his first British Open. Arnold Palmer has also been designing and is presently working on a project in China. Severiano Ballesteros has designed a course in Japan, and in the Far East Peter Thomson has gained a considerable reputation for building. Of the British ex-professionals, Peter Alliss and David Thomas have been influencing the design of new courses in Europe.

The equipment

The golf ball, too, has a history. The first mention is of a feather-stuffed ball – in 1620. Because of the nature of their construction, balls were more often oval-shaped than round, which affected the way they behaved. Rarely were they consistent in size or weight.

When the properties of gutta-percha were discovered in about 1848, manufacture became simpler and the balls (gutties) were truly spherical. They were made in a range of weights, each golfer choosing which he thought was best for him or the conditions at the time. Before long it was discovered that dimpling the surface improved performance.

The next step was the introduction of the rubber-cored ball, which offered not only better performance but also made playing easier for beginners. This ball, too, came in a range of weights, but in 1921 the R & A and the USGA got together and agreed on a

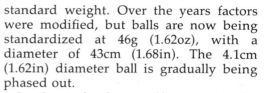

standard weight. Over the years factors were modified, but balls are now being standardized at 46g (1.62oz), with a diameter of 43cm (1.68in). The 4.1cm (1.62in) diameter ball is gradually being phased out.

In the early days, golfers were quite happy with one club (and often only one ball). It was not until the end of the 15th century that different clubs were craft-made for special purposes and eventually iron clubs were added to the original wooden ones.

The introduction of the gutty and then the rubber-cored ball also affected the design of the club. Lead to weight the wooden clubs and insets of various materials to face the driver were further innovations, as were steel shafts and laminated heads. All these new materials facilitated the production of identical clubs and so the 'matched set' was born.

This led to the manufacture of inter-mediate sizes and by the 1930s caddies were carrying round as many as 25 assorted clubs. It all became so ridiculous that the R & A and the USGA agreed to limit the number of clubs to 14, made up of woods, irons and a putter (see the section in this book on equipment).

The course

And what of the golf courses? These started as links, just as nature created. As time passed, a few additions were made by players, although really no thought was given to design. In the latter part of the 19th century improvements were restricted to the construction of formal flat greens and ramparts of bunkers.

Slowly, however, more imagination was used and a breed of golf course architects emerged. At one time the number of holes varied, but in 1764 the course at St Andrews was increased to 18 holes and this

The arena at St Andrews in Scotland, including the 18th hole. You can see the television commentary box on top of the Old Course Hotel in the foreground. It was here that Alex made his first broadcast during the 1978 British Open championship.

became the norm. Because of space restrictions, some courses have only nine holes which for a full game are played twice.

Competitive golf

The history of golf over the last century or so has been very much linked to the growth in competition. In Britain, this has evolved from the first major tournament – the British Open championship – and international competition with the United States through the Walker Cup and the Ryder Cup.

British Open The R & A organizes this, the greatest golf show on earth, which was first held in 1860. Such is its popularity that there is an annual pilgrimage of the game's finest players from all over the world to compete in the championship, which takes place in July.

By tradition the British Open is always played on a links course and every year record crowds flock to the chosen coastal venue to witness the spectacle, while many millions more all over the world watch it live on television.

It was at St Andrews in 1921 that, ironically, a Scottish emigrant to the United States, Jock Hutchison, won the championship that virtually ended the British dominance of the event. Famous American players then came over and claimed the title – Walter Hagen, for example, in 1922, 1924, 1928 and 1929 and the most famous amateur ever, Bobby Jones, in 1926, 1927 and 1930.

From 1934 until the start of the Second World War, British players once again dominated, the immortal Henry Cotton winning in 1934 and 1937, a feat he was to repeat in 1948. Cotton's last victory was at Muirfield and it came one year after the Irishman Fred Daly had won at Hoylake. There have so far been only two British winners since – Max Faulkner in 1951 and Tony Jacklin in 1969.

A young Australian from Melbourne, Peter Thomson, arrived on the scene in the early 1950s and won the British Open at Royal Birkdale in 1954. He won again there in 1965 and between those victories took the title no less than three times – in 1955, 1956 and 1958.

In 1960 the American superstar Arnold Palmer came to Britain to try his luck in the British Open. He played St Andrews in the centenary championship, finishing second to Kel Nagle of Australia, and vowed to return. He did and won the next year at Royal Birkdale and again the following year at Troon. Not only has he played every year since, but he has also been instrumental in bringing every top player from his country with him. In the 21 championships since Palmer's last victory, no fewer than 14 have been won by Americans – with Tom Watson winning five times.

Walker Cup In 1921, when Hutchison was ending the British Open championship run of Britain's star trio of James Braid, J H Taylor and Harry Vardon, a similar fate befell the British amateur team playing the United States at Hoylake.

The home players were quietly confident of victory when they set off, but had they known more about two young members of the American team – Bobby Jones and Francis Ouimet – they might not have been quite so sure of themselves. Jones was destined to become winner of a grand slam comprised of the American Open, the British Open, the American Amateur and the British Amateur championships all in the one year, and Ouimet won the US Open. The American team won 9-3.

In the 29 Walker Cup matches played so far, including the first one, Great Britain and Ireland have won only twice – in 1938 and 1971 – and have drawn once – in 1965. Despite this record, the harmony that exists between the two governing bodies – the R & A and the USGA – and the good fellowship enjoyed during the matches, will ensure that the Walker Cup games are here to stay for a very long time.

It was a year after that first match – in 1922 – that the president of the USGA, G H Walker, presented his cup, which is

The first British Ryder Cup team with Samuel Ryder (hatless and with his dog) setting off to play in the United States. The journey by train and boat from London would probably not have appealed to today's players. The 1983 team flew by Concorde, while the caddies went by ordinary jet.

now competed for every two years in May, alternately in Britain and the United States.

Ryder Cup In 1927 the first Ryder Cup match was held in Worcester, Massachusetts, USA between teams of professionals representing Great Britain and Ireland and the United States. A great deal has changed since those early days when Samuel Ryder, a seed merchant from St Albans in Hertfordshire and a golf fanatic, presented a trophy to be played for every two years. The Ryder Cup takes place in September and the match alternates between Britain and the United States in the same year as the Walker Cup.

In all, 25 matches have so far been played, the Americans winning all but four, one of which was halved. Since 1979 a change in the rules has allowed the inclusion of European players. As the playing section of the British PGA had become the European Tournament Players Division, this was only natural. It allowed people of the calibre of Spain's Severiano Ballesteros to take part and, although the European team has not yet won, the result is getting closer each time. Only one point separated the sides in 1983 – and that match was played in the United States.

Like the Walker Cup, the Ryder Cup has stood the test not only of time but of one-sided results and still it continues. It does so because there is a great pride in representing one's nation in golf and because of the incomparable friendship that exists between the game's competitors.

The world of golf

The young, and often very rich, superstars of modern professional golf owe a great deal to their predecessors, many of whom were very forward looking. It is doubtful, however, that these early players could possibly have envisaged the status to which professionals would rise or the enormous financial potential that now exists for their profession.

Professionals came originally from the ranks of the caddies, the best of whom would give some instruction and had the ability to repair and, in some cases, make clubs. The outstanding caddies were given permission to play on the course of a club or society and were offered some facility, such as a hut or similar premises, in which they could set up a workbench and carry out their skills for a retainer.

In 1879 a well-known Musselburgh caddie, Bob Ferguson, borrowed a few clubs and used them to win his first professional tournament. He was then given a set of eight by a patron and with these he won three British Opens in succession.

It was about that time that a good deal of Britain's most famous courses were being laid out, many of which were designed by the top professionals of the day, who became resident at those clubs. By making clubs, repairing others, giving lessons, selling whatever equipment was available and then playing in challenge matches and competitions, they were establishing an accepted way of life that was to be followed until the 1970s.

The Professional Golfers' Association (PGA) was formed in 1901 when a group met to discuss their dissatisfaction at the way they were being treated by their clubs. J H Taylor, who was a great champion of causes as well as having three British Open

Golf's triumvirate – James Braid, J H Taylor and Harry Vardon – who championed the cause of the professional at the turn of the century.

titles to his credit, and his colleagues Harry Vardon and James Braid were quick to promote the formation of this association. They played their first PGA tournament in October of that year at the Tooting Bec Club in South London, with prize money of £15. The association then grew in numbers and strength.

There is no longer such a club, but a cup is still awarded each year to the British player who is a member of the PGA and who has the best single round in the British Open championships.

Competitive golf became an important part of their lives. The normal procedure for club professionals was to play in tournaments on the Wednesday and Thursday.

Las Brisas, venue for the 1983 Spanish Open. This magnificent course was designed by the American Robert Trent Jones.

The top 40 or 50 qualifiers would finish the event by playing 36 holes on the Friday. This meant that everybody could be back at their clubs for the weekend to look after the members there.

Professionals at one time had to be attached to a club, either as a full professional or an assistant, for five years in order to qualify to play in other than open or overseas championships. This meant, for example, that the Scottish professional Eric Brown was winning the Open championships of Europe yet had to wait five long years before he qualified to play in domestic tournaments.

The PGA split

In the mid-1960s tournaments switched to a Saturday finish for several reasons, one of which was television coverage. Neverthe-

Eric Brown, known as the 'Brown Bomber', never lost a singles against an American in all the Ryder Cup matches he played.

less, the fields, instead of shrinking, grew as more and more youngsters entered the profession.

With the larger fields it became necessary to establish pre-qualifying, which meant those not in the top league had to play a preliminary round on the Tuesday, often on a different course, to prove they were fit to play in the major event. Tournament finishes were then moved to Sunday and, instead of two rounds on the Saturday, there was a single round each day, allowing television to show the closing stages on both days.

It was becoming obvious that a professional could no longer compete and look after his own club members at the same time. Nor, on the other hand, could someone who wanted to concentrate on playing for a living divide his attention between this and giving lessons and looking after his day-to-day duties in the club.

Midway through the 1970s the split came. Those who administered the tournaments and those who looked after the affairs of the club professionals had been based in offices in the Oval Cricket Ground at Kennington, London. The European Tournament Players Division was established and stayed on at the Oval, while the others moved to The Belfry, a hotel at Sutton Coldfield that boasted two championship-length courses – The Brabazon and The Derby, the first named after the former president of the association and the other after the association's current president, Lord Derby.

The ETPD, since renamed the PGA Tournament Players' Division, has now also moved from the Oval, to the Wentworth Golf Club in Surrey. Its membership has grown not just because of the large European influx but also because of the easing in the method by which a golfer may turn professional.

By having a handicap of one or better, any amateur can apply to enter a PGA Tournament Players' test-of-ability event. These are held once a year, with two separate weekly sessions, normally in Spain. Anyone finishing in the allocated spaces earns a player's card and he may then enter for all official events and will have to compete in the pre-qualifying stages of those events. Once he makes the final day's play, he does not then need to pre-qualify for the following event. If he makes the top 60 at the end of the season, he is not required to pre-qualify during the following year.

After a very poor season, if a professional's winnings are below a set figure, he must go back to Spain to earn his card again. Otherwise he cannot compete in official events.

Other young men, who join the profession as assistants at a club, become attached to the PGA and are registered at The Belfry. They then complete a three-year apprenticeship before qualifying to apply for the post of professional. They have a final examination in all aspects of running the job, as well as passing a playing ability test, which demands both skill and courage. Then their future career relies on qualifying.

They, like their employers, may compete in three major events without going to Spain for a card. If they can earn sufficient prize money, the current figure being £1500, from the three events, they can also gain a card.

No youngster who first joined the Tournament Players' section, even though he has played for several years, may take a full club professional's job until he has passed the examinations.

Progress made the parting of the ways necessary, but it is evident that both divisions work very closely together, since it is only natural that many of the competitive players will wish to convert at the end of their playing career. Some club professionals find the security of their position relieves the pressure and they become such improved golfers that they make the grade and join the ranks of the successful tournament stars.

The PGA circuits

A large contingent of young professionals leaves Britain's shores during the months of January and February bound for the African continent. Those taking part in the two circuits there are not only PGA card holders but also those who have failed to obtain a card. These players enter in the hope that their performance in either tour will place them high enough in the money earners' league to qualify them for a European card on their return.

One of the tours is in South Africa while the other, known as the Safari Tour, takes place in Nigeria, Kenya and Zambia. In addition to the visiting professionals, the South African Tour is supported largely by professionals from that country. Gary Player returns home, along with Nick Price, Mark McNulty and many others who make their living travelling the world circuits. The competition is very fierce and it is fairly unusual to have a 'foreigner' win any of the events.

The Safari is quite different, for there are not many local professionals and the winners are usually from Europe. The local golfers are, however, rapidly improving and should soon make their presence felt. It was in the 1982 Nigerian Open that England's Peter Tupling created the world record for a 72-hole event with a total of 255. South African players and those who play in South Africa are not allowed to travel north for this tour.

The European circuit begins in April and, strangely enough, starts in Africa with the Tunisian Open. After that the players move to Madrid in Spain, across to Italy for their Open and then to the French Open. They finally arrive in England in May for a series of tournaments building up to the British Open in July. Throughout each season they make trips back abroad – to the Scandinavian Open in Sweden and also to the German, Dutch, Irish, Swiss, Spanish and Portuguese Opens.

It is a very busy schedule of events in which the European players are joined by

Left: The professionals' annual circuit ends in the Caribbean, where there are some delightful courses. This is the short 7th hole at the Sandy Lane Golf Club in Barbados.
Below: The big three in 1983. Larry Nelson (below left), who is running into form at a comparatively late stage in his life, with the US Open trophy at Oakmont. Tom

Watson (below right) with the British Open trophy which, incidentally, he dropped. His win at Royal Birkdale was his first in England; the previous four Open successes were in Scotland. Severiano Ballesteros (bottom) receiving his second Green Jacket after winning the US Masters at Augusta. Keeping up the tradition, the previous year's winner Craig Stadler helps him on with it.

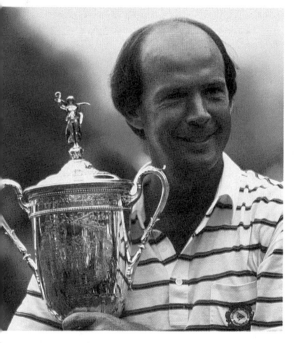

professionals from many other countries. The Australians support the circuit well, as do the South Africans, and there is now a fairly large group of young Americans.

In the United States, which has the largest and most competitive circuit, there is also a 'school' through which young players must qualify to gain their player's card. Those who do not qualify find that, by spending a couple of seasons on the European Tour, they gain enough match experience to get their card when they return. One such American is the promising Corey Pavin.

It is the ultimate desire of every young professional to make the American Tour and Europe has proved a very good training ground for this ambition. Many of the winners of the American majors have come through in this way. Gary Player, who struggled to survive in his early years in British golf, is one of the most successful. More recently, there has been Severiano Ballesteros, who not only won the very first American event he entered but has also claimed one of their biggest tournaments – the US Masters at Augusta – and not just once but twice, in 1980 and 1983. Graham Marsh of Australia has also won in the United States, as has David Graham, who has now settled there after learning much of his craft in Europe. He has claimed two of the American majors – the PGA championship in 1976 and the Open in 1981.

Hopefully it will not be long before more young British players win there again to follow the footsteps of Tony Jacklin. In 1968 he won at Jacksonville, then took the Open title in 1970, the first Briton to do so since Ted Ray exactly 50 years earlier. Since then only Nick Faldo has won – that was the 1984 Heritage Classic.

The majors

Most golfing countries have their own Open championships and a lot of these carry considerable prestige. The Canadian and Australian Open championships are two that many of the top players travel to,

as well as the World Match Play championship held at Wentworth in Surrey. The latest 'big one' – the Sun City in Bophuthatswana – started in 1981 and was then worth a million dollars; it has since grown even more in stature and prize money.

The four championships that make up golf's 'Grand Slam' are the US Masters, the US Open, the British Open and the United States PGA championships (in order of when they are played each year).

Towards the end of September, as the European season comes to an end, the Asian and Japanese Tour is in full swing. Many of the successful players make their way there, since the prize money rivals that of the United States Tour.

They move from there to the Australasian Tour, where they again compete for large amounts of prize money culminating in the Australian Open, which attracts many American competitors. The players then cross over to New Zealand, in particular for their Open.

Those with the strength and will left can finish the competitive year on the South American Tour, playing in the Open championships of Chile, Argentina, Brazil, Venezuela, the Caribbean and Colombia – and still be home in time for Christmas.

Ladies' golf

The world of professional golf is not exclusively for men, since the development of women's circuits throughout the world has spread from the United States to Europe and the Far East.

In 1950 the Ladies Professional Golf Association was formed in the United States, with such illustrious players as Patty Berg, 'Babe' Zaharias, a former athlete and Olympic champion, and Louise Suggs competing in nine events that year. The following year the circuit had 14 events and during those first two seasons 'Babe' Zaharias won 13 of them.

In those early days the players did more than just play golf. They set the courses, made rulings and handled the publicity

and accounting themselves. This is a far cry, of course, from the multi-million dollar set-up of the current LPGA, which is now housed in permanent headquarters in Texas, where it has professional staff to run all its tournaments and various promotional activities. In 1983 the 200 LPGA players were competing for a total prize money of seven million dollars.

With the development of the LPGA, several stars have emerged. Kathy Whitworth joined the circuit in 1959 and is still competing. She has won more tournaments than any other player, her victory in Hawaii in 1983 bringing the total to 84.

Jo Anne Carner, who joined the circuit in 1970, is one of the longest hitters in the ladies' game, a fact that helped her become the leading player in 1983. Along with Miss Whitworth, she was one of the earliest members of the 'Million Dollar Club', having earned that amount so far in her illustrious career.

In 1978 a young lady from New Mexico took the LPGA by storm: Nancy Lopez, in her Rookie year, notched up nine tournament wins, including a then record five in a row. She set new standards for Rookie earnings, official money and scoring averages and was named Rookie and Player of the Year. In 1979 she broke her own earnings and scoring average records, winning nine events *en route* to her second Player of the Year award. It was her outstanding performances that helped the LPGA to enhance its standing in the world of sport and to expand its current status as the supreme test for women golfers.

Meanwhile in the Far East, mainly in Japan, ladies had started to play professionally and by the late 1960s a circuit was in existence. But, as in the United States, it took a few years to blossom. Indeed, it was not until the leading Japanese player Chako Higuchi went to the United States in 1977 and won the LPGA championship that the Japanese became fully aware of just how good some of their players had become. The circuit has now expanded.

Jo Anne Carner, the leading money-winner in the US in 1983, is one of the few players to win more than a million dollars in prize money.

The last circuit to be formed for women professionals has been the Women's Professional Golf Association in Europe. The circuit began in 1979 and from the initial promise of 12 two-day events then, the circuit in 1984 has approximately 15 major four-day events, plus a televized tournament in which the top American and Japanese players will compete. The nucleus of the circuit is made up of British players, but the WPGA can also boast members from Sweden, Spain, Sri Lanka, Germany, South Africa and Australia.

Golf equipment

At one time, virtually all golfing equipment was sold by club professionals and a few major stores with sports departments. Then only the basic necessities were stocked: sets of clubs; balls and tees; studded shoes; waterproof cotton clothing; umbrellas; golf bags, mainly designed to be carried; and some very expensive golf gloves for those who could afford them.

Many of the professionals, who could not afford to stock all these items, supplied their customers through golf equipment catalogues. The golfing boom, which in Britain started in the mid-1950s, put an end to this type of selling. Cut-price competition was mainly responsible, although catalogue sales were also hit by the fact that manufacturers were taking longer and longer to deliver.

The leisure industry had arrived. People had more money to spend and more time to pursue sporting activities and golf, catering as it does for all ages, probably boomed more than most. The days of playing in a collar and tie and wearing trousers that were too old even for gardening were gone. Many new items appeared on the market and golf shops sprung up everywhere. The younger professionals rose to the bait.

Shops at all the major golf clubs are now more like fashion houses and it is often hard to spot a club, particularly in some of the shops in the United States. Shirts and slacks, many sporting the club's crest, have become the main business.

Golfing extras are now available in abundance, thanks to the arrival of the golf trolley in 1950. Because golf bags no longer had to be carried, they grew in size and were made with cavernous pockets, all of which apparently had to be filled. Extra holders were added to the bags to take not only an umbrella but also a seat-stick!

A standard full set of woods and irons. The remaining club in the set is the putter.

Among the additional paraphernalia available nowadays are towels with which to wipe the ball, and bag-tags to show off where a player has been – or would like to have been! There is room for neck-scarves; mitts for when it is cold and visors for when it is sunny; specially designed tins of sweets; cards you can write on without a pencil; holders to prevent your card getting wet; ball cleaners, either manual or those attached to the trolley wheel so you can clean the ball while you walk to the next tee; and trolleys with seats on so you can slow down play even further. Other gadgets include those that will clean the club face, tighten shoe spikes, repair pitch-marks and even open a bottle. There are portable rakes to remove marks in bunkers and telescopic gadgets for retrieving balls from water.

With trolleys jammed full of every imaginable piece of equipment, the tyres were naturally enough causing damage on the course. So wide-wheeled versions were introduced, making all previous models obsolete. Finally fashion turned full circle when once again it became popular to carry golf bags rather than wheel them around.

The clubs

These have undergone dramatic changes over the years. From the traditional wooden shafts and club heads, in the 1920s and 1930s shafts were made of steel. Then, for a while, aluminium was used until several million discerning golfers noticed that their idols were not using this type of shaft and it was immediately dropped. Next came the carbon fibre shaft – and with it a huge increase in price. When people realized that the torque factor of this shaft resembled that of hickory and only a few wristy players among their heroes were still using it, this type was also scrapped. Titanium came and went and steel is now back in fashion.

Golf equipment

Even at the completion of the swing there is movement in a carbon fibre shaft, which only a few players such as Manuel Pinero are prepared to risk controlling to gain extra yardage.

After the change in shaft, it was the turn of the club head. Instead of a set of clubs consisting of traditional woods and irons, metal woods were introduced. Despite their name, these clubs do not have a single piece of wood in them. Many professionals believe they achieve better results with these 'woods', claiming that they play longer and make it easier to get long fairway shots away. The ability to place most of the head weight very much closer to the sole of the club has helped.

Although some professionals have introduced the odd metal wood into their set, most have refused to budge from their trusty persimmon woods. For a while it seemed inevitable that wooden heads, which take time and skill to make, since much of the work is still done by hand, would give way to metal ones. The latter can be made in a mould, which should produce more accurate results.

Fortunately, however, the wooden club-maker will have a job to do for a long time yet and for two reasons. The first is that the boom in the golf industry has resulted in a fair amount of rubbish being produced by manufacturers who have come and, thank goodness, gone. The other is that the 'sweet' feel of striking the ball with a superb piece of wood takes a lot of beating and so far no substitute has been found.

As for the heads of the iron clubs, it is only natural that manufacturers should continue to change the design in their search for perfection. This they did until mass-produced cast heads flooded the market. Many were poorly designed and full of gimmickry aimed at catching the eye rather than improving performance. Current designs have reverted to the more traditional style.

Towards the end of the 1970s not only the public but also the makers noticed that none of the well-known and expensively contracted players were using the models in current production. They had gone back to the sets they had been using up to 10 years previously. The outrageous had run its course and the simple, straightforward blade made by craftsmen was on its way back into favour.

Fortunately most of the recognized manufacturers survived the flood of cheap products and were the first to return to the production of models that could be played with. It is pleasing that after seeing old chipped sets in tournament players' bags for a period of years, sparkling new models are now being used on which these players – and the general public – can rely.

Above: Shaping laminated blocks on the lathe.
Below left: A master craftsman at work. Charlie Thompson has worked as man and boy at the Ben Sayers factory in Scotland and is now the foreman. Alex worked as an apprentice under him. Although the lathe will cut the basic shape of the club head, it still needs the craftsman to do the final shaping.
Below right: Putting lines on the face of a wooden club.

Golf equipment

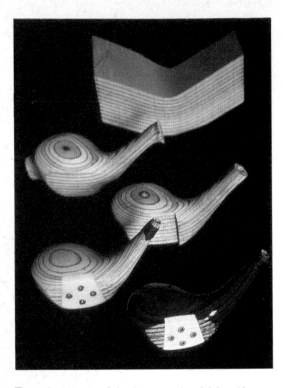

The various stages of shaping a wooden club head from a laminated block.

Choosing clubs

At one time golfers could take round the course all the clubs they wanted and in some cases two bags were needed in which to carry them all. The authorities finally decided to limit the number of clubs to 14, including the putter, and it was then that clubs began to be numbered in sequence according to their loft.

Before clubs formed part of a set, individual ones had been given delightful names. Many clubmakers were reluctant to let these die out and so stamped the old name on the back of each club, as well as the number on the bottom. Where, for example, we now have Nos 1, 2, 3, 4 and 5 woods, there were the 'driver', 'brassie', 'spoon' and 'baffy', which came between the No 4 and the No 5.

The modern set of irons are numbered from 2 to 9. According to the amount of clubs carried and the ability of the player, there are three other irons – a No 1, a pitching wedge and a sand iron. The traditional names for the irons were: No 1 and No 2 – 'driving iron'; No 3 – 'long iron'; No 4 – 'mid iron'; No 5 and No 6 – 'mashie'. Something between the modern No 7 and No 8 was the 'mashie-niblick' and the No 9 and pitching wedge the 'niblick'.

Other single-purpose clubs, which finally disappeared with the introduction of steel shafts, included the 'jigger'. This was a shortish-handled club with the lie normally reserved for the less lofted clubs; but it only had the face loft of a No 4 iron. It was used for running-up shots, which were definitely part of golf on a windy seaside links course.

Some iron clubs were made with a good loft but a head not much longer than the size of the ball; these were called 'rutting irons'. They were designed to get the ball out of the rut made by a cart-wheel, for in the days when the club was made there were no rules allowing the ball to be lifted. Clubs were even made, with gaps like the teeth of a comb, to get the ball out of water. It was assumed that the water would pass through the gaps and so create less resistance to the hit.

Some very lofted irons were made with concave faces to help get the ball up and out of the deepest bunkers. When, in the 1930s, the concave-faced club was made illegal, the famous American professional Gene Sarazen designed the forerunner of the modern sand iron. Its broad flange made it suitable for use in sand, but difficult in tight grass. It was the South African Bobby Locke who promoted a thinner-soled club with similar loft that became known as the pitching wedge.

With the introduction of numbered clubs, which were matched into sets, players were able to obtain clubs that matched each other in both feel and swing

The principle of hand-forging iron club heads has come back in fashion. Here the blacksmith shapes an iron bar.

Golf equipment

weight. The ideal full set for an average player would be: Nos 1, 3 and 4 or 5 woods; Nos 3, 4, 5, 6, 7, 8 and 9 irons; a pitching wedge and a sand iron. With the addition of the putter, this brings the total number of clubs to 13, leaving room for a player to add a No 2 iron – or even a No 1 when he has reached a sufficiently high standard.

When the No 2 wood was more common, it was simple for a beginner to split a set, whether used or new, with a friend who was also starting. One would have the odd numbers and the other the even ones. With the more lofted No 1 wood, there are now very few No 2 woods about. So a part-set usually includes No 1 and No 3 woods, then either the odd or even irons.

Until recently it was possible, after starting with a split set, to add the other clubs at a later date. With modern methods of manufacturing and marketing, clubs are subject to more frequent changes and the days of building a set in stages are over.

What is essential, regardless of the cost, is that clubs are suited to the player. Several factors determine this:

- the weight of the club
- the flex of the club
- the lie of the club
- the loft of the club
- the thickness of the handle
- the length of the club

With a new set, you are entitled to expect all these aspects of the clubs to suit you. With a used set, most of these can be altered by a skilled professional to suit. But if those aspects of the club that need changing are at the top of the list, the costs involved could prove impractical.

The weight This refers to the dead weight, the overall weight of the club. It also refers to what is called the swing weight, which is a means of comparing every club in a matched set so that each, regardless of the different shapes and lengths, swings with a similar feel of weight. The variation of swing weight here or there is very slight, since half of one swing weight measured is equivalent to a £1 note or $5 bill being rested on the club head. This means very small adjustments can be made to adapt a club to an individual player's needs. With standard clubs, a light swing weight is classified as D0, medium as D1 and heavy as D2. Incidentally, a lady's club would have a lower swing weight – C9.

To produce a constant swing weight through a set, it is necessary to have the dead weight of the longest shafted club much lighter than the shortest. Although manufacturers can create similar swing weights, they have their own theories on the actual weight of clubs.

As an average, a driver would be 370g (13oz), gradually increasing through the set of woods to the No 5, which would be about 397g (14oz). From the No 1 iron at 397g (14oz), there would be a gradual increase to the No 9 iron at 440g (15½oz). The wedge and, particularly, the sand iron could be made heavier according to the manufacturer. But an average for the wedge is just over 440g (15½oz) and 454g (16oz) for the sand iron. Ladies' clubs are a fraction lighter.

You may think that a fraction of an ounce here or there would not make any difference. But when the club head is doing over 160km/hr (100mph) at the bottom, it makes a very big difference.

The flex Shafts are made with varying flexes, since weaker players can get help from the more flexible ones. When hickory shafts were in use, the manufacturer would sandpaper down more of the wood so that the shaft became weaker and therefore more flexible. In a sense the same thing happens today, for the steel shafts in ladies' clubs are much slimmer than the men's. When the shafts have to be stiffer, they are made from broader tubes.

Shafts are manufactured in five grades of flex. A tight standard in the flex is maintained by the companies that make clubs, although tournament players in particular do have a preference for make.

The stiffest shaft is classed as 'X' and it would take a very strong tournament player to use this. Even he would save it for just his driver and maybe his No 1 iron, where total rigidity helps under pressure.

Next comes the 'S', which is commonly used among professionals and fairly strong players. The 'S' stands for stiff. 'R' is for regular and means what it says; most weekend golfers should use this grade.

Then there is the 'A' shaft, which is ideal for the stronger lady golfer or club player who is not as young as he used to be. It is a gentle shaft, without being too whippy. The 'L' shaft is just right for those ladies of average strength and smallish hands, for the movement in the shaft allows the club head plenty of momentum without the need to hit the ball that much harder.

There are two ways of altering the flex of a shaft, both of which should only be carried out by an experienced professional. To stiffen a shaft, the club head, whether wood or iron, has to be removed. The head is then reamed to take a wider part of the shaft and the bottom of the shaft cut off accordingly and refitted.

Because it is tapered, the farther through a shaft is pushed, the stiffer it becomes. The club will then need an extension plug at the other end to bring it back to normal length. This means the grip has to be refitted as well. With an odd club like a driver this adjustment would be practical; for a full set of used clubs, however, it would not make financial sense. If a new set requires this type of adjustment, then some bad advice was given – and taken – when the set was first bought.

It is simple enough to increase the flexibility of a shaft – by lengthening the club. This might appear pointless, for few people want a longer set with whippy shafts. It is, however, probably advisable for a very tall player who needs longer shafts to lengthen a set that has stiff shafts; this would bring them to the equivalent of 'R' grade flex.

The lie This is vitally important since using clubs that do not have the correct lie for your physique is like playing the entire round from the side of a hill – uphill or downhill, depending on whether the clubs lie flat or upright.

No matter how unsuitable an angle the head of the club is set off at, an inexperienced player will attempt to place the bottom edge of the head level on the turf when setting up. This could well mean that he adopts a completely wrong posture and hand position.

A flat-lying club will drag a tall player over, bringing his shoulders far forward and causing his hands to lower towards his knees. The opposite will happen when a shorter player uses an upright-angled club; his hands and wrists will rise and his spine will become erect, immobilizing his swing.

Strangely enough, although both swings start badly, nature will take over and attempt to correct the situation mid-swing. The results are shown in the divot mark and the flight of the ball, particularly when an iron club is used.

As the tall player straightens up and his shaft comes into the correct line, the deepest part of the divot is made from the toe end of the club. The ball will fly to the right as the toe of the club, going deep, is slowed up and the heel is projected forward into the ball.

Shorter players move into the ball with their hands travelling in a lower plane than they started in, so the heel of the upright club digs in, turning the toe end into the ball. The divot is deep at the inside and the ball is pulled away to the left.

Even though a new set has been tailored to suit an individual, it should be brought back to the professional's shop after a few weeks of use so the faint scratch marks of the ball on the club face can be studied by an expert eye. From these it is possible to judge how the club is reacting to the swing. If necessary, the lie of the club will have to be altered slightly. It is vitally important that the club suits the individual and not the other way round.

PGA professionals are trained, during their apprenticeship, to alter the lie of a

Golf equipment

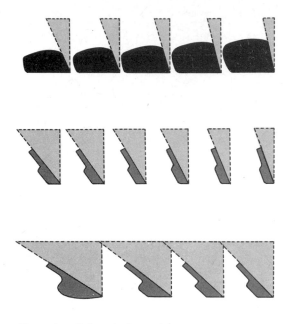

The angles of loft on the faces of the range of clubs (from right to left): top row – Nos 1, 2, 3, 4 and 5 woods; centre row – Nos 2, 3, 4, 5, 6 and 7 irons; bottom row – Nos 8 and 9 irons, pitching wedge and sand iron.

club so that it will suit the individual player. This cannot be done at home.

The loft There is a standard set of loft angles on the club face for every set of clubs, although slight variations are used by some professionals to make the ball go farther. The normal loft angles are:

	Club	Loft angle	Name
Woods	No 1	12 degrees	Driver
	No 2	14 degrees	Brassie
	No 3	16 degrees	Spoon
	No 4	20 degrees	4 wood
	No 5	24 degrees	5 wood
Irons	No 2	19 degrees	
	No 3	23 degrees	Long iron
	No 4	27 degrees	
	No 5	31 degrees	
	No 6	35 degrees	Middle iron
	No 7	39 degrees	
	No 8	43 degrees	
	No 9	47 degrees	Short iron
Pitching wedge		52 degrees	
Sand iron		58 degrees	

Years ago drivers were made with as little as 6 degrees of loft, which rendered them unusable for many average players, who bought a No 2 wood (brassie) instead. Now drivers have gone to 12 degrees, most players can use them and the No 2 wood is almost a thing of the past.

Many professionals have their clubs made a shade more powerful by having the loft reduced a degree or two. They also have their powerful No 3 wood reduced to 14 degrees to help them play more powerful shots into the wind. Top players often use a No 1 iron, which is not included here since this club is exclusively used by expert players, who adjust it to whatever they prefer in order to keep the ball low.

For the average club player the normal lofts are ideal. For the beginner, who may be buying some old clubs, it is essential that the driver is not too old or lacking in sufficient loft.

To add loft to a driver is a very skilled job, for in its original state this club possesses what is known as a 'four way roll'. This means that there is a slight bow on the face from heel to toe, as well as one from roof to sole. It is one of the mysteries

The four-way roll that is put on the face of all wooden club heads.

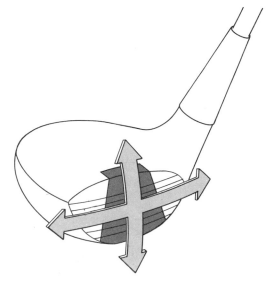

of golf why a wood has a bowed face in two directions, although many reasons have been suggested.

The most sensible one is largely proved by the tee peg marks streaked across the sole plate of the club. You would think, after a perfect hit, that these marks would be straight. But they never are. They run diagonally across the plate, suggesting that the club face is still fractionally 'open', although the shaft and head are perfectly on course. The slight curve on the face provides the equivalent of a straight contact point when striking the ball.

Right or wrong, there is obviously a very delicate curve on the face and without it the ball would not fly off sweetly, nor would it travel as far.

It requires more than an enthusiastic amateur at his garage workbench to alter the loft and get it right. Many experienced professionals, when asked to add loft to a very good club, are reluctant to file the actual face and increase the loft by removing the sole plate and filing the wood away from the back of the club. This causes the face to lean back.

The thickness of the handle This is a simple matter to alter, where necessary. The modern moulded rubber grips are made in two thicknesses – ladies' and men's. If a lady golfer has large hands, she can either have a men's grip fitted or, if the shaft of her club is very thin, more packing can be added under the grip to thicken it.

When a man needs a thicker handle, it is a case of adding more layers of tape before fitting the grip. Should he have very small hands, then a ladies' grip can be fitted, even though a bit of persuasion is needed to get it over the thicker shaft.

There is only one problem when different thicknesses of grip are fitted. Thinner grips make the club head feel heavier, while thicker grips make it feel lighter. If this does cause a problem, the weight of the club should be altered accordingly, for the correct thickness of grip is essential to the swing. Fat handles definitely dull hand

action and slim ones encourage it.

You can fit grips at home. You will have to cut away the original grip, clean off the old tape and wrap on new tape to achieve the thickness required. You then use a spirit to produce a solution on the surface of the tape to help you slide on the new grip. When you are putting on additional tape, take care that the new handle does not stick halfway down. If you do not get the grip fully down, it can creep up the handle during the 24-hour setting period. Sometimes it pays to give the clubs to a professional to do this job, since it costs little more than the price of buying the equipment needed to do it yourself.

The length Many beginners worry, particularly if they are fairly tall or short, that getting the correct length of club will be difficult. They are then pleasantly surprised to find that hardly any difference exists between the lengths of sets. This is entirely due to the lie of the clubs. A tall player will use clubs set more upright, which brings the handles higher up from the ground. For the shorter player, the handles of the flatter lying clubs are that much closer to it.

There are odd exceptions, for example when a player is particularly tall or has very short arms. In this case the clubs may need to be longer. Clubs should not be shortened, except for small children. An adult who is very short should have the angles of the heads flattened out to suit. Shortening the shafts would make the player a very short hitter of the ball, since the swing arc would be greatly reduced.

To lengthen clubs, the grips have to be removed and a length of good quality dowel fitted. The fit must be tight and there should be at least twice the amount of dowel inside the shaft as above it. Extending clubs by more than 2.5cm (1in) can be dangerous, since great strain is put on that particular part of the club when it is swung.

Lengthening a club adds a good deal to the swing weight and increases the flexibility of the shaft. With woods this can be rebalanced by removing the sole plate and taking out some of the lead weight that is under it. Very little can be done with irons, other than grinding the metal from the head, which requires great skill.

To shorten a club, the grip must be removed and the required length cut from the shaft with a hacksaw. Here the swing weight of the club is reduced and the shaft stiffened. Lead may be added to bring back the feel of the woods and lead tape stuck to the iron heads.

Although there may be slight variations between manufacturers, the standard length of men's clubs is as follows (ladies' are 2.5cm [1in] less):

Driver	109cm/43in
2 wood	108cm/42½in
3 wood	107cm/42in
4 wood	105cm/41½in
5 wood	104cm/41in
1 iron	99cm/39in
2 iron	98cm/38½in
3 iron	97cm/38in
4 iron	95cm/37½in
5 iron	94cm/37in
6 iron	93cm/36½in
7 iron	91cm/36in
8 iron	90cm/35½in
9 iron	89cm/35in
Pitching wedge	89cm/35in
Sand iron	89cm/35in

The putter

Since golf began, manufacturers have produced special putters which, because of their looks but mainly for their feel, caught the golfers' imagination and became the big seller of their time.

The famous Willie Park, who hailed from Musselburgh and was the winner of the first British Open in 1860, was renowned, as was his son afterwards, for making great putters. So a 'Willie Park' putter was the one to possess.

Most of the Scottish clubmakers chased the market and a design called the 'Gem' was popular for a while. It is still made to

this day. Ben Sayers produced a 'Benny', which was regarded as revolutionary because it had a squared-off handle, matching the square edges of the blade. The feeling that everything was right-angled made for greater accuracy. According to the 1984 Rules of Golf, the cross-section of all grips must be round, with the exception of putters; so the tradition has remained.

In more recent years American models came to the fore. They specialized in centre shafts, which were not legalized in Britain until the early 1950s. The 'Bulleseye' was the best and is still widely used, both by amateur and professional players.

Right: Even a player with the skill of Severiano Ballesteros still requires the perfectly balanced putter – the Ping. Below: The Ping putter is probably used by more competitive golfers, both amateur and professional, than any other.

Golf equipment

In the mid-1960s a putter came on to the market that looked like a bit of plumbing gone wrong. It was called the 'Ping', because of the noise it made when it struck the ball. However it had more than a noise. It had a fantastic balance and its design afforded it a large 'sweet spot' with which the ball could be struck. It is still used by more professionals than any other make.

The 'Ping' set all the other manufacturers off in search of the secret and the better makes of putter have improved enormously as a result.

You can only select the right putter once you have developed a good striking technique. Initially, provided you choose one of the branded models – and lighter and shorter if you are a lady golfer – you are safe. As the years go by, you will have plenty of fun selecting another, more suitable putter.

Sometimes, unfortunately, putters are selected in desperation, since all golfers go through problem periods in their golfing life. Some club professionals have in their shop a 'sin bin' full of old putters, where for a set fee you can dispose of an enemy and select a new friend, temporary though it may be.

Maintaining clubs

Preserving the polished finish on the wood heads improves their appearance and also preserves the wood by protecting it from the elements. A shiny iron, with the grooves on the face regularly cleaned out, seems to make the ball fly more crisply. Maintaining a set of clubs in good condition is, for many people, one of the pleasures in golf.

Wooden clubs Often more than £100/$150 changes hands when a persimmon wood is sold, particularly if it is a vintage Macgregor club of the old Tommy Armour type. Even though such clubs are well over 25 years old, the blocks from which many were originally made were so hard and durable that some tournament players will pay a ridiculous price for one.

The latest innovation to putting – the Basakwerd putter, which was introduced in 1983. It may be just a short-term fad.

Persimmon is a type of ebony tree found growing in parts of America, Australia and Japan. Although it is still used to make clubs, it is not given the time to season that it used to. The great boom in the game used up the old blocks and the younger ones that had to be used were prone to break up because they were unseasoned.

It was then that layers of wood were glued and compressed together to make the blocks from which club heads were fashioned: if one layer was faulty or broke up, it would be hidden among the others and fully supported. This practice worked and still does, for it produced the closest feel yet found to compare with persimmon – and these laminated woods are much cheaper, another point in their favour.

Scientific processes used to quick-dry wood are being applied to younger persimmon with some success. But it is nevertheless necessary to look after the more recently made clubs. Should they get wet during a round, you must dry them thoroughly and store them in normal conditions and temperature. If you leave them inside wet headcovers, the wood is bound to swell. This goes for all types of wooden clubs.

One of the important areas on a wood is around the insert – plastic or other moulded substance set into the club face at the point that makes contact with the ball. The extra hardness is to increase the effectiveness of the strike. The wood immediately around it takes quite a lot of punishment, both from balls hit just off centre and from the impact with mud and grass. As the varnish chips, the wood is exposed to the weather and very soon it softens and flakes. Similar things happen to the varnish.

The neck-binding, which used to be of twine and is now a form of plastic thread, can work loose and you should examine this regularly. The joint between the shaft and the neck of the club requires constant support, since the glue has long since dried out. Any movement will crack the glue and the head will loosen. If this goes unnoticed for a period of time, it will cause the neck of

the wood to split. So keep an eye on it.

The best treatment for woods – including the lines of the face – is regular cleaning and the application of a very thin coat of varnish. If damage has already started, you should take the wood back to its original state, first by scraping off the old varnish then sandpapering until the entire club head is perfectly smooth. First lightly varnish those parts that do not require colouring then, when they are dry, stain the rest of the wood the desired colour and varnish over it.

When the insert is badly damaged or the head turns on the shaft, the club professional can replace the insert and refit the head. His staff are also expert at restaining clubs and can restore them to their original finish. They can also put back the maker's name on top if you want.

Iron clubs You need do little to look after irons, other than wiping them dry when they are wet and not allowing them to lie about damp. Moisture can get under the plastic ferrule and cause the base of the

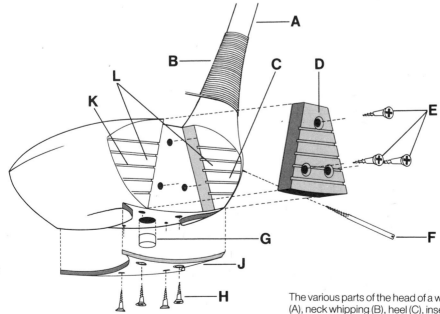

The various parts of the head of a wooden club: the shaft (A), neck whipping (B), heel (C), insert (D), face screws (E), neck screw (F), lead weight (G), sole screws (H), sole plate (J), toe (K) and face (L).

Golf equipment

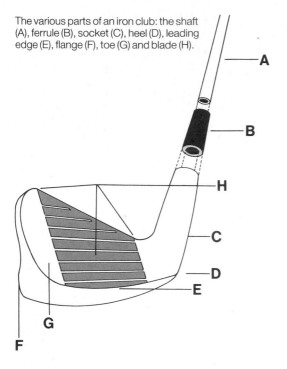

The various parts of an iron club: the shaft (A), ferrule (B), socket (C), heel (D), leading edge (E), flange (F), toe (G) and blade (H).

shaft to rust just where it enters the head, at the point where all the strain is taken.

You can buy a set of plastic covers which fit neatly on to the heads and are easily removed and replaced when playing. Like the wooden club head covers, it is worth the effort of replacing them after each shot. Most of the damage to iron heads is caused when they knock together as you take them in and out of the bag. It must be said, however, that while wood covers are essential, iron ones are not.

You should clean out the grooves of the club faces, particularly after practice sessions, for the mud will have been compacted by many hits. These grooves are a definite aid to back spin and help tremendously on wet days when the ball is inclined to slide when struck. If you watch the professional's caddie, you will see him clean the grooves before replacing the iron in the bag.

Shafts and grips If club shafts are left damp, tiny rust spots will eventually

appear on the chrome plating. Although little else is necessary than to wipe them, a very occasional polish with non-abrasive chrome cleaner will bring up the shine.

The rubber-moulded grip will look after itself for several months before it requires a scrub with hot soapy water. The older it gets, the quicker it will dry and become shiny and the more often it will need scrubbing. A tournament professional will go through two or three sets of grips each year. Those players who practise a lot will use more.

Leather grips used to be standard, but they are hardly ever used nowadays. One reason for this is that they are very expensive to fit, being twice the price of rubber ones. What is more, they have to be replaced sooner, unless they are treated frequently with leather oil. It is not that they fall apart when neglected; many are still seen on antique clubs. But they become very shiny and slippery, especially when it is cold. Arnold Palmer, who always preferred to use leather grips, was often seen rewinding one during a round.

Other essential equipment

A large number of gimmicky items are available for the golfer, many of them fun and some quite useful. But certain pieces of equipment are absolutely necessary.

Golf bag This varies in size according to its purpose. You should always have one, whether you carry it on your shoulder or wheel it around on a cart, from which you can take the clubs out easily. Tugging clubs from the bag will severely damage the handles and a set of grips can be more expensive than a new bag.

You can get a small version known as a 'Sunday bag' which takes fewer clubs. It has a small pocket for balls and tee pegs. All-the-year-round golfers will need a pocket large enough to carry some waterproof clothing, a cap and perhaps a towel, as well as the balls and pegs.

You can get a bag that is small and light enough to carry, yet has a frame inside that enables it to be placed on a golf trolley without collapsing in on the clubs. Whatever the size of bag, if it has to be carried make sure it has a well-padded sling: a thin one will cut into your shoulder.

Waterproofs The market is full of superb and genuine waterproof suits. The days of cotton ones, which were too heavy to swing in, even when they were dry, have gone. Flexible, lightweight, plastic-type materials, through which the makers claim air can pass but not water, are now commonplace. They are obviously better, since tournament players are regularly seen wearing them. Until recently, although some would wear the overtrousers, very few would bother with the jacket because it restricted movement.

The new suits not only keep a player dry, but also fold up very small and can be tucked in the bag. It does pay, however, to air them now and again, otherwise the material may crack.

Golf shoes The choice of good golfing shoes was widened with the advent of the rubber-studded models. At first these were frowned upon, particularly in the United States. When Scotland's Sandy Lyle turned up to play in his first American tournament, he was ordered to change from rubber to conventional spikes. He had not brought a spare pair with him, so had to buy some more. But even the Americans now allow shoes with rubber studs.

When the grass is a bit greasy and muddy, there is no doubt that well-spiked shoes are better, since they offer more substantial support for the feet. Many players still prefer them. A good sound footing helps the swing and there is nothing better for a player's physical condition than firm support over the many miles he walks.

Golf glove You must ensure you get the maximum amount of grip with the left

The modern lightweight waterproof suit not only keeps you dry but allows you freedom to swing the club. In this instance, Hale Irwin is putting one on for protection before backing into a thorny bush.

Golf equipment

As golf bags get bigger and heavier, so the caddies have to be younger and fitter. There is also a trend to be fashionable. This is certainly so with Craig Stadler's caddie, seen here loaded up with equipment.

Spiked golf shoes are still preferred by most professionals. Here an assistant professional replaces the set of spikes.

hand (or right hand if you are a left-handed player) when striking the ball – and a good golf glove definitely helps. The great Ben Hogan did not wear one, neither does Bill Rogers, another winner of the British Open. However it is difficult to think of another competitive professional who does not.

A more expensive, good quality glove will outlast two cheaper ones. It is wise to keep the plastic bag it comes in – at the end of each round, put the glove back in the bag so the moisture is retained longer in the glove. Keep a worn glove with you to use on really wet days, since heavy rain can ruin a glove, even though you dry it with a towel later. One method of restoring a dry glove is to rub hand cream into it.

There are cheaper waterproof gloves that have proved satisfactory. One made of snakeskin – sold in many parts of Europe and particularly in Britain – is very practical in the wet.

Golf cart In Britain this is called a trolley and it is in Britain that the best-balanced models are probably made. Some countries produce much fancier designs, but these are a lot heavier to pull.

There are only a few really good trolleys on the market and the others should be avoided since they do not stand up to the wear and tear they receive. The best may be

the most expensive at the time, but the length of service they give is well worth the additional cost.

Tee pegs When tee pegs replaced mounds of sand as a means of teeing up the ball, they were available in all shapes and sizes. The most famous was called the 'carrot', which described its shape. It was almost impossible to break one of these because of the thickness of the stem. However, it was quite possible to lose one. The peg was quite expensive, especially when compared with the free sand provided in square boxes at the side of the teeing area, so a hole was drilled through and a tassle of coloured wool attached. Rubber pegs were made, but these were too cumbersome, and plastic became the standard material.

Some of the better players have switched back to wooden pegs, and the advantage of these is that they do not mark the face of wooden clubs. On some American courses these are given out free or provided in a box at the side of each tee. Unfortunately used pegs litter the ground immediately in front of the teeing area since, because they are free, few bother to pick them up.

Golf balls Along with clubs, balls are the most important part of the equipment; and there is a huge selection of makes in a range of compressions. Soon there will be no choice of size, since the original 4.1cm (1.62in) diameter ball is certain to be phased out in the next few years. The 4.3cm (1.68in) diameter ball now being adopted will, however, retain the original weight of 46g (1.62oz).

There have always been different compressions, created by the tension of the long strands of rubber when wound round the core of the ball. The normal ball was known as 90 compression and the tighter and harder one 100 compression. Balls could have been made tighter still, but the R & A and the USGA have regulated how fast a ball can leave the club face; this has been set at 76m/sec (250ft/sec).

The traditional wound ball has now been joined by some with larger solid centres,

around which less strands of rubber are wrapped, and others with no strands at all, which are completely solid. The advantage of these balls is that they can fly farther. The disadvantage comes with shorter shots, such as pitch shots, for it is very difficult to create the same amount of back spin on these balls compared to the wound ones. When putting, too, the actual strike feels a lot harder, and the 'sweet' feel you get with the conventional ball is lost.

In many countries a tournament professional who does not normally like the solid ball will produce one just when the hole is very long or when he is playing directly into the teeth of a gale. Elsewhere this practice has been banned and the type of ball played from the first tee must be used throughout the round.

Many lady professionals, not normally the long hitters, use the solid ball because they are happy to gain the extra distance, even at the expense of a better feel and more control when playing shorter shots.

The dimpling on the balls has gone through continual changes. The depths have been altered and the dimpling has gone from round to square to triangular to hexagonal and back again to round. It is common knowledge that a ball with dimples that are too shallow does not lift and one that has deep ones lifts too much.

Dunlop has produced a ball called the DDH, which is quite revolutionary in the pattern and distribution of its dimples. It was designed as a dodecahedron, a figure

Here you can see the development of the golf ball's surface patterns from the feathery to the new Dunlop DDH. The balls are (from the back) feathery, gutty, chisel-marked gutty, two examples of early moulded surface patterns, the bramble pattern, the lattice or mesh pattern, an early dimpled ball, the Dunlop 65 and Dunlop's new DDH pattern.

with 12 identical pentagonal sides. With many other balls, where the outer shell is made in two halves set together, the join has either to intersect dimples or to form a complete ridge without any.

With the new DDH ball it is possible to have 10 'equators' passing round it without touching a dimple. The dimples are set in clusters in matching patterns, but of varying sizes. This ball has been tried and tested and looks very likely to stay at the top in popularity, certainly until research produces something better.

Most of the golf balls that have survived the very tough competition come from reputable manufacturers, mainly because the golfing public knows how a good ball should feel. Although some of the poorer makes look the same, they lack the quality.

What is important is to choose the type of ball that suits your individual needs. For the average player common sense would definitely suggest using the standard 90 compression ball. Most makers produce a top model of that compression, as well as a less expensive one.

A long-hitting young man should use the 100 compression ball, but be prepared to switch back to the 90 on cold days, for the rubber in the ball does not warm up in these conditions. Common sense, however, does not always prevail. Those shorter ladies who should be using a softer ball but have experienced the benefit of the extra distance the solid ball can achieve will not give it up.

For the really discerning, there are also two types of outer skin – one made from natural Balata and the other from man-made Surlyn. Top professionals claim that with the former they get more back spin – and that even applies to the rubber-wound ball with which most of them play.

The golf swing

In the last half-century a complete transformation has taken place in the world of sport. Games have changed from being a source of healthy exercise to today's overriding need to win, which can reach terrifying proportions as competitors drive themselves to the limits of endurance.

Equipment is needed in all sports and manufacturers are involved in a constant struggle to produce equipment that will make players perform better than ever. Professional golf is no exception.

Fortunately the game has a few steadying influences to keep it on an even keel. The various governing bodies, such as the R & A, the USGA and the PGAs, ensure that nothing is allowed on to the market that might be detrimental to the game. Every new style of golf club and ball, for example, comes under heavy scrutiny. If the authorities are satisfied that new designs are not in the interests of the game, they are listed as illegal and may not be used in any recognized event.

Within the sensible guidelines laid down by these governing bodies, golf equipment has changed a great deal since the 1930s and the techniques have altered even more. Clubs, for example, are now better balanced and more consistent and practical in their design.

Each club is matched for swing weight to the others in the set. More care has been taken with the angle of lie to see that it suits the individual. Shafts are much lighter and this has meant an overall reduction in the weight of the club. Drivers are made with a more generous loft; most now show about 12 degrees, whereas in the 1930s some had as little as 4 or 5 degrees. The pitching wedge has been invented, sand irons are lighter and putters with centre shafts have been made legal.

The classic swing of Jerry Pate, probably the most uncomplicated swing in golf today.

Important as these modifications to equipment have been, however, the changes in the technique of swinging have been even greater.

In the 1930s the steel shaft was taking the place of the hickory and the technique involved in swinging a club with this shaft was very different, although this was not noticed by everyone at the time. The early steel was of inferior quality and there were many critics around who were determined to stick to what they knew. When, after half a century of examination and change, one compares the swing of that era with the swing of today, it is easy to see how wrong they were.

Golf came to a halt in Britain during the Second World War, but possibly in those six war years more was learned about manufacturing than at any time before. It was not long, therefore, before better equipment was being produced and with it a new golf swing.

Typically it was the professionals in the United States who made the first dramatic changes to the golf swing. They had been experimenting before the Second World War and of course were still playing competitively when other nations had stopped. Britain's best player of the day, Henry Cotton, visited the United States at one stage and tried out the new swing. But he was not in favour and went back to his own style, which he continued to do well with, winning the British Open championships in 1934, 1937 and 1948.

What a great pity it was that, apart from a Ryder Cup visit every four years, the American professionals did not start playing on the British side of the Atlantic in large numbers until the 1960s. Then Arnold Palmer came to the British Open, went back and opened the flood gates through which the best players in the world have since come annually. If they had come earlier, we in Britain might not

51

The golf swing

The design characteristics of the old long-headed club, bound to a hickory shaft, created the historic shape of the traditional golf swing.

have gone on playing and teaching the swing techniques of the 1930s with their foundations built on the traditional club with the hickory shaft.

The swing had first been developed around the original equipment, the major part of which was not so much the clubs as the ball. This was made of leather, stuffed with feathers. It was packed very tight, since it took about two 'top hats' full of feathers to fill each ball. The clubs were made to hit this ball using a sweeping technique and were longer and more shallow-angled than those of today.

The longer head of the club, which was bound and glued to the shaft, and the fact that this was made of hickory combined to cause the club head to roll from 'open' in the back swing to 'closed' on the through swing. The need to sweep at the ball made it necessary to sway the body – and that is

where the 'Scottish sway' came from. If you learned your golf in Scotland any time between 1539 and 1939, you were taught this sway. Unfortunately the habit went on for a few years after that.

The technical advances made more than 100 years ago, including the strengthening of the ball's structure, and subsequent improvements enabled the design of clubs to be changed. Being able to bore through the head to fit the shaft, for example, must have been a major breakthrough and caused great changes in the swing. There was less sway and hand action improved and the strange versions of holding the club were gone forever.

Harry Vardon, who for many years was resident professional at the South Herts Golf Club, designed a hold that has been accepted as the orthodox grip now taught all over the world. It used to be claimed that as many as 99 per cent of all professionals used it. With the current breed of players, and the more recent changes in the evolving swing and equipment, a similar percentage are still using this grip, but with slight modifications.

In the bronze cast of Harry Vardon's hands, which hangs in the club house at the South Herts Golf Club, the left hand is sufficiently over the handle to have almost three knuckle joints showing. Modern swinging has reduced this by at least one knuckle; the average professional shows two, while some of the very strong players show only one.

It is not, of course, the knuckle count that is important, but rather the response of the wrist action in the swing that those who show fewer knuckles have developed. The left wrist joint now arches at the top of the back swing; in Vardon's day it definitely cupped under.

The sway has been eliminated and the preference is now for a direct shoulder turn. The wrist action has been simplified, with the left wrist being cocked on a truer line to the plane of the swing.

The ball, soon to be fixed at 4.3cm (1.68in)

diameter, is produced in different compressions and possesses different qualities of performance. This enables those who are inclined to hit high shots due to a swing fault to use a low trajectory ball, and low hitters to use one with slightly deeper dimpling, which helps lift it.

Although it may seem unfair to some to gain help from technology, the technique for hitting the bigger ball, which can still go sideways regardless of the height at which it flies, does need to be more consistent. So there are also disadvantages to overcome.

The shafts, like the ball, have improved too and now couple strength with lightness. This has enabled the overall weight of the club to be reduced and the movement of the swing to be cut back. So swings are, on the whole, shorter than before. A long back swing used to be commonplace, but now Ben Crenshaw is one of the few players who spring to mind that still use it.

With the directness of the swing it became possible to think of a consistent

It is rare for players whose wrist action operates 'square' to the swing plane to overswing in the back swing. Ben Crenshaw is one of the few who does.

This shows the old Scottish sway (left), which was developed over generations when players used hickory shafts, flatter-lying clubs and feathery balls. Compare it with the swing of today.

swing angle, which could be described as 'being on plane' – an expression used by the legendary Ben Hogan in the 1950s. It could not have been used in the days of the hickory shaft, because then the club head was rolled into the back swing, the arms being taken around the body on a shallower angle than that on which they would swing the club through to hit the ball.

At a point about waist high, a change of direction was made and the cock of the wrist brought the club upwards into the striking position. So there were two directions to the back swing and two distinct movements, but no angle of plane since it would lie somewhere between the two.

The Australian Peter Thomson won early on in his career because he was one of the least complicated players in the game and he swung 'in plane'. His was the sort of simplicity that is fairly commonplace today but stood out when he came on the scene.

He made a great contribution to golf by illustrating the fact that, with such simple movements to complete, it was best to prepare the swing from a position very close to that of the strike. For many teachers that was the moment the expression 'address the ball' became 'set up to the ball' and almost all of the good players now do so. This is one of the reasons why we are producing winners today at an age which a few years ago would have been thought of as a fluke.

Learning from the professionals

Advances made in the golf swing mean that it is easier for instructors to teach and less complicated for players to learn.

It is a foolish person who takes up golf without the advantage of some coaching. Unfortunately those who do can appear, at first, to be making better progress than the ones receiving proper instruction. But it is not long before the coached players catch up and overtake the others. Then the difference is all too obvious as the gap between them widens.

Certain disciplines are absolutely necessary. They may require some patience to develop, but the reward of keeping to them is well worth while. Without studying and mastering the basic guidelines, you can never hope to make consistent progress.

Many people who start on their own believe, when they hit a good shot, that by continual playing they will hit the shot regularly. That is not the case. The shot is a fluke and will only happen rarely.

A lot of players are influenced by the fact that top professionals have varying swings, yet all are successful. What they are looking at are those aspects that are done differently. What they miss, and what really matters, are those that are the same.

Several aspects of the swing, religiously adhered to by tournament professionals, have become standard techniques. These have been tried and tested under the very toughest conditions and are there for the benefit of all students of the game to follow. It is on such aspects that a good foundation can be laid and a platform established from which, with natural flair and talent, a very high standard of play can be achieved or, with more average talent, a consistent standard can be enjoyed.

The professionals' swing routine

Every golf shot has its individual requirements, yet all shots incorporate a three-part routine – set-up, back swing and through swing.

The set-up is how the player, once he has decided what he wants to do with the ball and has chosen his club, sets himself to deliver the necessary strike.

The back swing is the preparation, by the combined movement of hands, arms and body, to get the club into the right position and on the correct angle to strike the ball to the target.

Arnold Palmer was one of the first to demonstrate the strength of swinging with the left wrist cocked 'square' to the swing plane.

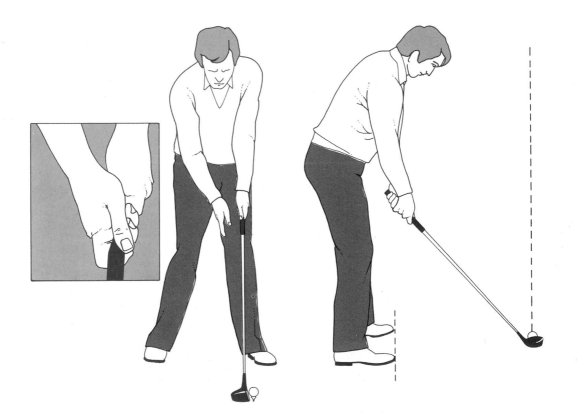

The through swing includes the transfer of weight and the swinging of the arms down and through, so that the hands can take the club head to, then through, the ball and continue on to the appropriate follow-through position.

The set-up

A very high percentage of swing faults are created by setting up incorrectly. For this reason experts are prepared to spend a great deal of time perfecting the set-up, which is particularly important to ensure the right movements for deliberate spin.

It is noticeable how many of the top players establish similar set-up routines. This is not by accident, for players are prepared to copy what others benefit from – and knowledge is freely shared among the game's great rivals.

Phase 1. Aiming the club, positioning the ball and taking the stance Standing directly behind the ball or at least leaning over so he has a view from the ball to the target, the professional looks along what is called the 'ball-to-target line'.

Holding the club in the right hand, approximately the width of the left hand down from the top of the handle, he offers the club head to the ball, aiming squarely at the target. Simultaneously he places the right foot as near as possible to the position it will take up as he makes the swing.

Where he places the right foot is one of the keys to good swinging, for it establishes the leg and hip at right angles to the ball-to-target line and contributes to the accuracy of the shot. He has to bear in mind that if he normally splays his feet, the right one will be turned outwards.

Since 90 per cent of mistakes in the swing result from faults at the set-up stage, the following procedure is well worth learning. Having established the ball-to-target line and the type of shot required, take the club in the right hand and line it up to the ball and the target. At the same time place the right foot as close as possible to its correct position. Then bring the left side of the body into line and place the club in the left hand. Let go the right hand and then position it correctly in the grip, lifting the left shoulder and flexing the right leg inwards.

Phase 2. Bringing up the left side and taking up the grip Having completed the first phase and after looking to check along the target line, the professional goes through a combination of movements.

He brings the left side of the body and the left foot into line and, at the same time, brings the club forward with the right hand and places it in the left hand at a point opposite the left thigh. This gives the necessary strength on the left side to achieve a wide swing arc. By raising the left shoulder slightly and matching this by flexing the right knee inwards, he gives the left side a greater feeling of strength.

Only at this point does he put his right hand in its exact position on the handle of the club.

Phase 3. Settling into the correct posture, the waggle and the forward press Posture in the golf swing consists of leaning the spine over, according to the club being used, to enable it to help guide the angle at which the swing moves round the body – called the 'swing plane'. The posture also refers to how the player holds his head, which is crucial for helping to maintain a central position during the swing and for the distribution of weight on to the feet and legs so they are capable of both mobility and balance.

Professionals always ensure that the body line is established prior to flexing the legs, otherwise the swing could be seriously out of the correct plane.

Waggling the club has two purposes. With it the professional demonstrates, by a few back and forward movements from the ball, how the swing is about to be shaped. He also brings suppleness to an area that normally, under pressure, would become static. He waggles the club using his hands, wrists and arms, although with longer clubs he may bring in some shoulder and knee movement.

The forward press could be construed as being part of the back swing, for it is a movement used to initiate that. It involves a combined push of hands and wrists,

The golf swing

There are three ways of taking the club head into the back swing. You can roll it 'open' from the swing plane (A), keep it 'square' to the plane (B) or turn it 'closed' from the plane (C).

The ideal direction is 'square', when the turn of the shoulders blends in perfectly with the part-rotation of the forearms, allowing the hands to prepare the wrists on the direct swing plane. This way the right elbow will not fly upwards and outwards, nor be jammed into the right side. Your hands should never be behind the club head when setting up. If they are, you have no option but to roll the club head 'open'.

together with the right knee, towards the target. With the recoil from that, many professionals start the back swing.

The back swing

The back swing describes the movement that brings the club to the point above and behind the player from where it can be swung powerfully and accurately through the ball. The term 'back swing' tends to convey the idea that the movement is a complete swing in its own right, but it is not. Professionals show it is just the preparatory stage of the full swing, but they do not 'swing' from the ball to the top with anything like the freedom they engage in the through swing.

In the preparation, which is a better description of the movement, the swing of the club head guides its direction and gives it tempo and rhythm. For the professional, it is a calculated movement for position and angle of swing plane, incorporating a strong awareness of balance.

This preparation is, in a way, like drawing back the elastic on a catapult or the string of a bow.

Starting the back swing Moving the club back from the ball often confuses amateur players, since the club head appears stuck to the ground. The professionals overcome this by taking the shaft of the club forward and placing it in their left hand when they set up, so the club head is already ahead of the arms as the back swing starts. Those players who have their hands behind the ball are forced to drag the club along the turf until it clears the ground.

The preparation The hands are first into action, although the response from the arms and shoulders, which provide the span and strength of the swing, is almost instantaneous. A great deal is accomplished in this combined movement, as the hands determine the strike angle while the arms

To engage his very full shoulder turn in the back swing, Tom Watson is prepared to bring his left heel well clear of the turf when swinging.

and shoulders provide the swing base.

The wrist joints are used by the hands to gain the correct position and the forearms are partially rotated. This determines both the direction of the swing path and the angle of the swing plane.

In a normal shot the left wrist cocks, bringing the club shaft from a position in line with the left arm at the set-up to an angle of not less than 90 degrees from it. The right wrist is hinged back and the elbow pointed downwards as the right hand prepares for the work it has to do during the hit.

To prevent this preparation for striking the ball turning into a snatch or involving a tight spin or twist of the body, the hips, legs and feet are brought into the movement. They come into action a fraction afterwards and contribute to the width and turn of the arc by guiding the balance of weight and preparing it for the transfer through, when the ball is hit. The left knee and ankle are used to maintain the level of the swing and prevent the shoulders from tilting off the correct line, which would take the swing out of its plane.

The result of these combined efforts is that, with one movement and in a single direction, at the top of the back swing the club shaft lies almost horizontal and parallel to the ball-to-target line. The shoulders are turned 90 degrees from their starting point at the set-up and a similar minimum angle exists between the left arm and the shaft of the club.

When the majority of professionals swing, the enthusiasm to achieve a full turn, even in the gentlest of swings, causes two outstanding characteristics. The professionals use both of these, for different reasons, to help the down swing.

Firstly, the head turns slightly to the right and also tilts fractionally so that the left side of the face turns to the ball. This helps the professional start his down swing slightly inside the line of swing taken when the club was brought up. The average player does the opposite.

Good players often try to guide the down swing of the club on a path inside that of the back swing. This is really only an impression, however, for the fact is that the centrifugal force of the down swing tends to have the opposite effect. It is, nevertheless, an advantage to try to counteract any outward throw of the club.

Secondly, when the body weight tries to override the right knee in the back swing, it prompts the hips to move to the left – the first movement of the down swing.

The through swing

This swing is in three parts: the down swing, the strike and the follow-through. They are described under the one heading because, with the best players, the movements flow so effortlessly through that the actual strike is indistinguishable as a separate action from the swing.

The professional's objective is to get through to the completion of the follow-through in one movement, as he is well aware of the danger, even with his high standard of play, of hitting at the ball rather than through it.

The down swing The last parts of the body to move into the back swing – the hips and legs – are the first into the down swing. Many professionals claim their very first movement is a lateral shift of the left hip in the direction of the target. For this to happen, however, they would be among those

There should always be the impression that the arc of the down swing is inside the arc of the back swing. Here Lee Trevino, whose back swing climbs fairly sharply, has looped into his down swing to give that impression.

players who do not lift the left heel off the ground. Gymnasts who have studied the golf swing claim that if the left heel is raised, it is impossible to move just the hip. Therefore the left hip, leg and foot must move in unison, often aided by the reaction of the body weight as it moves on to the right knee during the back swing.

The other reaction that occurs here is that as the lower half sets off, the swing weight of the club head is still pulling in the oppo-site direction. The result of this is that the angle between the arms and the shaft of the club becomes even narrower. It is at this point that the shoulders and arms set about their task of swinging the club down and through the ball. Their initial effort is to pull at the club and form a very acute angle, as the right elbow is forced close to the right side of the body.

As the professional starts the down swing, his concentration is on the swing path he wants the club to take as it travels towards the ball. With a normal full shot, he tries to bring the swing arc down on a path just inside the one the club came up on. He does this because the combination

The golf swing

As the body weight shifts sidewards to the left, the club head is swung down towards the ball on a more descending arc than that of the back swing. This means the base of the arc is forward of the ball and the strike sequence is 'ball then turf'.

the down swing is almost whip-like. Many claim they are unaware of this hand and wrist activity at all, even though it does happen. If it did not, how else would the leading edge of the club come back into line at the strike?

With the professional, the strong lateral shift of weight causes the down swing to be narrower than the back swing. The result is that the base of any full swing is moved several inches forward from the starting point. This is why, with iron shots, the club head is still travelling down the arc when it strikes the ball, why so much back spin is put on the ball and why a divot is made forward of where the ball lay. This does, of course, allow the player to have the

The forward movement of the arms and body provides an extension at the base of the swing which permits the club head to remain on the target line for several inches after contact has been made with the ball. This is perfectly demonstrated by Gary Player, whose club, although some 60cm (2ft) beyond the point of impact, has still not passed the line of his left arm.

of body weight transferring to the left, the natural turn-back of his shoulders and the centrifugal outward throw of the club head later in the down swing will drag the down swing away from him.

The strike This occurs an instant before the professional brings the shaft and club head into line with his left arm, which at the top of the back swing was trailing by more than 90 degrees. The firmness of the strike is boosted by the right arm and the right hand, which has been doubled back against its wrist joint, straightening out. At the same time the forearms, which have partly rotated during the back swing, turn back to their original position.

Strangely enough, professionals are more aware of their hands moving the club head into line to strike the ball when playing softer strokes such as pitch shots. With full shots, the reaction of the shaft late in

For consistent swinging, it is very important to keep the angle of the spine constant throughout the swing. When you are practising, you should be aware of it at the set-up, at the top of the back swing and finally at the end of the follow-through.

ball well forward in the stance for many of his shots.

Today's professionals know that, even though the days of hitting past the braced left side are gone, there still has to be some resistance at the point of strike, through which the hands and the club are squared up. This is achieved by holding the head firm above where it started, with the left side of the face and neck tensed.

The follow-through In a major event, the pressures of the moment tend to make it appear that professionals pay little attention to their position at the end of the swing. Often you will see them leaning, as if to influence the flight of the ball, even though they cannot. If you watch them in practice, it is a very different matter, as they hold the final position long after the ball has gone.

By doing this, they can check on the angle of the swing plane round the body at the end of the swing. Ideally they should have kept the same angle of the spine they had at the set-up stage and maintained through the back swing, which helped dictate to the hands and arms the direction they should have driven on after the ball as they came through the strike. Even the eyes should be at a similar angle to that of the swing plane as they follow the ball.

Professionals do not keep their head down for very long, however, since this can affect the through swing. The stopping effect created by keeping the head down encourages the right hand and forearm to turn over the left hand and forearm, closing the club face too sharply. The longer the back of the left hand and forearm travel on square to the target, the more chance there is of the ball being sent straight. The natural turn of the body will bring the club face over soon enough.

This part of the follow-through, immediately after the strike, is known as the extension, where the professionals momentarily straighten out the curve. This is feasible, since the golf swing is not a true circle. With a perfect circle, it would not be possible to produce any power in the shot. There is a great deal of forward drive at the

The golf swing

Above: Jerry Pate at the end of the perfect swing. Although his body is arched fully through, his head has maintained its original central position, as he demonstrates the perfectly balanced finish.
Below: Who says you should not hit hard? The unmistakable high-handed finish of golf's greatest personality – Arnold Palmer.

Nick Faldo proves that it is not necessary to keep your eyes glued to the ground. Here his swing arc continues on a perfect plane as his head turns to allow him to watch the flight of the ball.

base of the swing and much of this is done by the right leg and foot as they share in the legwork, after the initial movements of the left leg and foot at the start of the down swing. That is why in many follow-throughs you see the player's right hip so far forward and the right heel so well clear of the ground, almost dragging the toe of the shoe forward.

It is the extension in the follow-through that carries the left arm on up to its eventual high position at the end of the follow-through, where it will still support the club shaft. With its contribution over, the right leg relaxes, with only the toe of the foot remaining on the turf. The outside of the left hip and leg now support the body.

A closer look at the swing

There is so much the amateur golfer can learn from these disciplines, which the professionals have virtually standardized. Even complete beginners should attempt to build up their swing around them, particularly those of the set-up, from where so many other movements follow.

Aiming

It is the club face that is aimed, with the body aligned to it, and not, as practised by many amateur players, the other way round. So the leading edge of the club face has to be placed very accurately against the ball. This is why continual reference is made to it as the setting-up takes place.

Even in the modern swing, when the head and eyes are encouraged to turn through with the swing when playing longer shots, it is still essential to create a firm 'barrier' through which the club must pass. This is best achieved by keeping the head central through the swing.
Except when playing very short iron shots, if you put too much emphasis on keeping your head down (inset) your left wrist may buckle early into the through swing and, as a result, the ball will be turned to the left.

The golf swing

The stance

The position of the right foot is important. When you first approach the ball, your right foot should be as close as possible to its final position for the shot. To do this, you will need to decide on the right distance of the stance from the ball and from what point opposite the stance you will play the ball.

Under normal circumstances, your decision will be made by the choice of club, for you should have already determined with practice a regular distance between the stance and the ball for each club – and should always stick to it.

Distance from the ball The exact distance you stand from the ball is, to a degree, a matter of personal preference. The farther away you stand, however, the greater the effect on the angle of the swing plane if you do not get the posture right.

There is a very simple way of checking what it should be. Having adopted the correct width of stance for the club you are using, place the club head against the ball and lean the shaft back until the top of the handle touches the left leg just above the knee cap.

Judging this distance does become automatic, although you should check it fairly regularly. Soon you will be able to position your right foot accurately every time.

Ball position There are two ball positions. One is known as the 'professionals' choice' and, although intended for advanced players, is the simplest to adopt. The other, more complex position is recommended for beginners for reasons that will become clear. Whichever you choose, you must become very familiar with it. This is because the width of your stance for individual clubs and the position of the ball in relation to your stance must be accurate to within a fraction when you initially position your right foot.

Fortunately the width of the stance (depending on the club) does not change, regardless of which method you adopt. You will need the widest stance when play-

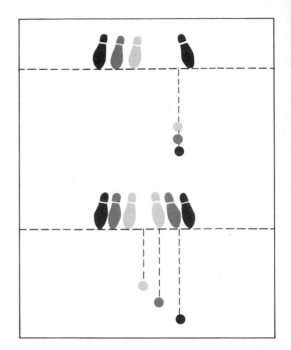

The professional's choice of ball position (top), where the ball is always opposite the left heel and the right foot is brought closer to the left as the length of club used gets shorter. The ball position recommended for beginners (bottom), where not only does the width of the stance reduce as the clubs get shorter, but the ball becomes more central in the stance. Establishing the correct ball position is vitally important for any shot.

ing with the wooden clubs; this should be about as wide as the length of your walking pace. With the long irons, bring the feet just a shade closer together. When using the shorter clubs, which require a much narrower swing arc, stand with your feet a little more than half the distance apart required for the woods.

The position favoured by many professionals is with the ball played from a point opposite the inside of the left foot, regardless of the club being used. Only the width of the stance and the distance from the ball, both dictated by the type of club being used, vary.

With the more complex position, you vary the point opposite the stance from where the ball is played. When playing with a wood, this should be opposite the inside of the left heel. Gradually move this point back as you play through the set of clubs until it is opposite the centre of the feet for all the short irons. With the exception of certain low shots, or with awkward lies, you should never bring this point behind centre.

Although the single ball position would seem ideal for the beginner, it can contribute to many of the major faults in the swing. Firstly, when lining up the body, he will find it is very easy to open up the shoulder line from the target. The result is that the swing path will be across the ball.

Another reason the beginner is better off with the second type of position is that he does not have the professional's ability to move the lower half of the body forward during the down swing. The professional can drive the base of his swing arc far enough to the left to strike with a short iron from opposite the left foot.

The professional can also line up to a ball off his front foot, yet still maintain his head position above the centre point of balance. The beginner tends to lean to the left to get his head over the ball and the point of balance goes with it.

Feet and hips The initial positioning of the right foot as it goes in with the club head helps you bring your left side into line at the set-up. With your right leg at a right angle to the ball-to-target line, it is very difficult to bring the left foot and hip beyond it.

It is most likely that the stance will remain slightly 'open', with your feet and hips aiming off to the left, and this will help good swinging. The supporting resistance in the right hip helps control the back swing, while the freedom of space you get with the left hip being slightly 'open' helps the through swing.

If you bring the left side up into perfect line with the right, your stance is 'square' – and this is most acceptable. When your left foot and hip come forward so far that a line drawn along the toes or the hips points

When taking up your stance, first introduce the blade of the club head to the ball and position the right foot (A). For an 'open' stance, bring the left foot up short of 'square' to the target line (B). For a 'square' stance, put your left foot on the target line (C) and for a 'closed' stance beyond the target line (D). The 'closed' stance is the hardest to achieve and it is necessary to draw the right foot back slightly as you place the left foot forward of the ball-to-target line.

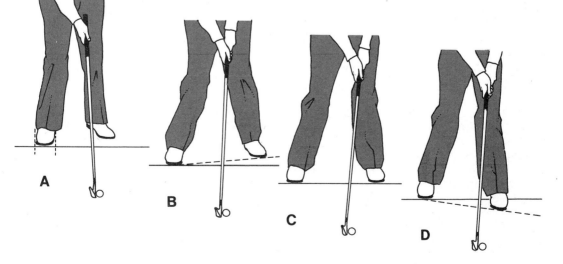

The golf swing

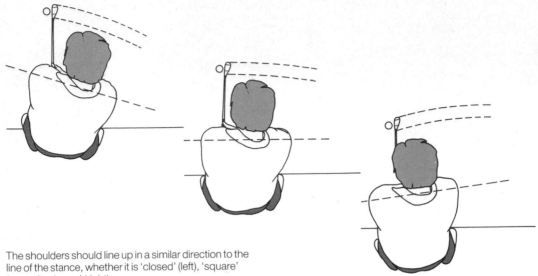

The shoulders should line up in a similar direction to the line of the stance, whether it is 'closed' (left), 'square' (centre) or 'open' (right).

Using the driver, where your reach is longest and you take up a wide stance with the ball forward, you can see the angle of the shoulders at its steepest (left). As you use shorter clubs and your stance narrows with the ball more central, the angle of the shoulders is reduced.

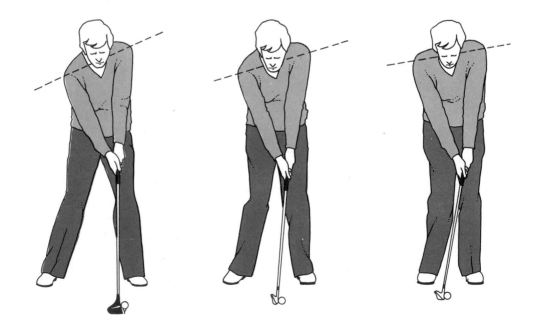

well right of the target, the stance is 'closed'. This type of stance can severely hamper the through swing. To direct the ball to the target, you must then turn the club round the hip using either the hands or the shoulders – and often both.

The shoulders You should go through the process of setting-up very smoothly, ensuring that one part leads easily to the next. This way the left shoulder will come forward into line, bringing the left hand and arm into position. This will be very close to the position the left shoulder, arm and hand need to be in when the club actually strikes the ball and exactly where the hand takes the club.

The shoulders are responsible for determining the direction of the club's swing path, so it is very important they get into line. With a normal shot this is square, with the right and left shoulders parallel to the ball-to-target line.

As your posture rises when longer clubs are used, the left shoulder will be higher than the right one. When using the driver, often to hit a ball that is teed up very high and far forward in the stance, you will find the left side of the body is several inches higher than the right. At the opposite end of the scale, when only a pitching wedge is used and the ball is farther back in the stance, your shoulders are virtually level, although always at a slight angle.

Bringing the shoulders over is the crucial factor in achieving a good posture, for here you must tilt the spine sufficiently to help provide the correct angle of the swing plane. Only after doing this should you flex the legs to complete the posture and introduce mobility into the swing. If you flex the legs first, you will bring the spine into a vertical position and adopt the wrong swing plane.

It is at this point in the set-up that you should apply the grip. By the very nature of the shot, subtle changes will be needed as the club passes through the hands. So you must level the leading edge of the club to the ground to find out what it is going to do. Some foolishly form their grip before setting up. Many club players even take up the grip with the club held in the air, often pointing directly upwards, as though the same grip will suit any type of shot.

The Vardon Grip

Teaming up the hands on the handle of the club is, without doubt, the most important single factor in the game of golf. You should practise this at every possible opportunity, even with a rolled magazine in the office or a poker in the sitting room at home, until it becomes second nature.

Although the position of the hands on the club is still referred to as the Vardon Grip (after its originator Harry Vardon), some slight changes have been made to his original style.

For example, most players now see two knuckle joints on the left hand as they look down, although with the very strong tournament professional only one may be visible. With the Vardon Grip, when swinging was a wristier business, three knuckle joints would normally be seen.

Many of the younger players are choosing to interlock the little finger of the right hand with the forefinger of the left, whereas in the original version it overlapped.

Nevertheless it is still called the Vardon Grip and the benefits are many. Although perfect opposites, the two hands are teamed together in such a way they can still perform entirely different functions, but in complete harmony. At the top of the club, the grip provides perfect support and strength to withstand the leverage of the swing. Below, the right forefinger and thumb have a sensitive enough feel to provide the most delicate of touches.

Left hand In the left hand, three parts are used to take up the grip: the upper palm of the hand, the callous pad and the fingers. As the handle is pressed against the callous pad, the end three fingers curl up from beneath, while the upper pad compresses from above. When pressure is applied by the fingers and the palm, it is felt in the

The golf swing

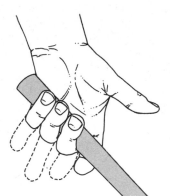

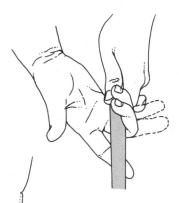

The correct procedure for applying the Vardon Grip. With the back of the hand facing the target and the club head square on the turf, make sure the handle is at the correct angle across the palm of the hand for the length of club you are using (top left). The end fingers press it into the palm. Once you have positioned the left hand, apply the right one (top right). First

position the fingers then close the palm over the left thumb. The V formed between the forefinger and thumb of both hands (centre) should point upwards – just to the right of the player's face. Overlapping the little finger of the right hand (bottom left) or interlocking it (bottom right) is then a matter of choice, although the former is recommended for beginners.

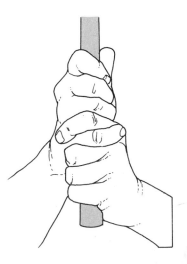

back muscles of the arm, as far up as the elbow. These carry the weight of the club when the leverage is at its greatest, at the top of the back swing, when the change in direction is made, and support it through the point of impact.

This still permits the hand to cock back against the left forearm, which is the primary function of the hand, as it prepares the angle between the arm and club shaft.

Although Gary Player's left wrist has cocked 'square' to his swing plane, the blade of the club lies 'open' from it. This can only happen when a left-hand grip is engaged that shows one knuckle joint or less.

Right hand The right hand is the natural throwing hand and its role in the swing is entirely different from its partner. To ensure that the right hand is supple enough to control the acceleration through the ball

The golf swing

and sensitive enough to have the right feel for the shots, especially those delicate chips and pitches, the club is placed in the fingers and hardly touches the palm at all.

With the back swing, the right hand gives way entirely to the left and the wrist joint hinges back on itself. This does not mean that the right-hand grip is slack, just that the wrist joint is supple.

Much of the work of the right hand, especially in the powerful shots, is involuntary, as the leverage at the start of the down swing forces the wrist even farther back. Then the hand straightens out naturally towards the point of impact. It is in the delicate pitch, bunker and short-iron shots that it comes into its own, where the combination of feel and timing is vital.

'Harry Vardon's hands.' The bronze cast which hangs in the club house of the South Herts Golf Club illustrates the most widely used grip, which has stood the test of time.

Overlap v interlock When it comes to bringing the two hands together in the grip, we actually have one finger too many. The basic question is whether the little finger of the right hand should overlap the forefinger of the left hand or interlock with it, which many younger players prefer.

One type of grip that used to be suggested for children and ladies with small hands begged this question, since it involved keeping the hands separate. This would enable them to wrap their fingers around the handle, and it was felt by doing this they could put more strength into swinging the club.

All this practice achieved was to make the hands work not as a team but independently. The result was that they overswung the club in the back swing and slapped with it at the strike as the right hand overtook the left.

Many years ago, when it was recognized that the closer together the hands were the more consistently they operated, the left thumb was stuck out to the side and did not come in contact with the handle at all.

When a move was made to bring the left thumb back in, to prevent the hands from being prised apart, it was housed on the handle beneath the palm of the right hand. To achieve this, the small finger of the right hand had to be sacrificed and taken off the handle. Over the years, it has both overlapped on to the forefinger of the left hand and interlocked with it.

Until Jack Nicklaus was seen using the interlock, and copied by his many admirers, the overlap that had held its place in the grip stakes since the 1930s was the method to use.

Today the interlock seems to be favoured by younger players. Many claim that, having small hands, which Jack Nicklaus has, they benefit from the interlock. It is certainly better than separating the hands. People with very small or very weak hands should, in any case, have slimmer handles fitted and use lighter clubs.

The advantage of overlapping comes at the set-up stage, when the club is placed in the left hand. It then becomes like a fixture, to which the right hand is added. With the interlocking method this feeling of strength is partly removed since the front section of the left hand has to open up to allow the little finger of the right to fit under the forefinger.

Where the experts who favour interlocking take care to give priority in their right-hand grip to the fingers, many less experienced players, striving to get that little finger more comfortably housed, end up with the handle in the palm of the hand. The positioning of that one finger should be for the benefit of the other nine.

Taking the club to the left hand

If you do not take the club to the left hand when setting up, this will seriously affect the way your hands work in the swing. By bringing the left hand back to the centre of your body and then gripping the club, you will create a kink in the left wrist. Although the position of the hand on the club may feel comfortable, the line of the left arm will point far off to the right of the ball.

Before you can make any preparatory movements between the left arm and the shaft of the club, which is what the back swing is there to do, you must get the club head in front of the line of the arm. From the kinked left wrist position, your first movement will be to operate the hands and wrists independently of the arms and body. This is the surest way to swing with too much hand and wrist action and insufficient shoulder turn to cope with it. Since the body will start its down swing movements well before the hands and club, you will normally end up slicing with the 'open' face of a trailing club head.

As you bring the club towards the left hand, this must maintain its position opposite the left thigh and not try to come back to the centre of the body.

Looking directly down, you should see the knuckle joints of your forefinger and middle finger. This determines that the back of the hand and forearm are, like the leading edge of the club, aiming directly at the target. Neither should move off this line while you are forming the grip.

The fingers must point downwards according to the club being used. With the high left-sided posture required for a driver, where the left hand extends some six inches from the thigh, the fingers should be directed straight downwards. In the case of the short wedge or pitch shot, when the hand nearly touches the thigh, the fingers could point somewhere behind your heels.

Short thumb With each type of shot played, the handle of the club will cross the palm at a different angle. This is known in golf by the length the thumb extends down the club. The more angular line taken by the handle of the driver creates a shorter left thumb, helping the shallower swing plane. Here the line of the arm and shaft are virtually the same.

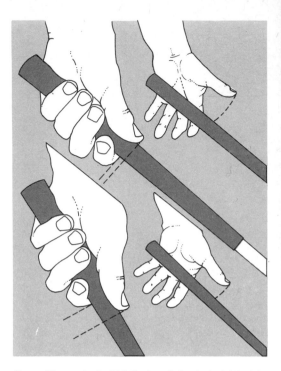

Above: The angle at which the handle lies in the left hand does vary slightly depending on the length of the club being used. When using a wood (top), with the left hand and arm extending out from the body to take up the grip, the angle of the handle through the palm and fingers is at its greatest, with the thumb of the left hand only slightly down the grip from the forefinger. This is the short thumb grip. When using a shorter club (bottom), the left hand is very close to the left thigh and the handle is almost at right angles to the palm and the thumb farther down from the forefinger. This is the long thumb grip.

Left: To achieve a simple, direct swing back from the set-up, the left arm and shaft should be in line, viewed from the front. If you take the left hand back to position it on the handle, the wrist joint will be kinked and the forearm turned and you will roll the club head as you start the back swing.

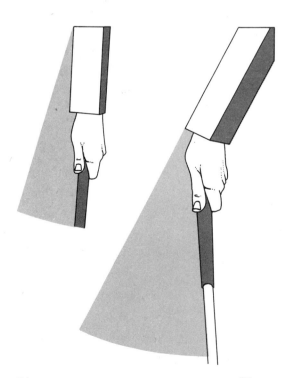

Long thumb With the body well over the shorter length club, however, the handle lies squarer across the palm, so the left thumb extends farther down it. This helps the wrist to move more sharply into the upright swing plane required by that type of club.

You can recognize these variations in the grip of the left hand by where the club leaves the front of the hand.

Take special care when applying the right hand to the handle of the club, since an incorrect grip can take the forearms and shoulders out of line and affect the path and plane of the swing. Ideally the forearms should be parallel to the target line (top). A strong right hand position (bottom left) lowers the right elbow. So the back swing will start inwards too sharply and the swing will be flat. With a weak right hand (bottom right) placed over the top, the right arm can be higher than the left and cause the back swing to be picked upwards and outwards. The swing will then be too upright.

Adding the right hand

When adding the right hand, you must not change the angle of the left-hand hold. Bring the right to the left, with its palm and fingers directly facing the target, and take up the grip with the fingers. You must avoid the temptation to gain a stronger hold by dropping back the hand so you can use the palm. During the swing, the right hand must work as if hinged at the wrist and you will need a strong sense of feel and suppleness to achieve this. You can only get this by gripping with the fingers.

The right hand is affected slightly by the changes in the left-hand hold, but in the case of longer clubs, it must never cause the right forearm to be higher than the left. Only on the short shots, where the swing is steeper, will the right hand sometimes be slightly on top of the left hand, with the wrist arched.

The right forefinger should extend round like a hook to cradle the handle, with the thumb just off to the left to support it. Together these form a hollow under the pad of the thumb, offering a perfect fit for the thumb of the left hand, which is situated right of centre, on top of the handle.

The hand and wrist action

There is an old saying that 'you can only be as good as your hands'. You only have to watch Severiano Ballesteros, who probably has the finest hand action in the game, to agree with this.

The Spaniard insists that his skills were learned when, as a boy caddie near Santander in Northern Spain, he played every type of shot using the only club he pos-

sessed – a No 3 iron. Had his club been a lofted one, he might not have turned out to be the player he is. To make the ball rise with those little pitch shots with only a No 3 iron loft was incredible training.

Creativity is very much part of the role of the hands in golf. For while they prepare the wrist joints and forearms so that together they can transmit power to the swing of the club head, they also guide the club into its swing path and direct it on to its swing plane. Although the basis of the

The golf swing

swing path and swing plane comes from the shoulder line and the posture of the body, the actual search belongs to the hands and fingers.

The shorter the shot being played, the more important the sensitivity and skill of the hand action becomes. The basic full shot can be produced fairly regularly by repetitive practice, going through the routine of set-up, back swing and follow-through. But the cunning little cut-up shot from a tight lie requires more than just habit. You should try to develop a sense of feel and touch that could, when necessary, take the club out of plane, turn its blade off line and then clip the ball off the tightest lie.

In the time it takes for the arms to swing up and the body to turn, in order to make the top of the back swing the hands must have completed their preparation. Fortunately the design of the grip permits both hands to work in perfect harmony, so that they can perform their very different tasks simultaneously.

When the hand action is square in the back swing, as the left wrist cocks the thumb is brought back towards the radius bone of the forearm, the back of the hand remains in line with the forearm, which is approximately the line of the swing plane.

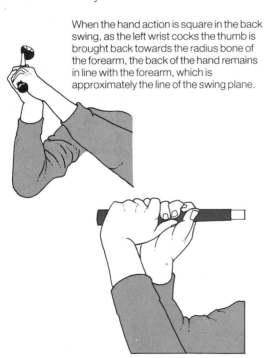

In the back swing, where the left wrist cocks the right wrist must hinge to prepare for its role in accelerating the club head through the point of impact.

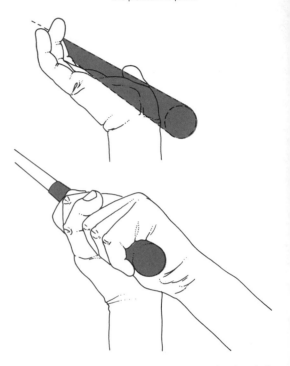

The left wrist cocks back, with the left thumb in line with the radius bone in the arm, rather in the same way it would when holding a hammer. The main difference in golf is that it is working on a swinging arm that is also partially rotating and the ball is being struck sideways.

You must cock the wrist at an angle of not less than 90 degrees. With powerful shots you would increase this, as the leverage of the swing movement makes the angle much more acute. If you fail to achieve sufficient angle in the wrist, the shoulders will play a greater part in the strike of the ball than they should. If you cannot make this angle, then you should examine your method of gripping.

By keeping the finger grip supple, you can hinge the right hand back towards the forearm, just as you would when applaud-

By being conscious of maintaining the swing plane throughout the down swing, you will achieve a smooth and direct line of attack on the ball and a good through swing.

By swinging too upright and out of plane, your shoulders will come into the down swing too early and you will strike across the ball (left). With too flat an arc (right), your swing will be trapped on an 'in-to-out' path and the club face must be rolled to strike the ball. Otherwise the ball will be pushed straight away to the right, with the club head trapped on its 'in-to-out' path.

ing. Although the finger grip itself is fairly firm, the hand is still flexible. So the wrist can take a fairly submissive role, while the hand contributes to supporting and guiding the swing arc.

Into the hit As the body unwinds and the arms swing down turning towards the base of the arc, the left wrist will start to uncock and the right hand and wrist will straighten out. If you straighten the hands too soon, the swing arc will be 'outside' the ball-to-target line. On the other hand, if you fail to straighten them in time, the club will swing well 'inside' and could lock on to an 'in-to-out' path, knocking the ball to the right. This action is commonly called 'blocking a shot'.

Whether you are playing an aggressive drive or a gentle short iron shot, by straightening out at the right moment the hands will be on their original line through the ball. The lateral body movement, which gives the base of the swing a bit more width than you could get with a perfect circle, enables the hands to work on together for several inches through the ball. The movements of the hands should not feel separate.

You do not have to help the right hand, since the right arm will extend beyond the left as it straightens.

The delicate shot If you are playing a tiny lob shot, perhaps in a bunker or from a fluffy rough, when you might take the club upright, out of plane and then bring it down across the ball, you will be very conscious of the right hand. In fact, your left hand can be virtually inactive during such a shot. You will need to flick the blade under the ball and you can only do this with the fingers of the right hand past the left wrist.

The arms and shoulders

In the golf swing the arms and shoulders must work as a perfect team and should be thought of as such. But this does not mean they travel in the same direction, since they are not locked together. Many

The golf swing

professionals move their arms and shoulders at different angles according to physique, the length of the club and the angle at which they prefer to attack the ball.

The teamwork is in their instant reaction when the hands take the club from the ball. Whatever the shot being played, whether it is the half swing of a pitch shot or the full swing of a drive, the arms and shoulders contribute equally. They should reach their position at the top of the back swing at the same instant, turn for home simultaneously and keep perfectly in line to back each other up when the ball is struck. Then they must continue in harmony well into the through swing, at the end of which the arms yield into the follow-through.

The arms With the shoulders well forward and the hands low and close to the left thigh in the set-up for a short iron shot, the arms are dominated by the fairly sharp break of the wrists that occurs when playing with that type of club.

When longer clubs are used and the spine becomes more erect and the hands move up and away from the thigh, the arms play a greater part in the shaping of the swing arc. The farther out they have to reach, when using the driver, for example, the greater the area covered by the back swing before the wrist break begins to show. This is why the swing plane is steeper for short clubs and shallower for longer clubs.

As the arms move into the back swing, they are not there just to widen the swing arc. They also help to boost the power in the strike.

You gain much of the strength from the arms by turning the forearms as you make the swing. This has caused a good deal of confusion over the years, since both right and left forearms turn from the upper arms during the back swing, straighten out at the point of the strike then turn a similar amount in the other direction during the through swing.

The confusion arose when the golf swing changed to having the left wrist cocking true to the arm. How, many asked, would the club face return to the straight position on impact with the ball unless the right hand passed the left and the wristy swing was preserved? In fact, all that is needed to bring the club face back is to return the partially rotating arms to their original position – and that takes place naturally.

To understand this partial rotation, hold your arms out horizontally, with the palms facing each other. Then turn both forearms, from the elbows down, until the back of the left hand and the palm of the right hand face upwards. That is exactly how much they turn when going back. The reverse movement of the forearms takes place during the through swing.

This used to be thought of as rolling the club face from 'open' to 'closed' and it would be if the movement was ever against the turn of the body. But while the forearms do this, the shoulders are also turning – at exactly the same time and by the same amount, keeping the movements together.

Early and late hitting Often the errors of hitting too early or too late are blamed on the hand action. You will hit too early if the club head gets to the ball in front of the hands and arms and consequently you will pull the ball to the left. In contrast, you will hit too late if the club head is left trailing and you will then push the ball off to the right of the target line.

Efforts to cure the first by hitting at the ball later or the second by hitting at it sooner will not work. Early hitting occurs when the forearms start their counter-rotation in the through swing too soon. Late hitting is where, for some reason, the forearms do not turn back and the club head is led, rather than driven, through the

This sequence shows how closely related the body turn is to the hand and arm movements. The shoulder turn begins as soon as the back swing starts and is completed by the time the hands reach the top of the swing. At impact, the shoulders have virtually returned to their set-up position, then the entire trunk of the body turns through into the finish. There are no breaks in this movement, which should be done with some freedom.

The golf swing

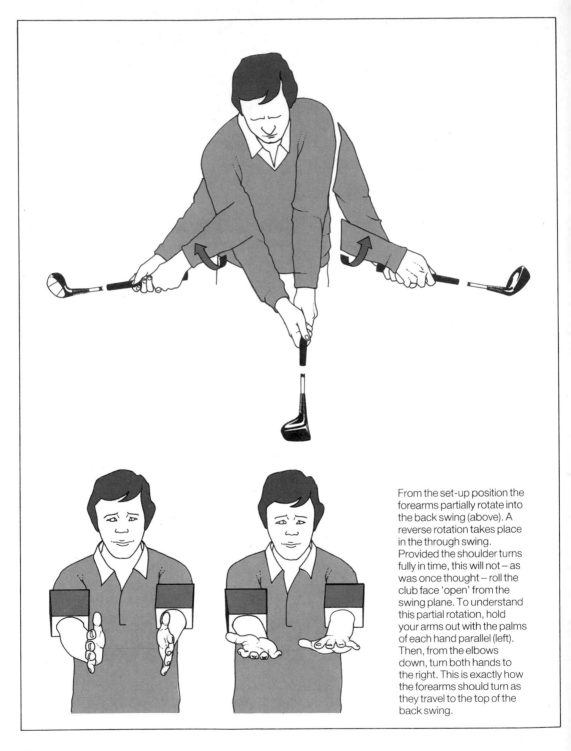

From the set-up position the forearms partially rotate into the back swing (above). A reverse rotation takes place in the through swing. Provided the shoulder turns fully in time, this will not – as was once thought – roll the club face 'open' from the swing plane. To understand this partial rotation, hold your arms out with the palms of each hand parallel (left). Then, from the elbows down, turn both hands to the right. This is exactly how the forearms should turn as they travel to the top of the back swing.

ball at the moment it makes contact with it.

You will see many professionals, between shots, swinging their arms and shoulders into practice back swings, with their empty palms working in parallel to turn the forearms into line, then reversing the process through to the other side. Ballesteros does it all the time. He knows the value of the strong relationship between the arms and the shoulders.

The shoulders Another point that caused confusion was the angle on which the shoulders turn. At one time it was believed that if a line were drawn from the right shoulder across to the left when a player was at the top of his back swing, that line would run to the ball. But it did not, unless the player dropped his left shoulder and as a result ruined the swing plane.

It is now recognized that, like the rest of the swing's first movements, the shoulders are preparing to help return the club through the ball. At that stage the muscles that will pull are those under the upper left arm and around the shoulder blade. At the point of impact, where the right side of the body comes into its element, it is the upper muscles of the right shoulder that will be driving the club through. So the 'preparation' is geared to those two functions.

Take a photograph of any of the best professionals, showing them at the top of their back swing. Draw a line on it from the ball, through the underside of the left shoulder, then across the top of the right. This is the correct turning plane of the shoulders.

It is quite enough for the shoulders to have to turn; they should not have to point downwards, too. It is, therefore, the basis of good posture to have the spine on the correct tilt for each club, so that you can establish the correct turning plane.

The feet and legs

The feet and legs make a huge contribution to the swing. Not only do they generate the proper transfer of weight but they also give

To check the correct angle of plane at the top of the back swing (left), imagine a line from the club to the ball; it should pass across the top of the right shoulder and under the left. Those who try to get the top of both shoulders in line with the ball will cause the shoulders to tilt and consequently misdirect the line of attack.

The golf swing

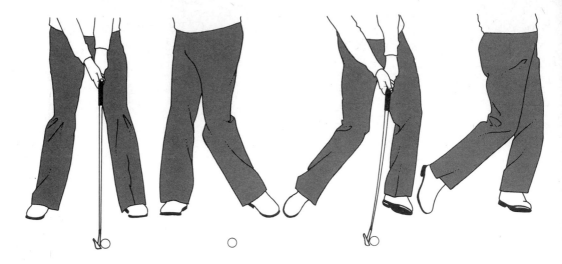

the swing much of its tempo and balance.

As the back swing carries the body weight towards the right side, the right leg takes it, while the left leg prepares for the transfer of weight on the second stage of the swing. What is obvious among the best professionals is how level the knees work during this process and this is one of the keys to a balanced swing.

The natural inward movement of the left knee cap, which helps the body turn, causes the leg to bend and, common sense would suggest, become shorter than the right leg. This in turn should cause the left side of the body to drop. With many amateur players the left side goes down and the right hip socket projects outwards, where it becomes totally immobile and can therefore make no contribution to the down swing. The professionals find a way of keeping the pelvis almost level and they use two distinct methods to do this.

Some lift the left heel off the ground; this, in effect, puts both hips the same distance from the ground. This is the simplest method. With the second method, the right leg has to be kept flexed, even bent, although it is taking the weight during the back swing.

The stabilizing effect you get by having your knees working as near level as pos-

Good foot and leg work plays a major part in the swing, not only to transfer weight correctly to add power to the swing but also to help the balance and tempo. What is noticeable among the best players is how level they keep their knees throughout the movement. Many achieve this by raising the left heel during the back swing.

sible helps to let the hips rotate, first to the right with the back swing, then round to the left with the through swing. This means you need give minimum thought to the hip movement, which in the back swing is governed by the position and flex of the right leg and then guided into the through swing by the initial feeling of a lateral shift of weight.

The through swing Just like the other aspects of the golf swing, the first part of the foot and leg work is preparatory. It should be done in one movement and as smoothly as possible, for any violent move into the back swing will have the effect of jamming the right leg back at the knee joint and will take all the fluidity out of the change of direction.

The greatest contribution is made when you are playing down and through the ball. As the left side starts the down swing, there is only a fraction of a second before the right leg and foot push their way through towards the target.

It is essential that you get the right knee

well into the swing as the club head nears the ball. Apart from adding power to the strike, this enables the hips to continue their rotation. If not, you will make the error that the professionals fear most, when the right shoulder and side of the body ride over the left and turn the club face in on the ball.

You can almost control the flight of the ball by the entry of the right knee into the down swing. The earlier it kicks in and brings the right heel clear of the ground, the higher you will send the ball. Such movement can also help fade or slice shots.

Keeping your right foot on the ground and the right knee back, which is normally done from a very wide stance, helps to create lower-flighted and hook-type shots.

The swing plane

Swing plane describes the angle at which the arc moves round the player. The correct swing plane depends on the physique of the player, the length of club he is using and, in the case of uneven ground, the degree of the slope.

Normally a tall player would be expected to swing on a more upright plane than a shorter player. However, if the taller man chooses to use longer than standard clubs, this would not be the case.

Anyone using a set of clubs with the standard reduction of length between the longest (the driver) and the shortest (the wedge) will swing on a shallower plane with the longest, gradually becoming more upright as he swings each club through the set. Fortunately this does not mean he must learn 13 different angles (the 14th club of the set is the putter). The effect of playing with shorter clubs is to pull the spine forward; this helps the posture adjust the angle of the swing.

Normally out-of-plane swinging is caused by the posture being in an incorrect position. By holding the hands low at the set-up, you will bring the spine too far over and cause the wrist action to operate early in the back swing. By doing this, you will lift the club shaft nearly vertical from the ground and end up swinging with an upright swing plane.

If you stand back on your heels before adopting the normal spine position, so the spine is too erect, you will arch your wrist joints when you set up to the ball. High wrists delay the hand action so much that the shoulders and arms will try to take over the swing. Without the guidance of the hands, however, they create a very flat swing plane.

Swing plane and the modern swing Because the modern swing allows the hand and wrist operation to function without the back of the left hand leaving the line of the left forearm, it is possible for a player to feel that he is swinging on a straight line. Although the golf swing is on a curve, the side elevation of the arc can be seen as a straight line, from its lowest point at the ball and its highest in a direct line through the base of the player's neck, which is approximately the line along which the left arm would be viewed when the top of a back swing has been reached.

In the days when the principle of hitting the ball involved swinging the club head very much from 'open' to 'closed', the back of the left hand would be out of line with the left arm by as much as 45 degrees. This meant that the back swing took two directions, the first inward and the second, when the wrists cocked, upwards. Then there could be no direct line of back swing.

The great players who are recognized as simple swingers are definitely the ones who have found the most direct line, due to their respect for the angle of swing plane. They are usually those whose left wrist cocks against the left forearm without leaving its line. This is known as swinging the club 'square' to the plane.

Some years ago swinging 'square' to the plane was confused by many who tried to swing 'square' to the target line. Not only did it cause a great deal of confusion but it also damaged their swing.

Swing plane and the through swing The

The golf swing

Above left: Tommy Horton, an exponent of hand and wrist golf. His left wrist cocks 'open' from the swing plane.
Above centre: Jack Nicklaus' left wrist cocks 'square' to the swing plane.
Above right: Lee Trevino arches his left wrist so that it cocks 'closed' to the swing plane.

swing plane applies to the entire swing and an awareness of it can protect you as you swing the club through the ball. The spinal angle, which is probably the greatest contributing factor in guiding the swing plane, should be maintained all the way through the swing and still be apparent at the end of the follow-through.

Shorter players, who swing the club on a shallow plane around the body, should finish the follow-through with their hands fairly low. For such people any effort to swing upwards to gain a high finish would be totally wrong. Only those with an upright swing plane should finish high up in the follow-through.

The golf swing

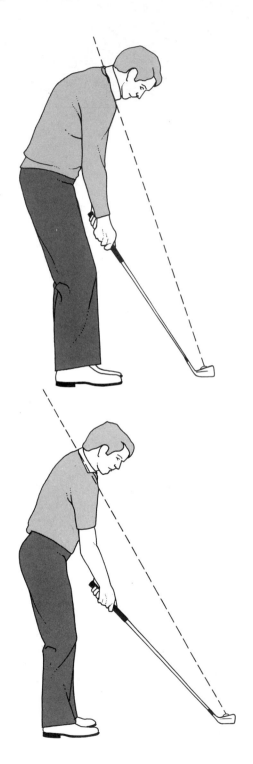

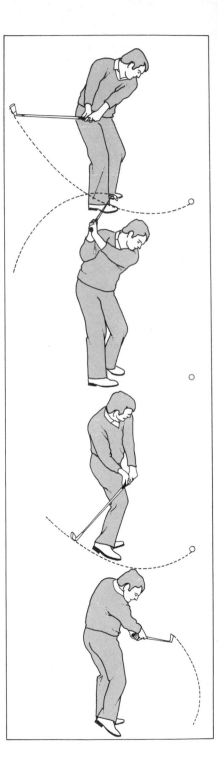

Here you can see the three basic swing paths and how they are determined by the line of the shoulders, which in turn are affected by the position of the ball in the stance. The swing paths are (from left to right) 'in-to-out', 'direct' and 'out-to-in'.

Swing path

Many references are made to the direction in which the club head moves in terms of its swing path. When the club starts its back swing and is turned quickly inwards, this is often called an 'in-to-out' swing path. When the club is picked up too sharply on the back swing, this is called an 'out-to-in' swing path. Unless these directions are repeated as the club head travels down and through the ball, they are merely directions of back swing. And the directions do not necessarily have to be repeated. When you commit such a fault, you are likely to end up with a loop, which can

A tall player using an iron with the correctly set club head will swing in an upright plane (top left). A shorter player, also with the correct club, will use a shallower swing plane. The sequence on the right shows the old swing, before the value of swing plane was really understood. The first movement took the club inwards to hip height. The second, with the wrists cocking into an 'open' position, brought the club upwards. So that the shoulders did not take over from the weakened wrists in the down swing, the arc dropped down behind the body. Finally, for the club face to be 'square' at impact it had to be rolled through the ball. This meant four directions – and four movements. With the modern swing, the amount has been halved.

create the very opposite down swing.

The swing path is the direction in which the club head travels as it approaches the ball in the down swing, then the direction it continues on immediately after the strike in the through swing.

To understand the reference made to the swing path, you must imagine the ball-to-target line. Then the ground between the line and the player would be called 'inside' the line and that beyond the line 'outside'.

When the expert decides a certain swing path is required, for example to play a curve shot, he will guide the base of his swing from one side through the ball to the other side. To do so he will definitely alter his shoulder line accordingly, prior to swinging, since the shoulders direct the swing path.

To close the shoulders in order to guide an 'in-to-out' swing path, he will have the ball farther back in the stance. To produce an 'out-to-in' swing path, he will play the ball from the forward position so that he can open the shoulders.

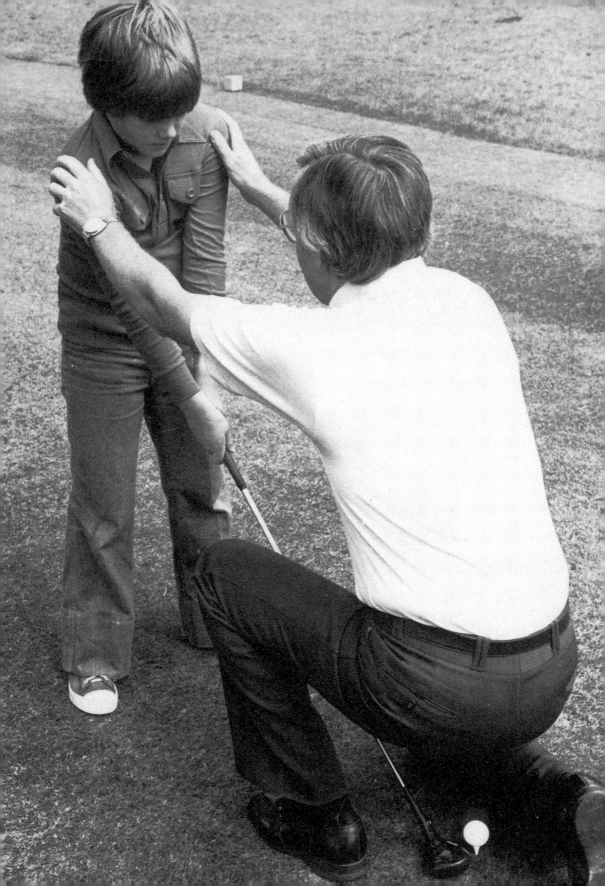

Developing a basic swing

Ideally you should start to learn golf under the supervision of a teaching professional or, failing that, someone who has a good style and has played for many years. It should certainly be a player who knows the pitfalls and how to emphasize the features that really matter.

Until you get into the habit, many of the initial positions feel uncomfortable, particularly the grip. This has the unfortunate combination of being both the most important part of the golfer's technique and yet the most awkward part to develop.

Although the basic sequence of set-up, back swing and through swing is one that the novice adopts within the first few months of playing, the starting sequence is even more basic. To allow for a margin of error you should start with a club that has a fair amount of loft, say a No 8 iron. Do not use anything more lofted, since shorter shafts tend to pull the shoulders too far over, leading to a chopping action.

Stage one
When you are developing your basic swing technique, there is a list of priorities that you should follow religiously, step by step. The procedure is as follows:
- positioning the ball
- lining up stance and body
- applying the grip
- the back swing
- the through swing

Positioning the ball As a beginner, you should start playing shots with the ball directly opposite the centre of your stance. When practising, make sure you choose a good lie for the ball. If the ground is hard, then use a short tee peg, and do not scoop the ball or you will spoil your swing.

Lining up stance and body You must

always have a target to aim at, preferably one that is completely out of range. While it is essential to hit towards something, even at this stage, distance is not so important.

It is a good idea to place a club on the ground to represent the ball-to-target line, just beyond the ball and pointing towards the target. You must get used to standing square-on to this. Your toes, knees, hips, shoulders and, most important, forearms should all be parallel to this line. At the same time learn to look towards the target by turning only your head and neck. If you twist your body while looking for the target, you will turn your shoulder line to the left and quite likely leave it there.

To start with you will shuffle back and

Even at this young age, certain disciplines are still necessary. Here Alex explains to his younger son David the importance of a good set-up.

To get used to lining up 'square' to the ball-to-target line, lay another club on the grass along this line when you are practising your swing technique.

Developing a basic swing

forth quite a lot to find the correct distance from the ball, but practice will take care of this. It is important that you get used to leaning the spine slightly forward to take the club towards the ball. Do not sit back on your heels and bend your legs.

Applying the grip Learn the Vardon Grip from the outset. Whatever grip you use at first you will feel uncomfortable, so it might as well be the correct one. It is most unlikely that a complete novice would find the ideal hold straightaway, but there are certain aspects of the grip you must master before you perfect the right technique.

Make sure the hands take up the grip slightly forward of, and not directly above, the ball. This will help you to adopt the correct posture because it immediately raises the line of the left shoulder above the right. It also provides one of the basic lessons about swinging – to swing forward through the ball and not flick under it.

You can practise the next point without a club. Point the fingers of both hands directly downwards with the right a bit closer to the ground because of the angle of the shoulder line. Then bring the palms, which should be parallel, together so that the thumb of the left hand fits perfectly under the thumb pad of the right, with its nail half-way down into the palm.

Having followed this simple instruction and determined that nothing will turn the hands out of their parallel position or split them apart, very little can go wrong when you put your hands on the handle.

The next movement, which quite naturally follows the change of the shoulder level, is to let the hands turn slightly to the right so that you can see at least two full knuckle joints of the left hand. In doing this, you must make sure that the leading

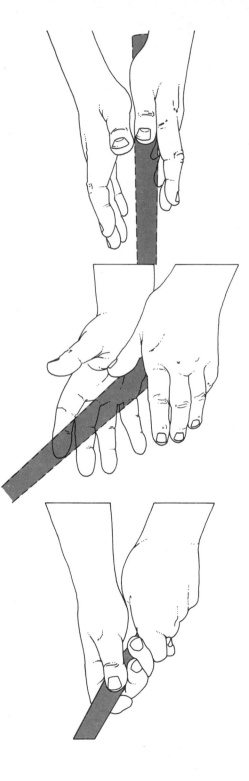

This is a simple method of establishing the right relationship of the hands on the handle of the club. Hold the palms parallel, then fit the left thumb beneath the pad of the right thumb so that it comes about halfway down the hand. This enables the fingers to take up a good position on the handle and the hands can then work together through the swing.

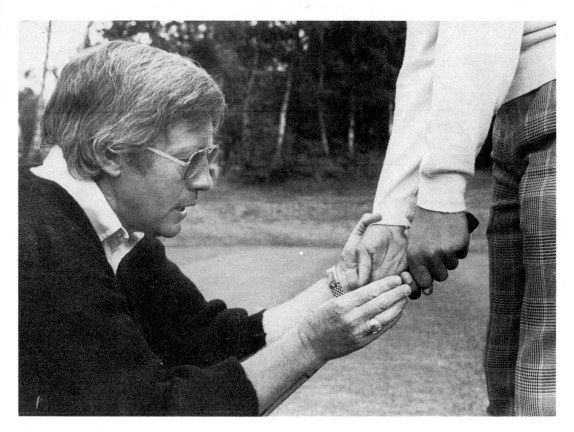

The most important single factor in golf is the grip. Here Alex shows a pupil the importance of gripping with the fingers of the right hand rather than the palm.

edge of the club head remains square-on.

There is no harm initially in exposing three knuckle joints, although in time your hands will turn back slightly, since it is essential to create a part-rotation of the forearms to the right. The benefit you will gain from this adjustment is that you can instantly relate shoulder turn with back swing movement. If you fail to do this, you will definitely strike the ball using only a hand and wrist action.

The top of the handle should fit snugly, low into the palm of the left hand. Beginners tend to let it slip into the centre of the hand. Then just the fingers of the right hand take up their hold, with the forefinger and thumb adopting a pincer-like squeeze. Finally the little finger of the right hand overlaps on to the forefinger of the left.

The back swing Bearing in mind that this part of the swing is a movement in prep-aration for subsequent swing actions, you must understand what the swing should and should not achieve. It is not a movement designed to lift the ball upwards; the person who decides that is the clubmaker, who put the loft angle on the club face originally. The purpose is to strike the ball towards the target with an uninterrupted movement.

Initially you should practise teaming up the hands, arms and shoulders to move the club first to the right then through to the left, since at this stage you should only be concentrating on the base of the arc.

Because you have deliberately twisted the left hand and forearm to show three knuckles, the direction the club travels

Developing a basic swing

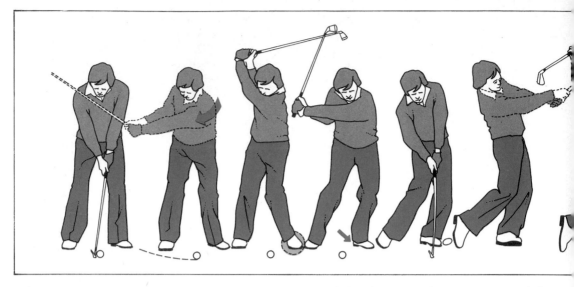

back will automatically be slightly inside the ball-to-target line. This should instantly prompt the shoulders to start their turn and cause a transfer of weight, which will pull on the left leg. As a result, your left heel will lift off the ground. Replacing this heel on the ground is a very good introduction to the through swing movement.

When you first attempt the swing, do not bring the club back more than hip-high. After you have played a few good shots, you will increase this automatically, through a combination of enthusiasm and pace of swing. Provided you have adopted a good grip, your wrist action will be self-building, although you may need to correct it later. Make sure that at no point in the back swing are your wrists rigid.

The through swing At this stage you should not think about down swing. All your concentration must be directed at getting the body weight transferred to the left foot and hip, and the arms and club through towards the target.

Natural instinct is at its strongest here and the young swing at its most vulnerable. The tendency is to stay back, with the body weight on the right foot, and attempt to flick the club head through under the ball with the hands and wrists.

Work hard at transferring your weight into the left hip as the initial movement. This way your hands, with the advantage of being lined up slightly ahead of the ball, will help swing the club head through the ball, rather than to it.

Once you have reached the follow-through position, hold it until the ball lands. Like the back swing, it should not be much more than hip-high initially, with the club head pointing towards the target.

When you can hit the ball away successfully, the length of the swing will start to grow. It is, however, an advantage to feel that the back swing is never more than threequarter length. This will help you to mould the eventual shape of the swing from the preparation stage to the completion of the follow-through.

Stage two

The clubs in the set fall into groups, and you can progress up through these once you have mastered the basic swinging technique. The clubs, as already mentioned, are grouped as follows:

Short irons – Sand iron, pitching wedge, No 9, No 8

Middle irons – No 7, No 6, No 5

Long irons – No 4, No 3

Once you have developed the basic movements of the swing (the dotted line shows their fullest extent), you can increase the arc gradually until you achieve a full swing.

Fairway woods – No 5, No 4, No 3
Driver

There are others you can add to a set, but these are not necessary or suitable for the average player. You need to be a very experienced player to use the long No 1 and No 2 irons successfully. There is also a No 2 wood, but this is rarely made today and would, for shots from the turf, only be of use to an expert.

Ball position Having started with one of the short irons, you will need to make one or two alterations as you progress up the set. The first involves the position of the ball. This should be progressively forward in the stance from its central position for the short iron until it is opposite the inside of the left heel when you are using the

Top right: The best way to measure the correct width of stance is from the length of your normal walking stride, from front heel to back toes. You should narrow the stance as you use shorter clubs and the swing is reduced.
Right: While the lie of each club is designed so that the top of the handle is always approximately at the same height from the ground, you must always alter the position of your hands to encourage the different swing planes required. Starting at about 5cm (2in) with the shortest irons, you should increase the gap between the handle and the left thigh to about 15cm (6in) with the driver. By doing this, your spine will be more upright and the swing plane shallower.

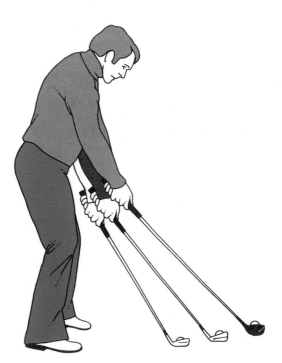

driver. It is, however, advisable to use a fairway wood when you begin playing tee shots until you have gained in confidence. **Width of stance and distance from the ball** You will need the widest stance – approximately shoulder width – when playing with the driver. This is equivalent to the distance between the toe and heel in a normal stride. Working down from the driver, you need to reduce the width of the stance to about two-thirds the maximum when playing with a short iron.

You have been given a good guide for judging the correct distance from the ball earlier in the book. Another aid, when playing with short irons, is to take up the left hand about 8cm (3in) from the left thigh. Here again, you need to increase this gap gradually through the clubs until it is some 15cm (or 6in) with the driver.

This is a good method of setting the distance, since it trains the player always to have the left hand forward in line with the left thigh. So many players bring the hands back to the centre of the body and consequently spoil their left-wrist position.

Developing a full swing

Once you have practised the basics of hitting the ball forward, using the loft of the club, start to develop a full swing.

You must introduce the hand and wrist action very early on, since once you grow confident of lofting the ball your enthusiasm will lengthen the swing – both back and through. Unless you introduce the correct hand action, you will bend the elbows.

Swing plane

Without having a clear mental picture of how the plane of the swing operates

This is an excellent way of practising the swing plane without a club. By pointing the left forefinger at the ball and swinging the right arm diagonally opposite the left arm, you will get a good feel of the correct swing plane. By varying the aim of the left forefinger, you will see how the angle of swing plane alters for different clubs. Swinging both arms back and forth helps footwork and tempo.

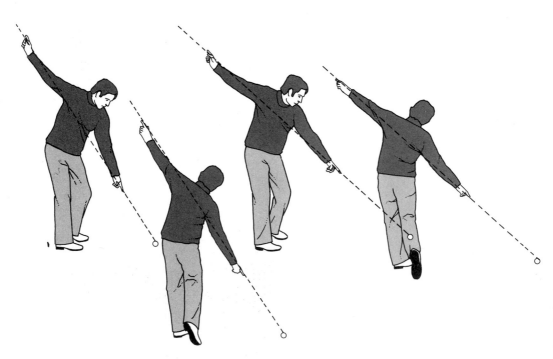

If the turn of your shoulders fails to match up with the turn of the arms and the cock of the wrists, then you will complete the arm and wrist movements without achieving any width in the swing arc. By continuing the swing, the left arm will bend.

around your body, it is extremely likely that with your initial efforts to cock the wrists you will change the direction and angle of the swing arc in such a way that inconsistencies will creep in.

One good exercise you can use to understand the swing plane can be practised without a club. Stand opposite a ball as though to use a middle iron and point the forefingers of both hands at it, making sure your spine is correctly tilted. Then swing the right arm upwards behind your body so that it points diagonally opposite the left, which you must keep aimed at the ball. By doing this you will set an angle of swing very similar to that required when playing the shot.

The character of the strike will change as the clubs you use get longer. From the set-up with the lofted iron (bottom), where the top of the club is very close to the left thigh and the shoulders are well forward, the swing plane is fairly upright. As you use longer clubs and reach farther for the ball, you raise the angle of the spine and the swing plane gets shallower and this is shown here through the back swing and into the through swing.

Developing a basic swing

Then swing the right arm back so that the forefinger points at the ball and at the same time swing the left arm upwards in the same plane. This will establish the angle of the through swing.

Swinging your arms backwards and forwards in this way is excellent training for the swing plane and also helps you to practise transferring your weight correctly from one foot to the other.

Follow up this exercise by standing a few inches farther from the ball, so that the angle of your outstretched arms becomes shallower. The effect of this will be to flatten the swing plane, just as you would when using the longer wooden clubs. From this move you can understand how the angle of the spine largely dictates the swing plane.

If the ball is positioned more forward in the stance, you must allow the left shoulder to rise slightly higher than the right, although this will mean flexing the right side and loosening the right elbow. If you try to keep the shoulders level, the right arm will rise higher than the left and affect the correct swing plane and path.

Wrist action The reason for cocking the left wrist and hingeing the right in the back swing is to produce sufficient angle between the left arm and the shaft to create acceleration through the swing.

When using a short iron, you will find the hand movement starts fairly early in the back swing. Many beginners worry about starting their hand and wrist action in case it picks the club up sharply. This only happens if you ignore the two major features of the swing – keeping to the swing plane angle and completing the shoulder turn. Without these, it would not matter whether your hands started early or late, since there would be no swing.

By practising the swing, you will develop the right timing for the hand and wrist action to blend in with the body turn and footwork. With a fuller back swing you can strike the ball cleanly and for a considerable distance.

When you can master the point at which the hands and wrists, coming down on the same swing plane, straighten up and release the club head into the strike, then you know your progress will be continuous.

Benefiting from the rhythm and movement of the preparation, the through swing will become the follow-through, where the body turns fully into the finish. This is where the swing plane exercises prove their worth, as the right foot comes up on to the toe of the shoe to allow your entire body to face the flag.

You must still maintain the follow-through pose until the ball lands. While you are waiting for this, check if the angle of the spine is the same as at the set-up and at the top of the back swing.

How longer clubs affect the swing

It is a mistake to spend too much time with short clubs. Even if you occasionally mishit when using the longer clubs, you should not rush back to the security of the No 8 iron. Because of the large margin for error with the basic learning club, faults could be escaping your notice.

With the hands and wrists set lower for the short irons, the wrist break into the back swing is earlier and this contributes to the narrower swing arc and steeper attack on the ball. With the longer clubs the hands extend farther from the body and the spinal angle straightens, resulting in a wider swing arc and less wrist movement.

As you progress through the groups of clubs, you will find each becomes more exacting. So there should be no rush to use the driver, for example, since a No 3 wood will give more encouraging results. The shafts get longer and the faces have less loft; and there is the temptation to hit the ball harder to send it farther. If you force the shot, you will narrow the arc of the down swing, rotate the arms too soon and smother shots with less lofted clubs.

As you work through the set of clubs and adjust the position of the ball slightly to the left accordingly, you must increase the distance you stand from the ball. At the same time, straighten the spine slightly. This has the effect of raising the left shoulder a little higher than the right.

If you do not make this adjustment, you will encourage one of the most common and damaging faults in golf. If you let the right forearm rise above the line of the left, this automatically confuses the starting direction of the back swing. The line of your arms will then direct the club outwards from the ball-to-target line, rather than slightly inwards, where it should be.

As a beginner, when you use the longer clubs such as the woods, it is sound policy to lower your right elbow slightly when setting up, so that a line across the forearms would point to the right of the target. This will definitely be a help when setting the shallower swing plane for longer clubs.

Hand and wrist action When using short irons, your hand and wrist action starts at almost the same instant as the swing. But with longer clubs, you will find as a beginner it is helpful to get the feeling of a wider back swing. An instant hand and wrist action, even with the correct swing plane, tends to restrict the body turn and use of the legs. Equally, with the fullness of the arc required with a long club, such as a driver, there is more time and space for the hands to get into action.

With the narrower and more upright movement involved in short-iron shots you are aware of the considerable hand and wrist action. As the length of the club shaft increases and the arc of swing flattens, the impression of sweeping takes over.

Beginners often worry that the wider arc of the club will cause a swaying motion, with the head going first to the right then back to the left. A slight sway never harmed any beginner and is certainly preferable to leaning the body weight against the direction of the swing, which is what often otherwise happens.

The best way to learn how to turn with the minimum of lateral movement in either direction is to practise the swing plane exercise using the pointed fingers.

Faults in the swing

There are many aspects of the basic swing that can go wrong, and the faults may have developed right from the start or crept in because you have neglected to have your technique checked by the club professional or a suitably qualified player.

This chapter examines many of these faults, not by picking them out at random but by taking the swing from its set-up stage and progressing through its movement. Any good teacher will admit that most of the identification and cure of faults begins and ends at the set-up, before a single muscle is moved.

Aiming the club

A common failing is to start the set-up by taking up the stance and grip then having a look at the target in order to aim the club head, instead of the reverse. If the body alignment is off, and it often is, you will probably turn the club head as a remedy, rather than using it as a guide.

In whichever direction you turn it, this will affect the swing path and the arc will work separately from the body line.

The ball position

If the feet are incorrectly placed, so the ball is out of position in relation to the stance, this will have a tremendous effect on the swing. Should the ball be too far forward, even though the feet are true to the target line, the shoulders will be turned 'open'.

Unlike the deliberate slice shot, where both stance and shoulders are turned 'open', here it is done just from the waist up. The body cannot turn properly into the back swing so the club swings back in an upright arc, from where it can develop little power, and so travels back across the ball.

With the ball too far back, the shoulder

Even tournament winning professionals can play bad shots. Here Carl Mason looks anxiously to see what has happened to a mishit ball.

line is 'closed' from the target. As a result, you will swing the club back on a very tight inward arc around the body. This is called a flat swing and it can do one of two things. Provided the swing stays short, the strike will be very much from 'in-to-out', which will push the ball to the right unless the club face is turned inwards, in which case it will hook the ball.

With a longer swing the hands, realizing that the arc is going into too flat a position for them to operate correctly, change the direction of the club upwards. That means the back swing has two directions, and if these cannot be reversed in the down swing, the club head will strike the ball from a very steep angle.

The grip

Without doubt the most important single factor in playing consistent golf is the grip. You should place the hands on the handle, with the palms parallel so that they remain happily together in the grip.

Weak left hand If the left hand is to the left of the handle, it will turn the left arm out of line and this will be too weak to support the back swing. This is known as the 'weak' position.

The immediate action of the left arm, as the back swing starts, is to rotate to the right to gain strength. The club face immediately turns 'open' and slices the ball, since it will probably remain that way as the strengthened left arm pulls through.

Strong left hand When the left hand is over the handle, with three or four knuckle joints showing, it has the opposite effect on the structure of the left arm. It turns the face inwards on impact, often violently, according to the number of knuckles showing.

Weak right hand When the right hand pushes well over the top of the grip, which can happen when the left hand is also weak, it operates with the left and rolls the club face 'open'.

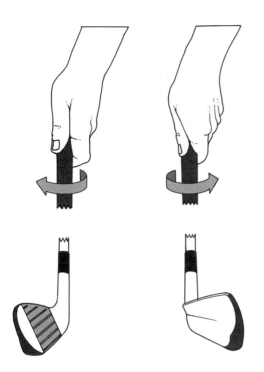

With a weak left-hand grip (left) you will not have enough strength in the hands to start the swing. You will then have to exaggerate the rotation of the left forearm and this in turn will roll the club face 'open'. If you fail to return the club face to the 'square' position, you will slice the ball. With a strong grip (right), where the hand is set so that more of the knuckle joints than normal are showing, the forearm can turn too much and too soon into the strike. When the blade of the club returns, the turning effect caused will result in hook spin on the ball.

If, however, the left hand is in a good position and the right climbs on top, the actual swing path of the club is seriously affected. The right wrist will rise above the left and cause the swing path to be 'out-to-in'. Very soon the shoulder line will alter to match as the right shoulder rises above the left shoulder.

Strong right hand This is the inexperienced player's favourite grip. Self-taught players always use their strongest hand to grip the club in the palm and curl the fingers up around the handle. The right forearm is turned off to the right and can

hardly wait to turn back at the point of impact on the ball.

Knowledgeable players realize that the right hand should work on a hinge basis, not on a turn, and to effect this the club must be taken in the fingers. By gripping with the fingers, the player gets more feel and accuracy in the shot, without any loss of power.

The 'weak' version of either hand is described as a slicer's grip, because with either the club face is turned 'open'. The 'strong' version of either hand will definitely turn the club face inwards.

The worst pairing is a 'weak' left and a 'strong' right. This provides such inconsistent results that self-diagnosis is almost impossible because of the variety of directions in which the ball may fly. A pull to the left is the most common result.

Stance and shoulder alignment

If the left shoulder and left foot fail to come into line, ensuring they are 'open' and to

You will weaken the right hand if you place it too far over the top (left). The pressure applied at the set-up (in the direction of the arrow) will reverse into the back swing and cause the club face to roll 'open'. It is likely to remain in that position through the strike and cause slice spin. The strong right hand (right) is favoured by most beginners because it gives the grip a feeling of strength. But because it is too far out of parallel with the left hand (with the pressure in the direction of the arrow) it reverses during the strike and turns the club face inwards, causing hook spin.

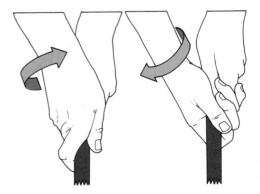

Standing the wrong distance from the ball will have a very damaging effect on the posture, particularly on the angle of the spine on which the swing plane depends. If you reach too far, you will pull the body forward and steepen your swing. If you stand too close, you will be forced back on to your heels, bringing the spine nearly vertical and flattening the swing plane.

the left of the target, the swing path of the club will be directed across the ball from 'out-to-in'.

As described in the section on slicing, should an attempt be made to keep the club face true to the real target, then it will be drawn across the ball and a slice shot will result. If, on the other hand, the player's sense of aim is out, like his body alignment, the ball will fly on a straight course left of the target.

Ciosed The setting-up procedure described in this book should prevent you from lining up with your stance and shoulders in the 'closed' position, which would result in aiming off to the right. If they are lined up 'closed', then the swing path will be 'in-to-out'.

If you do nothing to alter the club face from the swing path, the ball will fly straight to the right. Normally, however, those players with a 'closed' stance have a habit of turning the club head on impact. In fact, those who have always used a strong right hand, which turns the club in, automatically finish with a 'closed' line-up as a means of making two wrongs into a right. It works occasionally, but you will find it has little future.

Poor posture

The main faults in the posture are either standing too far from the ball or standing too close to it.

Too far Holding your head centrally is important for consistent swinging. If you have to reach for the ball, your head is lowered and therefore influenced by the shoulder movements. Your body weight is also moved so far forward that the legs have to strain to maintain the balance and are unable to contribute to the movement

of the swing, for which they are essential. Hitting the ball will then be left entirely to the hands and wrists, working on a very upright swing plane.

Too close Although less damaging than standing too far from the ball, this position forces you back on your heels to provide room to swing at the ball. By sitting back on the shot, you bring the spine towards the vertical, and this can have a disastrous effect on the swing plane. The ball is very difficult to hit from a plane that has been flattened by poor posture.

Other swing faults

The majority of faults happen when you set up to the ball and these have been listed as they occur. There are others, however, that can occur after you have set up correctly.

Swaying

Lady golfers believe that, because of their figure, they are prone to lateral sway in the back swing and feel obliged to swing away until their arms are clear. This is nonsense, for if they were to incorporate a direct turn of the shoulders the moment they started the back swing, they would experience no physical handicap at all.

Among the players who sway are those who make the back swing in two separate movements. First they swing wide away to the right; then, when the club has reached its full extent, they cock the wrists to take the club upwards. The trouble tends to be that in reaching to their full extent they have committed the sway they want to prevent.

In a one-movement back swing, the hands and wrists prepare simultaneously as the arms swing away, so there is no feeling of extending away from the ball.

Letting go at the top

This is often put down to having weak hands, but there are two other more likely causes. The first is when, as in swaying, a tremendous extension is built into the back swing which effectively completes the

shoulder turn and stretches the arms to the full. It is then left to the hands and wrists to get the club into the correct hitting position. The club goes up and over and the leverage of the swing has to be controlled entirely by the end fingers of the left hand, which cannot cope.

The second, and more common, cause is a poor grip, where a 'weak' left hand allows the club to roll into the back swing. As the club head rolls 'open', it forces the handle against the fingers of the left hand, which are gripping and directing the club, until they give way.

Hitting early

Even top players worry about this fault which occurs because the lower half of the body has become immobile while going through and the hands have worked the club head through early to get the ball away. The shoulders go over the hips and the player ends up leaning into the finish of the swing.

It is rare among those players who emphasize the leading of the down swing with a lateral movement of the left hip. This delays the hands and shoulders and prevents them from going in early.

You get immobility in the lower half of the body when, sometimes by accident but often by design, the left foot is kept flat on the ground during the back swing. Unless you are extremely supple, this can make the lower half so static that there is little to motivate the start of the down swing.

Falling back

It would seem quite natural that hitting a golf ball with a swing that travels from the player's right to his left would bring his body weight with it, just as it does when a child throws a stone. Instead, many finish stranded back on the right foot, no matter how much they try to lean to the left.

So anxious are these players to lean on to the left leg that they do this as they swing back. The very pressure they put into the muscles above the left knee provides the

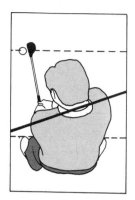

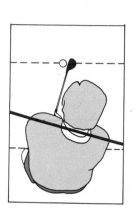

When the shoulders are set up 'closed' from the target line (right), you will be able to use a very full turn in the back swing. But the swing path will be 'in-to-out' through the ball.

When the shoulders are set up 'open' to the target line (left), you will be limiting the amount of turn available in the back swing and the club is likely to travel 'out-to-in' through the ball.

If the shoulders fail to complete their required 90-degree turn from the target line, the club cannot get into line (below left) and will point off to the left of the target – known as being 'laid off'.

If the shaft of the club lies across the target line at the top of the back swing, this is because the shoulders have turned too far (below right) or the left wrist has collapsed – or both. In the case of the latter, the right elbow rises sharply.

recoil that throws their body weight up and off to the right. Weight must be transferred in the direction of the swinging club, back and forth.

Club laid off

This describes the position at the top of the back swing where the shaft of the club, instead of lying parallel to the ball-to-target line, aims off to a point well to the left.

When this is pointed out, the player often attempts to adjust his wrist position to get his club to point correctly. This is using two wrongs to make a right, for the real cause is that the shoulders have not turned their required minimum of 90 degrees from the ball-to-target line.

There are many reasons for the shoulders not turning enough, but the first place to look is in the set-up positions. A ball too far forward in the stance can cause the shoulder line to be turned 'open' and the angle the shoulders are off at the start may be exactly the amount lacking when the top of the back swing is reached.

Players whose waistlines do not enable them to turn easily and who have not compensated by geting a bit of left-heel lift to ease the situation will never turn their shoulders the minimum amount required.

Club across the line

This fault occurs at the top of the back swing, when the club shaft points away to the right – the opposite of laid-off. It can prove a little more complex to detect, although it may be traced to the set-up, probably when a ball is played from a point far back opposite the stance, with the shoulders turned 'closed'. A back swing that is too inward will cause the shoulders to turn more and this can take the club out of line. Those who hook the ball tend to have more shoulder movement.

By letting the head turn so that the eyes can follow the flight of the ball, your swing plane can continue intact into the through swing. If you keep your head down and rigid, you may well buckle your follow-through.

However, there is a more serious cause, and that is when the left wrist has hinged too far 'open' from the swing plane and is nearing a state of collapse. The right elbow lifts out of position as it senses the weakness of the left wrist and threatens both the swing path and the swing plane.

Swinging out of plane

The correct swing plane should be determined by the physique of the player and the length of the club in use, although it will also be affected by the slope of the ground. Over the years many players have ignored the accepted orthodox methods and have chosen different types of swing plane instead.

Tom Kite and Ben Crenshaw are two American professionals who, although fairly short in stature, use very upright swings. Yet the up-and-coming Bobby Clampett, who is taller, prefers a flatter arc. They are among the players who differ, yet who use their choice extremely well. At club level, however, the angle of swing is

not always chosen out of preference but out of neglect and this can cause bad shots.

By swinging on too flat a plane, you bring the club head towards the ball from an exaggerated 'in-to-out' swing path. If you apply any forward aggression using the transfer of weight, you will trap the club head on that path and may push the ball to the right. Only by hesitating and giving time for the club head to square up can you hit shots straight.

If your swing is too upright, this will result in insufficient shoulder turn and the club is likely to be swung down across the ball on an 'out-to-in' swing path. As a result, your woods will slice the ball and your shorter irons pull it to the left.

Incidentally, Kite and Crenshaw, although upright, have very full shoulder turns which they acquire by lifting the left heel high off the ground as they move to the top of the back swing.

Head up

No golf book would be complete without a mention of 'head up', although relatively little is heard of this expression nowadays.

In the years gone by, the principle of hitting the ball was based on the club head starting the down swing 'open' and snapping 'closed' just at the right moment. The expression 'hitting up against the left side' described how the player, by being firm from the outside of the left ankle all the way up that side as far as the neck, created a barrier past which the accelerating club head would 'close'.

With such a technique, the slightest raising of the eyes soon undermined the braced left side, so players were trained to look directly down, often for several seconds, after the ball had gone.

Today, with the body turning, players work the club head through the ball more than at it. Keeping the head down can, therefore, restrict the progress of the swing unnecessarily. So the eyes are now encouraged to watch the ball. Nevertheless some barrier, or central resistance, is required and this is achieved in two ways. The head, although turning, still maintains its original vertical position and the spine holds its angle to preserve the angle of swing plane.

The best players will often turn their head very soon after the strike, yet their position is still held secure. This is how they gain the full follow-through that is seldom seen with a beginner, whose head is jammed down.

The perfect swing

The perfect golf swing is one that delivers the strongest and most consistently accurate blow, with every club in the set, into the back of the ball. This drives the ball directly forward towards the target, with no other spin than the back spin created by the loft of the club being used. Although this is the type of swing all golfers should search for, a near miss will provide a very satisfactory result.

There are two parts to the perfect swing. One gives the sense of feel and timing while the other provides a regular arc.

The first part is mainly the development of hand and wrist action, which provides the angle between club and arms needed to gain the acceleration of the club head through the ball. There is also a very strong relationship between the hands and wrists and the feet and ankles, for the latter also contribute to the feel, timing and tempo.

Part two is the turning movement, first one way then the other, of the arms, shoulders and body, centralized and assisted by the work of the feet, legs and hips. These provide the angled curve known as the swing plane, which is determined by the club being used and the technique suited to the physical capability of the player.

It is this second stage that allows scope for creative hand movement, and without it there can be no consistent performance.

Individual swings

There are several ways of swinging a golf club, most of which are used successfully by players at all levels. In many cases players have been taught to swing in a certain way, while others have adapted a swing that, although apparently less elegant in design, works extremely well even under pressure.

When Lee Trevino first appeared on the scene, his swing came in for much criticism. Yet after his meteoric rise to fame, he was accepted as one of the all-time great players and probably the finest-ever controller of the flight of a ball.

Ireland has a history of producing players with unorthodox swings. Jimmy Bruen, one of the best amateurs of his time, swung the club in a huge flailing loop, up and out, then down and in. Fred Daly, winner of the British Open championship in 1947, had a built-in sway that would be frowned upon today.

Harry Bradshaw, whose right hand almost engulfed his left as he gripped the club, came very near to winning the British Open at Royal St George's in 1949. In the final round his ball landed in a broken bottle from which, by today's rules, he would have been allowed to drop without penalty. Then he had to play ball and bottle. The stroke it cost him allowed Bobby Locke to tie and the South African went on to win the play-off.

Bobby Locke was four times winner of the British Open championship and a winner in the United States, which was quite an achievement since few visitors won there at that time. His swing caused the ball to hook so violently with each shot that he had to aim his body off to the right by some 20 or 30 degrees in order to land the ball on target.

The first American impression of him was that he was too weak in the left hand, to which he replied: 'Don't worry. I'll be picking up the cheques with my right.' And he did!

Ben Hogan, who is looked upon by many as having been the best player in the history of the game, will always be known as the man who built his own swing. Before he gained his greatest successes he

Throughout the history of the game the Irish have produced players with very individual swings. Currently the best Irish player, Eamonn Darcy demonstrates his particular version of the swing.

went through many lean years, winning barely enough to keep him going. Yet he worked on a technique of swinging that, although definitely artificial, produced a standard of accuracy that was unsurpassed at that time.

His swing, and the books he wrote on it, provided some of the greatest contributions to the understanding of modern-day swinging.

In the current era of professionals, Eamonn Darcy is the top Irishman and, like many of his predecessors, he has a unique personal swing.

The three methods

The shapes of golf swings fall into three distinct categories, all of which work well provided you choose the correct version to suit your particular physique – and temperament as well.

With each type, the movements of the various parts of the body must be correct for that method. Any attempt to change from one to the other in stages will fail, for they do not mix. That is why tuition is an essential part of beginning the game, whether you go to a teaching professional, read a book like this one or learn by copying others. If you are going to copy, make sure you imitate a good player of similar physique. There is no point in copying the mistakes of other players.

The three methods are known by the way the club face is turned by the hands and wrists during the back swing in relation to the plane of the swing. In order of age, or evolution, they are: 'open from the plane', 'square to the plane' and 'closed from the plane'.

This shows the three wrist and club face positions at the top of the back swing as they relate to the swing plane – (from left to right) 'closed', 'square' and 'open' – with the matching leg and foot movements required to get the club face through square at impact.

Open from the plane

To speed up the delivery of the club head, the hands and wrists roll open the club face as the back swing commences. The hands must feel for the correct amount of turn so they can whip the club head back at the ball. This technique is favoured by, and definitely correct for, older people and possibly ladies who are not too strong. It requires less turn of the body and, provided the shaft of the club is reasonably flexed, it can be done at a slow, gentle pace.

It is, however, most dangerous if used by a young, strong yet inexperienced player. With this technique, as the club is rolled back the arms move around the body in a shallow sweep and then the hands cock at the wrists to ensure the club travels on the correct plane.

At this stage there is a potential short-cut back to the ball. Whereas patient swingers take the time to reverse the process smoothly, the young and enthusiastic do not, and the down swing drives the club head on a much narrower arc than it did as it went back. This movement is described as a loop.

One of the major problems that has caused this technique to be discarded in modern teaching is that the club face has very little time to be absolutely 'square' as it nears its contact point with the ball. At the top of the back swing it is turned off the line of the swing plane, often by more than 45 degrees, and the original line must be recovered while the club head is travelling at its highest speed.

That is the whole object of the operation. Only a foot or two before impact it is still wide 'open', and by the same distance after impact it will be turned 'closed' by a similar amount. Hard-hitting professionals found such timing too demanding and the swing changed.

To play this type of swing, you have to turn the club back on the inside, cock the wrists to get it up, reverse the process downwards before the temptation to hit from the top becomes too strong, then hit through the ball. Four movements, four directions and therefore four very good reasons why the swing changed!

Square to the plane

There is every reason why players of average build and physical strength, male or female, choose a swing movement in which the hands use the wrist joints to prepare the club to hit the ball while working 'square' to the plane of the swing.

Most people are capable, with the co-operation of some footwork and good knee movement, to create sufficient turn of the hips to enable the shoulders to move 90 degrees from their original starting point. Balance this with the fact that the minimum required angle between the left arm and the shaft of the club, at the top of the swing, is also 90 degrees from their starting position and the golf swing appears like a mathematician's dream.

In only one movement, degree for degree, the shoulders turn and the hands cock the wrists in perfect unison, both arriving at the top of the swing fully prepared, at the same instant and both having travelled in the same direction. That direction has been guided by the player's awareness of the angle of swing plane, the key to the whole sequence.

The second stage of the swing movement – and with this method there are only two – is the through swing. The process involved in going up is put into reverse, not back to the ball but back through it, for in this case the aim is to get to the end of the through swing in one movement.

With a good basic training in swing movement, you can get the left hip and leg to initiate the downward transfer; then the angle between arm and shaft becomes more acute. This in turn causes a natural delay in the release of the wrist angle, so that it only straightens as the club passes through the ball.

With the 'square to the plane' technique, this simpler method of bringing the club back is the only form of hand action required and is much easier than using the open-faced method.

What the professionals like about this method of swing is that there are only two movements and only two directions to think of. Tom Watson plays well with it.

While having dinner with Watson during the filming of a celebrity series in August 1983, BBC Television's golf director Harold Anderson asked the Open champion what he thought about when he swung the club. Tom replied that he kept the swing much simpler than most, for he thought of it as only two movements. From set-up to the top he turned hands, hips, shoulders and feet all together, all in one. Then he turned the whole lot back again, all in one, to the finish.

Closed from the plane

If it is to be recommended at all, this method is only for the very strong and very fit. It is a means of hitting the ball very hard without the danger of slicing it, but it can result in a vicious hook shot if played with too much aggression. It may also play havoc with the back due to the great pressure it puts on the player's spine.

Its main advantages are that, as the swing goes back, the left hand turns the wrist under. It can only do this by a limited amount, so the back swing generally becomes three quarter length and the left-hand grip is tightened. This is in contrast to the 'open', rolling club that prises the fingers apart.

From such a short version of back swing the player must place more emphasis on working through the ball towards a strong finish; this gives him a greater sense of purpose. The chance of the club reaching the ball ahead of the hands is eliminated, so the player is more likely to achieve a good strike on the ball, and then the turf, when using the irons. Such is the direct turn of the shoulders into the back swing, as the wrists turn under, that the chances of swaying are very unlikely.

The advantages of this method appear to

be many, but so are the disadvantages. By closing the club face from the plane, the player has to ensure his arms are more upright during the back swing so the arching left wrist can find the required plane.

The danger of an arm swing such as this is that the shoulders might not turn sufficiently to gain the correct width for the arc of the swing. Those who have chosen this means of swinging then have to twist their spine deliberately to get more behind the ball – hence the back trouble.

If the left wrist and forearm are not well forward of the ball as the club head strikes, then the club face will lose several degrees and the ball will be smothered or hooked.

It takes a very strong man, one who can turn the lower part of his body out of the way so that his left hand can travel on unimpeded ahead of the club face, to use this method. There are not too many of these about in the amateur game, especially at club level.

Among the professionals, Bill Rogers is

Far left: Lee Trevino plays his golf using an 'open' stance.
Above left: Tom Watson with a perfectly 'square' stance.
Above: Bill Rogers, a very lightweight golfer, pulls his right foot back to create a 'closed' stance.

good at it, as is Hal Sutton, who has rocketed to the top of the money-winning list in his first years as a professional. Arnold Palmer was particularly good at it; even now, in his fifties, he still does it, although in a much gentler fashion, often tending towards being 'square' rather than 'closed'.

111

The spinning ball

Spin is a major feature of many ball games. A table tennis ball spinning from the bat's surface probably demonstrates as well as anything the effectiveness of deliberately striking across a ball's surface. Tennis balls, although larger and heavier, can also be turned, both in the air and when they bounce, by the player's skill in moving his racket across the surface. A football can veer in flight, as though it were out of balance, because of the side spin applied by a player's foot to one side or the other.

Unfortunately golf is not often looked upon as a spinning-ball game, except by those at the top level. This is probably because when the ball is hit by an expert it goes at about 240km/hr (150mph), more like a bullet than a ball. Golfers do understand back spin, since it is the ambition of every player to strike the ball so crisply with an iron that it will stop immediately on landing – or even spin backwards. It is, however, the application of side spin, by design rather than by accident, that can be a tremendous aid to players.

By knowing how to turn a ball in the air, from one direction to the other, a player can avoid trouble or, should he encounter any, have the means to play around it. Even more important, the knowledge of side spin makes the diagnosis of a swing fault a fairly simple matter. Once a player accepts that a persistent spin can be counteracted by engaging the opposite spin, he will achieve a happy balance very quickly.

Most of the tournament professionals prefer to play shots with some side spin. Some use the very slight left-to-right spin known as 'fade', while others use the right-to-left curve known as 'draw'. A good many like to draw tee shots with a driver, then fade iron shots to the green.

When you understand spin, this is a very good plan, since draw spin is an extension of the club head's arc around the body. This means you can hit the ball at full strength to gain the maximum possible length and the draw spin will encourage the ball to roll.

By fading iron shots, where the blade of the club is led slightly across the ball, you can spin the ball in the opposite direction to the curve of the arc. The shot will climb a bit higher, weaken more rapidly and land with little forward movement. Players are perfectly happy to accept the slight loss of distance in return for the extra control they gain over the ball.

Probably the greatest exponent of the curving flight is Lee Trevino, who openly admits that playing a straight shot would worry him, since it could turn off accidentally – either left or right. When Trevino nominates a cut spin or a hook spin shot, it is possible he could overdo or underdo the shot, but at least it will only turn one way. So there is something very positive about choosing a single flight. Trevino plays the majority of his shots with a slight fade, and this has virtually become his trademark.

Unfortunately this has encouraged players who suffer from slice spin to believe they are almost correct, since they misguidedly think their wild slice is just an exaggerated form of the Mexican's fade. Nothing could be further from the truth, for it takes a natural hook spinner to create a positive opposite – fade with control.

Hook spin v slice spin

The correct swing, with the club circling the body on a swing plane suited to the physique and with the shoulders engaging a full turn, should bring the club head back to, then through, the ball. At the base of the swing the club head should work from a point just short of impact, where it is still

Bobby Locke, four times winner of the British Open, played all of his shots with hook spin. Here you can see the excessive body turn necessary to bring the club down on an 'in-to-out' swing path.

'open' from the ball-to-target line, to 'square' at impact. Then, a short distance afterwards, the club should be closing from the ball-to-target line. If the slight 'open-to-closing' phase should convey any instruction to the ball, it is that it takes on some right-to-left side spin, along with the back spin provided by the loft of the club.

From this naturally powerful basis, the player may choose to counteract and swing towards the ball on a more descending line, leading the club face slightly across the ball while keeping the blade fractionally 'open'. This is the fade shot.

The slicer, whose down swing arc is very much away from his body hardly circling him at all, pulls the club head down and across the ball, with its 'open' face skidding across the ball. By trying to stop the amount of slice spin by closing the club face, he ends up pulling the ball violently to the left.

It should be the ambition of every novice and high handicapper to develop hook spin, even though it appears rather punishing to start with. It takes good golfing muscles to hook – but from the hook all things are possible. The slicing habit is a disease that allows no adjustment and should be got rid of as quickly as possible.

Whenever Lee Trevino decides that a longer drive is necessary, he squares up his stance, turns his shoulders more and applies a perfect draw spin. Natural slicers cannot do that.

Back spin

This is the true spin applied to the ball by the loft of the club under certain conditions. At the point of contact with the ball, the swing path must be absolutely true to the target line and the club's leading edge must be true to the level of the turf from which the ball is being played.

The greater the loft of the club the greater the spin imparted on the ball. This is the principle on which lofts are set, with the loft of a driver being the straightest and sending the ball the farthest. In contrast the

sand iron, the most lofted club, is capable of sending the ball almost vertical.

It is not just the loft of the club that produces back spin, especially the type demonstrated by tournament professionals, who bring the ball sharply to a stop when it lands on the putting green. It is also the angle of attack on the ball and the crispness of the strike. Club designers have a great deal to do with the angle of the strike, since they make irons with shafts that reduce in length as the loft increases. This brings the player more over the ball and creates the upright plane.

If you get the correct angle of attack on the ball, you can transfer your body weight well towards your left side. This brings the base point of the swing arc to the left of the ball. The order of contact is ball first, then the turf – the best means of increasing back spin. That is why a ball that has been slightly thinned, when the club enters the turf well after striking the ball, comes to a sudden standstill when it hits the green.

It is extremely difficult to impart sharp back spin when playing very short shots. Few players have the ability or courage to accelerate the club head sufficiently to create the spin when so close to the green. Normally you need a distance of no less than 27m (30yd). Fortunately the back spin achieved with the lofted club will be sufficient and, if you swing the club slowly, the sheer lack of forward momentum on the ball also minimizes the roll.

Minimizing back spin Once you have learned the art of side spin you can, after suffering from a few too many hook shots, go off to the practice ground and apply the cut spin technique to rebalance your swing arc. Equally, when slicing is the problem, by applying hook spin you will soon put the fault right.

Back spin is different, since in golf there is no opposite spin. To apply top spin, you would have to hit the ball above the centre of its circumference and this would result in the ball being sent along the ground and possibly suffering a fair bit of damage.

The only way of avoiding too much back spin is by minimizing it and there are two methods of doing this. The first is perfectly simple. Select a club with a lot less loft and, by holding it well down the handle, pretend that the shot being played is appropriate for a club of that length of shaft, rather than for a club of that loft. Also make sure the ball is positioned as if you were using a short club – back towards the centre of your stance.

This method is ideal when playing into a fairly strong wind, particularly from the tight lies found on seaside links. Often the shot you would normally play with a full wedge can be controlled in the wind by choosing a No 6 or No 7 iron.

You can use the second method – or the two together – when you also need a bit of run on the ball. It is ideal when you are playing out from under trees and are hoping to scuttle the ball along the turf. This involves reducing the hand and wrist action throughout the swing. Activity from the hands creates spin on the ball, so the less movement from them the less spin you will put on the ball.

You might find yourself in a situation where you need to play a pitch shot to the green, perhaps to climb up on to a second level, and need the ball to run. Because of a tail wind, flying the ball all the way to the top is out of the question, so this is the ideal time to reduce your wrist action.

Learning from a spinning ball

Concentrating on those shots that turn – right and left – in the air, much of what is happening to the shape of the swing can be diagnosed from the flight of the ball. So distinct are the patterns of movement that cause the ball to fly in various curves, that it would be perfectly feasible for a good teaching professional, watching only the flight of the ball, to describe several causes of the problem.

It is obvious that a knowledge of these patterns is a great asset to players of any standard, as adjustments can then be made

to the normal swing to turn the ball to the player's advantage. Equally, should a certain curve be plaguing a player, the problem can be diagnosed and corrected.

Applying side spin

For a ball to spin sideways, at the point of impact the leading edge of the club has to turn from or fail to turn on to the path on which the club head is travelling. In the first situation the club face is 'closed'; in the second the club face is 'open'.

When the club head is travelling directly to the target, it is on what is known as a 'direct' swing path. When it travels from inside the target line to outside it, this is called an 'in-to-out' swing path. When it travels across the line from outside to inside, it is called an 'out-to-in' swing path.

If the club face is true to the 'direct' swing path, the ball will be sent straight. If it is true to an 'in-to-out' swing path it will be pushed to the right on a straight line. On the 'out-to-in' swing path it will be pulled left in a straight line.

By contrast, the turning ball alters its flight according to the spin put on it. On leaving the club face it travels forward in the direction of the swing path of the club. Part-way through the ball's flight, the spin that was applied by the out-of-line club face takes effect and the ball then turns in the air. The amount of the turn is determined by just how much the swing path has differed from the line of the club face.

Side spin from an 'out-to-in' swing path
This also creates three types of shot. When the face is 'closed' from the swing path the ball sets off left and then turns even more in that direction. This is a pulled hook. If you use clubs with little loft, the turned-in head actually delofts even more, so the ball cannot lift and is smothered.

When the swing path is only slightly across and the face only partly 'open' from it, this is a fade shot which is used by many professionals to control iron shots. After flying off course just slightly left of the flag, the ball turns back towards it.

The spinning ball

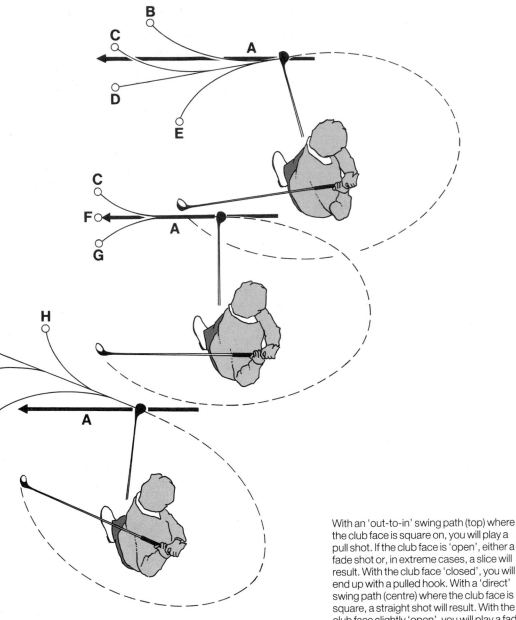

With an 'out-to-in' swing path (top) where the club face is square on, you will play a pull shot. If the club face is 'open', either a fade shot or, in extreme cases, a slice will result. With the club face 'closed', you will end up with a pulled hook. With a 'direct' swing path (centre) where the club face is square, a straight shot will result. With the club face slightly 'open', you will play a fade shot. Where the club face is slightly 'closed', you will hit a draw shot. With an 'in-to-out' swing path (bottom), where the club face is 'square', a push shot will result. When it is slightly 'open', you will play a pushed slice, while with the club face 'closed' you will hit either a draw or, in extreme cases, a hook shot.

Key
A = target line   F = straight
B = slice   G = draw
C = fade   H = pushed slice
D = pull   J = push
E = pulled hook   K = hook

The slice is the most common type of spin among beginners. Here the club head travels a long way from 'out-to-in' across the ball, with the club face left trailing in a wide, 'open' position. The ball sets off to the left then suddenly, as it gains height, curves away to the right as the spin takes effect. The more effort you make to send it left, the farther it will spin to the right.

Side spin from a 'direct' swing path This is the shot that appears fairly well hit and looks, to all intent and purpose, as if it is flying straight towards the green. Then, according to whether the face of the club was 'closed' or 'open', it turns in the air and misses the green accordingly – either left or right, a slight hook or a slight cut.

Side spin from an 'in-to-out' swing path This creates three types of shot. When the face is 'open' from the swing path, the ball flies along the line of the strike then turns it even farther right – a pushed slice.

When the swing path is only slightly 'in-to-out' and the club face only slightly 'closed' from it, this is a draw shot. Many top players prefer this shot, as the ball starts off just slightly down the right of the fairway then turns back to the centre and, on landing, gains some roll.

With the violent hook, the swing path is very much from 'in-to-out' and the club face turns sharply 'closed' on impact. The ball travels only a short distance to the right, then curves wildly away to the left.

One very important point to remember is that a ball flying to the right must not automatically be thought of as being sliced. Nor, indeed, need the one to the left automatically be thought of as being hooked.

With an 'in-to-out' swing path, the mother of all hook shots, provided the club face agrees, the push shot can go well to the right. As for the 'out-to-in' swing path, which provides the basis for all slice shots, should the club face be in line, the ball will be pulled to the left.

Perhaps those players who attempt to cure the 'shank' by applying a hook technique, believing the shank to be a form of slice, will now realize why this only aggravates the problem. Shanking is created by a flat swing bringing the club head in too much from the inside – and that is also where the hook comes from.

The spinning ball and club loft

When deliberately applying side spin to a ball on the turf, the secrets of success are never to attempt hook spin with a straight-faced club or slice spin with a lofted one.

Hook spin To achieve hook spin you need to get the club head travelling towards the ball on an 'in-to-out' swing path, with the club face turning 'closed' from it. The feeling is rather similar to a left-handed top spin shot in tennis, but in golf there is no room, other than when the ball is teed up, to get lower than the level of the ball before the strike.

To get the club head as low as possible without hitting the turf and then have it almost catching the ball on the upswing, there will be no loft in the shot if you are striking with a straight blade. The point of contact will be too high up on the ball and you will smother it.

By using a more lofted club you can lower the blade's point of contact on the ball. As the swing arc approaches the ball, with a shorter shaft the low point does not have to be that far from the ball. With a longer shaft you might catch the turf first.

Slice spin It is quite common to hear of players who hit directly left of the target with all their lofted irons, yet always slice with their straight-faced clubs.

The swing path they adopt is 'out-to-in' which, because of the combination of the steep attack from the shorter shaft and the back spin generated when the lofted club catches the ball well down, sends the ball directly left. This is a pull.

Then, when using a longer club, the face trails 'open', although the down swing is fairly steep. The straighter-faced club head will make contact higher up the ball and activate the side spin of the slice.

Using spin

Before you attempt to apply side spin to the ball, you must understand more about the swing path and the club face. Although it is the attitude of the club face that finally determines the spin, you must first learn about the swing path.

An awareness of the required swing path is the overriding factor when you set up to the ball. You must place the blade of the club behind the ball and aim at the target. The ball must be in whichever position opposite the stance suits the type of swing path for the spin required. It must also be in the correct position in relation to the stance to ensure the shoulders will turn on to the line of the swing path, for it is they who maintain its direction.

Shoulder alignment and ball position determine the wide part of the swing, whether this is before the strike, as in the case of hook shots, or after the strike, as with the slice. With the club face lined up to the flag, its leading edge will automatically be out of line with either of the off-line swing paths, so the ball is bound to turn from either direction.

Hook spinning

When playing a hook spin shot, the swing path should be 'in-to-out' with the club face 'closed'. The woods you can use for this shot are the driver, with a high tee peg, a No 4 and a No 5. The average player should play from the No 5 iron down through the set to the wedge. Better players may use No 3 and No 4 irons.

When setting-up, aim the club face at the target, with the ball at least 5cm (2in) farther back than normal opposite the stance. There is no need to close the stance. But you must close the shoulders so they line up to a point well to the right of the

target. Only when you have a violent hook shot would you need to draw the right foot back from square and toe-in the club face.

The shoulder line is what dominates the swing path of the club, along which the club will travel, both back from the ball and down to it.

As in the normal set-up procedure, you should not bring the left hand back because the ball position has been drawn in that direction. Keep it forward and lean the club to get to the ball. This is another reason why a fairly well-lofted club is essential.

Making the swing Using the 'in-to-out' swing path, clearly defined by the shoulder line, to determine the direction of the back swing, you achieve a shallower swing plane than normal and your body develops

The very aggressive downward and forward strike creates a tremendous amount of back spin when Johnny Miller plays iron shots.

By swinging the club head on an 'in-to-out' swing path, with the club face closing from that path, you can hook the ball around obstacles ahead.

Using spin

a much fuller turn. This is why the widest part of the hooker's swing is before contact is made with the ball.

On the return journey, you must bring the swing path back as close to its upward route as possible, to ensure that the club head crosses the ball-to-target line as it makes contact with the ball.

Because of this swing path, you will drive the ball on a line to the right of the target. But the club face, which was aimed at the target and is closed from the swing path, will cause the ball to rotate from right to left.

By exaggerating these points, you will achieve a great deal of hook spin. In this case use very lofted clubs, since the hands and wrists are likely to turn the club head inwards as it approaches the ball so far from the inside.

The divot By studying the divot, you can learn a great deal about your swing path and how the blade turns from it. With the hook shot, the blade enters the ground on the line of the swing path and creates a curve in the divot towards the target. The toe end of the club head will be the last to leave the ground.

Because the wide part of a hooking arc is before the ball, there is a danger you may strike the ground a fraction too early. This is why you should use shorter-shafted clubs and have the ball positioned backward in the stance.

When to apply hook spin Mild spin can be used to draw the ball, which the professionals often do when driving. The strength they generate by the full turn is brought into the back of the ball and its

When the ball is positioned backward in the stance (left), the shoulders tend to close from the target line and the full swing arc approaches the ball on an 'in-to-out' path. This will result in a hook shot as the club head turns through the ball. The divot shows the curving route of the club head. With the ball forward in the stance (right), the shoulders tend to pull 'open' from the target line and this limits their turn and the length of the swing. The club head approaches the ball on an 'out-to-in' path and here the heel of the club is still ahead as it leaves the turf. This shows how the blade is dragged 'open' across the ball, resulting in a sliced shot.

flight is like a continuation of the arc's curve around the body. Because they tee the ball up fairly high, they can position it forward in the stance. Average golfers should not be tempted to emulate this.

The full hook shot is particularly useful when you need to get around an obstacle, such as a tree, which is obscuring your view of the target and which you cannot go over. The ball will run on landing and you should allow for this.

Only attempt the violent type of hook with a very lofted club, since the turning-in of the club head would otherwise smother the ball. It is remarkable just how far a No 8 or a No 9 iron can make a ball travel as well as turn.

With the more lofted fairway woods, you can attempt the draw shot. A good time to use it is when there is a hazard or an 'out of bounds' area to the right of the fairway.

Slice spinning

When you are playing a slice spin shot, the swing path should be 'out-to-in' with the club face 'open' from the swing path. The woods you can use for this shot are the driver, from a low tee peg, and a No 3. As far as irons are concerned, you can play with Nos 1, 2, 3, 4, and 5 and perhaps No 6 if you are a very good player.

When setting-up, aim the club face at the target, with the ball positioned well forward opposite the stance. In this case the stance does turn 'open', along with the shoulders, so they both line up to a point left of the target. When you need to play a violent slice shot, your body line must be very 'open' and the club face turned out slightly. With this body line and the forward position of the ball, you will be well aware of the required swing path.

Making the swing As you begin the back swing, you will get the impression that the left shoulder is going under to maintain the direction of the swing path. The club climbs more steeply into an upright swing plane and the shoulders never achieve the normal 90-degree turn. The club does not

By drawing the club head across the ball on an 'out-to-in' swing path, with the club face 'open' from that path, you can slice the ball round obstacles, particularly when using straighter-faced clubs.

get behind the body in this position, but with this type of shot this is the narrow side of the arc.

The swing path of the club comes down and across the ball, crossing the ball-to-target line at the point of impact with the ball. The club face, 'open' from the line of the swing path, will then affect the side spin on the ball.

The section of the swing after contact with the ball is the fullest part of the arc. The club continues to a full finish, leading the body even farther away from the ball-to-target line.

Although the contact point on the ball is fairly high, which is ideal for the creation of side spin, the fact that the club face does not close over, as in normal shots, means you can lift the ball a reasonable height even when using the straightest-faced of clubs.

The divot This will be made across the

121

Using spin

ball-to-target line, but will not be oblong since the heel end of the club leads into and out of the ground. With longer slices it could look more like scraped turf than a divot and the first contact with the grass may be an inch or so after the ball.

When to apply slice spin Fade is one of the most controlled ways of flighting the ball. Unlike a straight shot, which may turn either right or left, the fade is bound to move only to the right. And it stops the ball very quickly when it lands, which makes it a favourite iron shot for professionals.

Strangely enough, when you need a fairly big curve, for example to turn the ball round a tree, then the straighter the face of the club the better, for the higher up the ball you strike the more the side spin takes effect. If the green lies too close for you to use a long iron in normal circumstances,

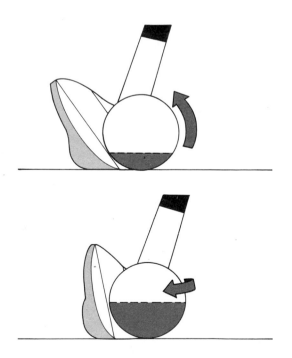

When the blade of the lofted club makes contact low on the ball (top), it will create back spin, the enemy of side spin. When the straighter-faced club makes contact high up on the ball (bottom), it will create side spin – and particularly the sliced variety.

you can grip this club down the handle and play with a part-swing. If you choose a more lofted club, you will only add back spin and nullify the side spin turn.

You can play a long slice with a straight-faced wood. Years ago it was the speciality of the brassie, now known as a No 2 wood, but this type of club is not as common today. Nevertheless, the modern No 3 wood is very powerful and, with a bit of cut spin, you can maintain the loft of the club face through the ball. This is useful when there is an 'out of bounds' area to the left of the green.

Many professionals use a driver from the ground. Yet however brave and skilful they are, because the minimal loft of the club cannot get to the bottom of the ball, they will almost certainly effect some slice spin. This is why they choose the driver when an 'out of bounds' area or similar problem lies to the left. They would not choose the driver if the trouble lay to the right.

Mild hook and slice spins

The simplest spins both to understand and apply are those that come from the 'direct' swing path. In this case, the swing used is the one for all straightforward shots, but with the body aligned to a point either left or right of the target. The curve on the ball, which returns it to the target, is created by turning the club face at the set-up stage.

You turn the club face by slightly adjusting the position of the handle in the grip – never by twisting the arms. If you close the club head too much, the ball will fly directly left and not on a curve. If you open it too far, you will add loft to the face. As well as turning right, the ball will loft so high it may not travel forward far enough.

When to apply mild hook spin Having driven to the left side of the fairway, you may find there are some trees very close to the path of your straight shot to the green. Risking hitting a branch is foolish, when by playing a mild hook shot you can flight the ball clear of the obstruction.

When coming in from the left, you may

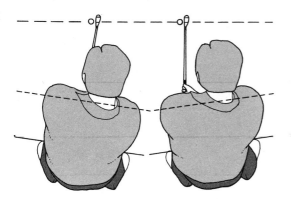

The simplest method of applying either hook (left) or slice (right) spin to a ball – and one that should certainly be used when you need only a slight amount of side spin – is to aim your stance and body line towards a point to the right or left respectively of the target to determine the initial direction of the ball. Then adjust the club in your grip so that it faces the actual target and swing normally.

find a cluster of deep bunkers directly in front of the flag. By aiming out towards the right side of the green, away from the hazards, you can bring the ball in over a safe route to the middle of the green. It is worth remembering, however, that by playing even slight hooks you increase the power of a club and reduce the back spin.

The mild hook is the ideal shot with a left-to-right wind, since it enables you to align your body directly to the green and let the hook spin argue with the wind. You do not have to choose an extra club, for by turning in the club head you will deloft the club and make the ball travel more powerfully anyway.

When to apply mild slice From a position down the right side of the fairway, where overhanging branches threaten to catch the ball in flight, it would be wise to aim slightly left to avoid them. You can do this by making only the slightest adjustment to open the club face. Bear in mind that the ball is bound to lose power and therefore choose one club stronger to play this shot.

Using mild slice is a very good way of controlling a ball against a strongish right-to-left breeze. Provided you choose one club stronger, you can still align your body directly to the green.

Warning about mild shots It is common knowledge that players who line up to a ball with the club face either 'open' or 'closed' are inclined to be guided into their back swing by the aim of the club head. The 'closed' face tends to cause a steep back swing, while the 'open' face encourages a flat roll away from the ball.

These faults usually occur when the aim of the club head at the set-up has been adjusted by the forearms, rather than by repositioning the handle in the grip.

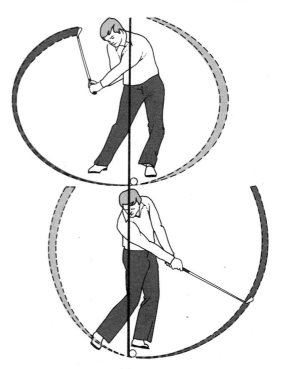

By imagining a line dividing two halves of an arc, a player who sets out to create hook spin on the ball (top) must be aware of his down swing and creative hand and wrist action being before that line, with the base of the arc coming just before the ball on an 'in-to-out' swing path. When trying to create slice spin on the ball (bottom), the player must be aware that the work is done forward of that line, with the strike down and across the ball and the base of the arc coming after the ball.

Using spin

Once you have set the club head on the desired line, however, you must concentrate only on a direct swing path.

Hook and slice arcs Once you can appreciate that the swing path is a major factor in spin shots and that the line of the club face, although very necessary, follows quite easily, then you must give priority to the position of the ball and the alignment of the body. These guide the swing into whichever wide part of the arc the particular shot 'lives' in.

By slightly exaggerating the swing to play a particular spin shot, some professional players demonstrate points that are very useful in learning how to play different spins. Having said that, however, there are few hookers who are not trying to fight the spin. After developing hook spin as youngsters, a lot of players are now happy to apply many of the cut spin techniques to gain better control.

Some years ago you could pick out Bobby Locke of South Africa or Eric Brown of Scotland, who with their huge shoulder turn into the back swing and their pronounced 'in-to-out' swing path generated a great deal of hook spin on the ball. Today

Lee Trevino discussing spin with his caddie Willie Aitchison during the British Open championship at Royal Birkdale in 1983.

Fuzzy Zoeller of the United States, although lifting his club quite sharply on the back swing, loops it back and delivers the blow very much on the 'in-to-out' swing path to hook the ball.

With those players, the widest area of their arc is from behind the body and they reach the low point of their down swing that bit earlier.

You need look no further than Lee Trevino for a player whose swing arc 'lives' forward, where the widest part of his swing is in his very extended follow-through. The base of his arc comes very late, at a point well forward and opposite his left foot.

Balancing the swing The patterns governing side spin are so distinct that any player suffering from hook or slice is accidentally applying some or all of the applicable ingredients already described in this chapter. The beauty of recognizing these is that the curving flight of the ball, whether mild or exaggerated, can be used to diagnose the fault in the swing.

By altering the ball position and body alignment, you can reverse the side on which the arc 'lives' and in working towards this you will eventually balance the swing into a direct swing path.

Just as the curving ball can be your teacher, the opposite curve can be the cure.

Improving your shots

The difference between the novice and the expert is that the novice can finish his round and spend the rest of the day happily remembering his one good shot. The expert, on the other hand, who expects to hit nothing but good shots, spends the time regretting his poor shot that cost him so dearly.

Golf is such an exacting game because it subjects players at all levels to pressure. Because the ball is stationary for each shot, no last-second reflex action is required to set it in motion; every move is premeditated. Nothing happens quickly on the golf course and there are many minutes between shots in which a player can dwell on a bad mistake. There are no colleagues to blame, since golf is a game for the individual where every weakness, whether in skill or temperament, is exposed. Poor shots naturally play a regular part in golf and each has a name.

In this chapter all the well-known faults are described and the causes and steps necessary to remedy them are explained. The information here cannot stop you playing poor shots, but at least it should help you understand what you are doing wrong and hopefully reduce the number of times you do it.

Topping

This involves hitting over the top of the ball and is the most regular mishit made by the beginner. It is due to lack of experience and only by playing regularly will the novice eliminate the fault, as he learns to get his eye in.

By deliberating over the swing, the beginner tends to tense up and loses any sense of feel. As a result, he takes the club head through the bottom of the arc with his

Telly Savalas, who has a rather unorthodox swing action, still derives as much pleasure from the good shots he connects with as he does from his lollipop.

muscles tensed. This effectively reduces the club's swinging length and he ends up topping the ball.

Another cause of the mishit is because the player tends to focus on that part of the ball he can see, which is the top, and that is what he hits.

The best way to eliminate topping is to use a very short practice swing just inches from the ball and manipulate the wrists to ensure the club head lightly brushes the turf, making a swishing noise. If your first practice swing is not satisfactory, try another since the second one is usually much better. Then go straight to the ball and apply the full swing, remembering the feel you got from the practice swing when going through the ball.

When experienced golfers top the ball, it can be a genuine case of lifting the head because the eyes are over-anxious to watch the ball on its way to the flag. When it happens regularly, it is usually when playing with woods from the fairway. The long shaft of the club causes players to use the shallower swing plane of the driver. But in this case the ball is not raised on a tee peg.

If you strike the ball above the centre, you will top it. This is the most regular mishit played by the beginner.

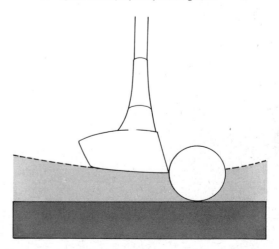

You will do no harm by going through the practice swing routine. Brushing the top of the turf will encourage you to get your hands higher in the back swing. With a more upright swing plane, you will create a lower base to the swing and the topping will stop.

Fluffing

Also called 'duffing' or, according to the Scots, 'sclaffing', fluffing occurs when the club head meets the ground before hitting the ball. It can happen with any shot and the shorter the shot the more damaging the effect will be.

Because of its flat sole, a wood will skid and may still give the ball a healthy blow. The longer irons may tend to dig slightly, but with their fairly shallow plane they will not gouge too deeply. It is the very lofted irons, coming from an upright plane, that

By undoing the wrist action too early in the down swing, the club head grounds before connecting with the ball, so the ball is fluffed.

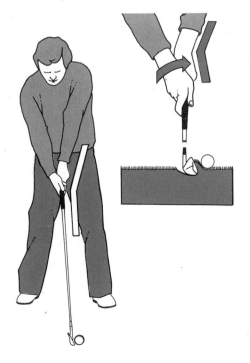

cause the most problems, digging deeply before hitting the ball and ruining its flight towards the target.

Small pitches and chips are also affected, because only a little strength is used and any connection with the turf virtually stops the club sending the ball forward.

The fluffed shot is caused by the right hand passing the left before the point of impact. This is commonly known as hitting early. It can happen as a result of nervousness, possibly when a touch of panic causes the swing to quicken. But it is regularly the fault of adopting a poor set-up position in the first place.

When a player lines up to the ball, instead of leaning the shaft of the club forward to meet the left hand, he brings the hand back to the handle and so alters the shape of the left wrist. The additional wrist action this causes throws the club head.

The best cure is to get the right set-up and aim to swing fully through to a good finish. The same goes for the chips and pitches, although with these shots you cannot have a full follow-through.

Toeing

Extreme toeing makes the ball fly virtually at right angles from the tip of the club head. This is caused when the swing travels across the ball from a very upright angle. It is the shot of a complete novice who is going through a spell of severe slicing. To cure it, you must shallow out the plane of the swing and develop a better shoulder turn to enable the club head to approach the ball from 'in-to-out'.

There is another version of toeing that happens even to very good, established players, who find the grass stain on the irons always well towards the toe end. Their drives often feel as if they had been slapped and there is a loss of power with all the clubs.

Again this is caused by early hitting, where the right hand passes the left before the club head strikes the ball. This shot is often partly fluffed, too.

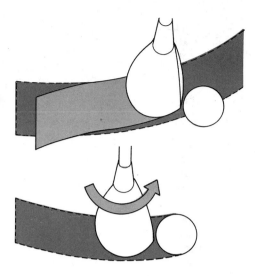

There are two ways of toeing a shot. The club may pass on the inside of the ball (top) because you have misjudged the distance of the ball from the body. If your right hand grip is too strong, you can turn the club face inwards quite violently (bottom).

mote it, because the method they apply is quite the opposite of that required.

Because the ball flies off to the right on the most violent curve, the inexperienced player identifies the fault as a form of slice, which it is not. A slice comes from the club head travelling from high outside the ball to low across it, so that the face of the club imparts side spin. The spin from the shank does not come from the club face drawing across the ball. It comes from the base of the shaft catching the inside of the ball, which it does when travelling from too low on the inside of the ball on the 'in-to-out' path of a flat swing, with the forearms still partly rotated 'open'.

Efforts to cure the 'slice' by positioning the ball backward in the stance and by swinging flatter, in the belief that a hook is bound to cure a slice, only promote the shank to the ball. In fact, it requires just the opposite to be done to effect an immediate cure – having the ball forward

When the lower part of the body fails to move through towards the target in the down swing, the top half goes over with the right side overpowering the left. The most common cause is a 'closed' stance, where the feet are incorrectly aimed away to the right. With this position, any lateral movement from the hips and legs at the start of the down swing sends the ball off target. So the right hand and shoulder take over to redirect the ball and the left wrist and arm submit.

The cure is to check the line-up by laying a club on the ground, aimed at the target, and place the feet parallel to it. From this unimpeded position you will, with the help of good footwork, have space to swing the lower part of the body through and will not have to hit early using the right hand.

Shanking

It is perfectly understandable why this type of mishit, where the ball is struck at the join of the socket and the blade, strikes fear into the hearts of most club golfers. All efforts to cure the fault only seem to pro-

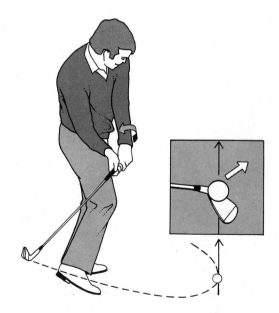

When the path of the down swing is too much 'in-to-out' and the plane is very shallow, your left forearm may lock and lead the socket of the club into the ball. This type of mishit is known as shanking.

opposite the stance and swinging the club higher in the back swing, then bringing it down slightly across the ball with the face of the club slightly 'open'.

The fault described is the version that comes in bouts. It is possible to shank occasionally from a perfectly normal swing by standing too close to the ball or, because of some anxiety, turning towards the target too soon. Then the club swings beyond its correct path into the ball and causes the socket to strike the ball. This version happens infrequently and there is no set pattern for the fault.

Ballooning

This is a particularly nasty form of tee shot which can damage the paintwork on the top of the club head as it sends the ball climbing to a great height, but with little forward distance.

With some players it happens infrequently and in that case it could be that the peg was not set low enough. This is often the case when a lofted wood is used on the tee and the peg is set at the normal height for the driver. The shallow head finds the lowest point of the ball and spins it back over the top of the insert.

Recognizing someone who balloons regularly is easy. Normally he does not use a driver. Instead he will tee off with a lofted wood, or iron, all the time. An examination of his wooden club heads will show that most of the varnish has been removed from the tops; in fact, they will be quite deeply scarred.

He will suffer from either, or both, of the following faults. His grip will be in the palm of the right hand, rather than the fingers, and the 'V' between the forefinger and thumb will point somewhere towards his right knee. He will swing the club at the ball from a very upright angle, probably

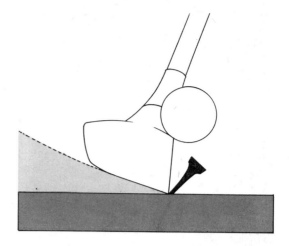

If you bring the club down on too steep an arc, you will balloon the ball.

caused by a complete lack of shoulder turn in the back swing.

Following these faults, he may have tried a 'closed' stance which, although it appears to aid the shoulder turn, really does no good at all.

Although the player who balloons may occasionally hit some very long shots, he will not enjoy striking with the 'sweet spot' on any club; all his shots will, in fact, be crushed.

The cure involves hard work and changing the grip, which will initially give a feeling of weakness. But this must be done. By practising part-shots, using a fairway wood and a moderately high tee peg, you should learn to sweep the ball away. You must keep the wrists inactive and train the upper part of the body to turn with the arms into the back swing, then through together to the finish.

Provided you sweep at the ball and do not hit at it, you will develop a smooth shallow arc with a wide base – and the ballooning will stop.

Other poor shots, such as slicing, hooking, pulling and pushing, are dealt with in the chapter on the spinning ball.

Golf has a great attraction for the world of entertainment. Two players who have learned much of their game from playing with professionals in Pro-Am tournaments are Dickie Henderson (left) and Bob Hope.

Playing from slopes

Playing from a slope means you are either going to hit from an uphill or downhill stance, or with the ball above or below the level of your stance. You may, of course, find yourself in a situation where a combination of these positions exists which makes the shot very difficult.

Uphill and downhill slopes are discussed under three categories: gentle, severe and steep. From gentle slopes you can still play power shots, provided you take certain precautions and make the necessary directional allowances. On more severe slopes you must give consideration to keeping your balance and positioning yourself correctly in relation to the ball. Here you should aim to play more conservative shots. On steep banks you must forget about trying to gain distance and concentrate on balance and clean-hitting.

Gentle up-slopes

Without doubt this is the simplest of the 'sloping lie' shots, since you will have the feeling that the ball is actually rising towards the club head. If you are not careful, however, this can result in one of the most common types of mishit – when the club crushes the ball into the slope rather than hitting it up from the slope.

The secret on gentle slopes is to persuade the club to travel up the slope, with the base of the swing arc parallel to the ground. To do this, you must lean your body not into the slope, as your sense of balance would suggest, but back on to the right leg so the upper part of your body is at right angles to the slope.

This body position will provide the best base from which to swing the club head cleanly through the ball. But it will have several other effects. Since it is difficult to

Arnold Palmer plays from heavy rough on the side of a hill and is careful to position his shoulders well over the ball to permit the necessary steep swing plane.

By keeping the bodyline as near right angles to the slope as possible does help in achieving a good base to the swing arc and clean contact with the ball. The trajectory of the ball will be altered, however, and a suitable club should be chosen accordingly. When hitting up a slope (above), the ball will fly higher and lose distance, so you should use a more powerful club. The loft will be reduced when hitting down a slope (below) and the ball will tend to fly farther, so a weaker club is needed.

Playing from slopes

transfer your weight forward in the normal fashion, your hands will be inclined to turn during the striking part of the swing. This causes the ball to move to the left in the air. Whichever type of club you use, the angle of loft increases and the ball climbs higher.

Do not argue with the fact that the ball turns in the air, but aim off to the right accordingly. Because of the additional height you are bound to get on the ball, to achieve the right distance you should use a club that would, under normal circumstances, carry the ball over the green when the shot is hit correctly.

No matter how determined you are to keep your body line at the correct angle to the slope, there will be a natural instinct to push the weight of your body up the slope and you could end up crushing the ball. So you should take up the stance with the ball fairly central. By swinging true to the slope and not into it, you can safely use any of the straighter-faced clubs in the set, woods or irons.

Gentle down-slopes

Once again you can be fairly bold when playing down a gentle hill, provided you adjust your body line to the left to get the feeling that the club head is swinging down it. You will need to lean this way to prevent the club head hitting the turf before the ball.

Here you need to use a club with a little more loft, for as you swing downwards you tend to drive the ball forward with a much lower trajectory. A No 5 iron, for example, will make the ball fly forward like a No 4 would normally do, so you must select your club carefully.

In this situation there will be a natural tendency for the weight of your body to move forwards down the hill with the strike. To take advantage of this, be sure the ball is positioned slightly forward in the stance.

As the weight of your body goes forward and down, the arc of the down swing into the ball is narrowed. The effect is to deloft the club and cause it to travel slightly across the ball on an 'out-to-in' swing path. With longer clubs, this results in cut spin on the ball, while with more lofted clubs you tend to pull the ball to the left. So you must make allowances accordingly.

Severe up-slopes

Because of the slope, balance is now more essential. If you try to hit the ball long distances, you are likely to pull it badly away to the left as you fall backwards.

When playing a shot in this situation, you must flex the left leg and lean into the hill, although this may cause the club to strike through the ball quite deeply into the turf. If you use a club with little loft, you will find you smother the ball as the face of the club compresses it into the ground. Loft is essential, even though it might result in the ball falling short of your target.

More experienced players are able to gain distance by creating the feeling that the back swing is travelling slightly down the slope. Then, as they hit through, they make a positive effort to swing the club through the ball and up the slope. By following the contour of the ground as far as possible, they avoid a heavy downward blow and can select a straighter-faced club. Less experienced players attempting this manoeuvre could find themselves falling backwards down the hill.

The ball must be positioned well forward in the stance and you should make allowance for the hooking flight of the ball by aiming off to the right.

Severe down-slopes

As you lean back and put the weight of your body on to the right leg, bending it to maintain your balance, the ground behind and above the ball is bound to get in the way of the down swing and the ball. So you must make sure the ball is positioned far back in the stance.

You need to make a definite change in your swing here. Deliberately steepen the back swing so you can strike the ball from a

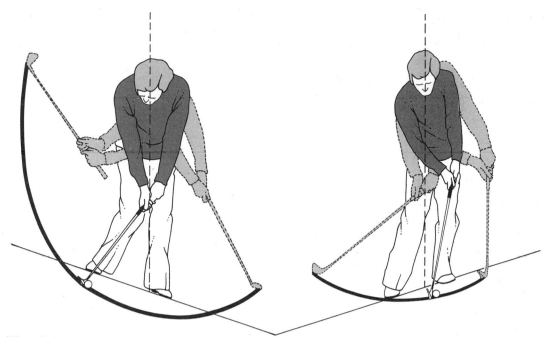

When playing down a severe slope (left), the body must be balanced almost vertically to the horizon, bringing the ground just before the ball into play. This means you will have to bring the back swing up sharply so you can swing down and through without hitting the ground first. When playing up a severe slope (right), lean the body forward and keep the back swing low and wide so that your follow-through can sweep up the slope.

very upright angle. The hands in fact control this direction and should start from a forward position opposite the left thigh.

Use a club with a good loft because the downward strike will be a crushing one and this should make the ball fly low and fairly straight.

Steep up-slopes

These are usually the faces of steep banks, grass bunkers or even sand dunes and are, hopefully, very close to the green since the ball will do little more than go up when hit. You cannot expect to go forward more than just a few yards in this case.

You may have to bend the left knee joint, often nearly to the chin, to ensure a firm balance, which is paramount. You can hold the lofted club right down the shaft, even to the point that the right hand is holding the steel of the shaft. The top of the handle will protrude beyond the left hand, but this will be pointing safely outside the left elbow and will not interfere with the movement of the swing.

Whatever your standard of golf, in this case you must definitely direct the club head downwards for the back swing. Your hands and arms will then pull up the hill, almost wrenching the ball from the grass rather than playing it. These shots, of course, are always played from rough grass since, had the grass been short, the ball would have been at the bottom of the slope and not stuck halfway up it.

The ball will fly almost vertically, so if you have to cover a fair distance you will need to strike it aggressively. Of course, if you play the shot too hard, you will be struggling to keep your balance.

Steep down-slopes

Once again from a very steep banking and with the same problem of thick grass

Playing from slopes

around the ball, this is one of the easiest shots to mishit. Not only is there the high bank between the down swing and the ball, but also a cushion of soft grass waiting to tangle up the club head. Hopefully the green is close by, since with this shot the ball will fly only a short distance forward. But should it land on the green, it will run forward because there is no back spin on it.

You can adjust your balance for this shot by bending the right leg. The ball may still be well behind and above the right foot and sometimes on the seaside courses the ball can be up as high as the player's waist.

Use the sand iron, since the angle of strike will cancel out much of the loft. The actual hit is nothing more than an up-and-down chop through the ball. Make sure it is always through the ball, for the grass will try to stop the club striking correctly.

If you are playing the shot towards a fairway, then choose the shortest possible direction. Risking an ambitious shot to gain length will often result in disaster. If

the shot is to a nearby green, allow for run, remembering that the ball is better off the bank and on the back of the green, rather than left in the rough, which might happen if the shot is too weak.

Sidehill lies

To play good shots from the side of a slope requires a good sense of swing plane. Simply being on the hill will affect your posture according to whether the ball is below or above the stance and will automatically alter the angle of the swing. You can only play confident sidehill shots if you are fully in control of all your movements.

The flight of the ball is bound to be anything but straight, since when you place the sole of the club against the slope, its facial loft is tilted accordingly. When the ball lies above the level of the stance, the spin you put on from the club loft will take it to the left. In the opposite situation, where the ball is below the stance, you will be flighting it to the right. In either case

With the ball only slightly above the feet (left), you should settle back as far as possible to make the swing plane shallower. When the ball is below the feet (right), lean forward to ensure an upright swing plane.

you will have to aim off, according to the degree of slope.

Good balance is essential, particularly if the slope is severe. Although you can play aggressive shots, especially when the ball is lying just above the level of your feet, the distance you achieve will largely depend on the control you have over the stroke.

Ball above the stance The swing arc must travel through the ball on a very shallow plane. If it is at all steep, the club will ground before it reaches the ball. You must adjust your posture to cater for this swing plane by getting the spine as near vertical as possible, which means sitting back from the slope. Depending on how steep the slope is, balance will allow you to do this to a degree. You might, however, need to reduce the length of the club by gripping farther down the handle.

When a slope is so severe that it is impossible to lean out, you will have to use a short-handled, very lofted club and play the ball just a short distance.

Again, with the ground level seeming to come up to meet the club head, you must position yourself with the ball towards the centre of the stance, even though the club is a wooden one.

With the club head tilted, toe end up, at address and during the swing, combined with the extremely shallow plane of the arc and huge shoulder turn, the ball is bound to turn to the left. You must therefore make sufficient allowance off to the right to compensate. A good way of doing this is to pick a secondary target, say a tree, a bunker or a building, and play to that. The ball will do the rest.

Ball below the stance Here your shoulders must lean forward as far as possible without you losing your balance. That is the only way you can strike the ball at the correct level, other than by bending your legs as much as possible on a severe hillside.

The toes and the calf muscles are very important as they carry your weight during

When the ball lies well below (left) or above the stance, good balance is essential. In this situation, you should forget about distance and concentrate on striking the ball accurately.

the very upright swing you achieve from your leaning position. The key to accurate hitting with this shot is keeping your head as steady as possible.

You will find your shoulder turn is limited and you will have to use your hands to guide the up-and-down movement of the swing. In this shot, probably more than any other in golf, the correct hand action is vital to get the club head to the bottom of the ball. It is so easy, with just a bit too much aggression, to top the ball. Make sure the ball is slightly forward of centre in the stance, because the half-shoulder turn and toppling body weight will drive the club to the left.

The lie of the club head should send the ball off to the right. This does not always happen, however, since you will often need a lofted iron for this difficult shot, the spin from which tends to hold the ball straight. With the milder 'hanging lie' – and here you could even use a wooden club – the ball will turn from left to right. In this case, it pays to select an object some yards off line and play towards that to allow for the turn.

137

The short game

The 'short game' refers to four basic types of shot. First there is putting, where the ball is rolled by the club, which has a near-vertical face, so that it remains on the grass throughout its journey. Secondly there is chipping, where the ball is lifted a minimum height then encouraged to run to the hole. The third type of shot is pitching, where additional spin is put on the ball to provide a minimum amount of roll when it lands. Finally there is the bunker shot, played from the greenside bunkers.

Although included in the list of 'short game' shots, putting and bunker shots have such individual characteristics that each has been given a chapter of its own. The shots from the grass, chipping and pitching, are dealt with in this chapter.

These shots are needed from the point

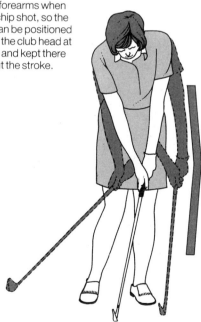

As with putting, you do not rotate the forearms when playing a chip shot, so the left wrist can be positioned forward of the club head at the set-up and kept there throughout the stroke.

Left: Severiano Ballesteros, a master of the short game, plays a delicate chip shot.

where the ball is only inches from the putting surface and the player considers it unwise to use the putter (although this club should be used if conditions permit) up to a good distance from the green, provided the player is within range of the full shot with his shortest grass club.

Missing the green by a small distance can happen regularly, even to the best of players. But this does not mean that a stroke has to be dropped. You only have to look at the putting averages of the top players to see that a single putt has often saved their score. This has been achieved by chipping or pitching close to the hole.

Getting 'up and down' is the expression for the two strokes used when a player misses the green but recovers successfully. To play a good 'short game' can bring an average player level with those who are much longer hitters, so it is an area worth a good deal of practice.

Chipping

You should only attempt to chip the ball when you cannot use a putter, no matter how good a chipper you become. It takes quite a brilliant chip shot to match even an average putt which hugs the ground.

Getting within a couple of metres (6 to 8ft) of the hole with a long chip is considered an excellent shot, yet to be that distance away after a long approach putt is thought of as average. Such is the proof that the closer you can keep the ball to the ground, the easier it is to judge distance.

Once you have decided to play a chip shot, you must choose the correct club. Do not make it a hard-and-fast rule to use just one club; you should let the circumstances dictate your choice. Look at the percentage of rough ground to be covered in the air compared with the length of putting green surface on which the ball may run out. Remember that, according to the loft on its face, each club offers a different percentage of 'carry in the air' to 'run on the ground'.

You must choose a club that has the straightest face to get the ball safely over the uneven surface, yet allows the ball sufficient distance in which to stop. The straighter the face, the less physical movement you will need for the shot – and this will improve the accuracy. The farther the ball is from the putting surface or the closer the pin to the edge of the green, the greater your choice of loft.

Many believe you can only chip the ball with the less lofted irons – Nos 5, 6 and 7 – after which the stroke becomes a pitch. This is not true, since you can play a chip-and-run shot using any iron. Only the flight specifications alter and, of course, the aggression of the stroke.

First place the blade of the club head behind the ball and aim either at the hole or to the side, according to the slope of the green. Hold the club lightly and low down the handle in the right hand. When you take up your stance, your feet should not be more than 30cm (or 1ft) apart. Stand with the ball just a fraction right of centre in the stance and bring the entire body alignment parallel to the ball-to-target line.

The next stage is crucial, for the entire character of the chip-and-run shot depends on it. Hold the left hand forward, at a point opposite the outside of the left thigh with the back of the hand facing the target. Then put the handle of the club into the left hand, which must not come back from its forward position to help take up the grip. Move the weight of your body with the club towards the left foot, where it must stay throughout the shot.

From the forward point of the left wrist, directly under the left shoulder, the left hand will hood into line with the slant of the shaft, which should be forward.

You must maintain the forward position of the left wrist throughout the stroke; and there is no partial rotation of the forearms. At no time should you let the hands flick the shaft of the club forward to break this slightly awkward position. If you do, they

will increase the loft on the club and change the character of the shot by increasing the height, which in turn will reduce the roll.

Apart from a slight rocking of the shoulders, according to the pressure being applied to the shot, there should be little body movement. In fact there is little movement in the entire shot, which is what makes it the safest shot in golf – after the putting stroke.

What you must master – and this can only be done individually with practice – is the percentage of flight to run each club offers (see diagram).

Only the loft of the club, and no action by you, heightens the ball. Even then because of the forward position of the hands there is always a lowish trajectory.

If you are using one of the very straight-faced irons, you need the minimum of movement to make the ball cover reasonable distances. This makes chipping an ideal shot for those two and three-tiered greens where the pin is at the back and the ball just off the front edge of the green.

Many players make hard work of a delicate pitch shot over a bank, risking the extra movements and skilful timing of this shot. By using the chipping method with a sand iron, you can still get plenty of lift and reduce the risks.

The chip shot is normally geared to getting the ball to bounce first on the smooth surface of the green. But when playing on a links course or a dry inland one, it is often a good idea to allow the ball to bounce short and do quite a bit of its running across the fairway grass. This is called 'bumbling' and is a good way of coming up and over an obstacle when there is very little room to hold the ball on the green.

This shot was partly responsible for bringing Severiano Ballesteros out of comparative obscurity. He played it from the semi-rough on the left of the fairway at the final hole in the 1976 British Open championship. When he chipped the ball, it ran up between two bunkers, then over some rough ground to within a yard of the hole, enabling him to finish runner-up.

Pitching

Once it becomes impossible to play a chip-and-run shot, you will have to start pitching. This either happens when the distance you have to carry the ball in the air requires a 'run out' distance that is not available or when you need to transfer your weight to achieve the necessary distance. Greater momentum is now needed and that is part of the pitch shot. The fact that you have to put more pace into the shot will help the timing and tempo of the extra, more flexible movements of the pitching action.

The physical movements required for a standard pitch shot are very similar to those for a full shot, but geared down according to the length of the pitch. The muscles used in the full shot of a wedge all function in the pitch, contributing equally to the required amount. You will have to find out what distance your minimum

pitch shot carries when you use the minimum equal amount of swing movements and you can do this in the following way.

Three factors are involved in building up through the range from the smallest pitch to the full shot. They are the length of the club, the width of the stance and the length and pace of the swing.

Using the normal set-up procedure, first place the blade of the wedge behind the ball and aim towards the target. On this occasion your right hand should be well down the club handle. Take up the stance with your feet only inches apart and the ball positioned centrally. Your stance and

This graph shows the approximate percentage of flight to run of the ball when playing a chip shot using different clubs. With a No 4 iron, you will get 10 per cent flight and 90 per cent run (A); with a No 6 iron – 25:75 (B); with a No 8 iron – 40:60 (C); with a No 9 iron – 50:50 (D); with a pitching wedge – 60:40 (E); and with a sand iron – 75:25 (F). Once you have learned this, you can calculate how to make the first bounce on the smooth grass of the putting green and make the most of the simplicity offered by the straightest-faced iron possible to achieve this.

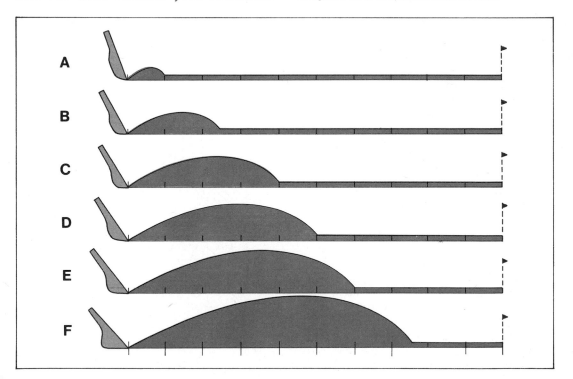

body alignment should be square-on.

Unlike with the chip shot, you must bring the left hand back to meet the right and hold the club shaft almost vertical, with just the minimum of lean forward. The weight of your body should only slightly favour the left side. With this grip, almost 5cm (2in) of the handle should be visible above the left hand.

At this point you will feel you can play this small shot with just your hands and wrists. After all the ball only has to travel a few yards. While you can do this, however, you must resist the temptation. To play the shot successfully like this would mean the hands working independently from the body and if you attempted longer shots, you would lose the accuracy.

As the hands move the club back the few feet required, the left side moves too. This allows the forearms to turn, the wrists to cock and the arms to widen the swing arc partially. You will feel the left knee flexing inwards, bringing the hip with it, and the pressure on the outside of the left foot will ease. This should happen in one co-ordinated movement, with all the parts of your body completing preparation together.

Provided your arm and body movements transfer back through the starting point and on towards the finish of the stroke, your hands and wrists may engage some feel as they accelerate the bottom of the club through beneath the ball.

The more skilful the player, the shorter the minimum pitching distance will be. Poorer players attempting a very short shot are likely to play the shot too slow and fluff it. They should increase the pace and settle for the fact that their shortest pitch will be that bit longer, until practice and experience reduce it. Because they continually fluff the shot, many higher handicap golfers prefer running-up shots, even though a pitch would be correct.

Once you have mastered the minimum length of pitch, you will soon make progress. By increasing the length of the club, the width of the stance and the length and pace of the swing in small but equal stages, you will extend the distance over which the ball flies. Gradually, after about half a dozen balls, you will reach the full swing and that final shot will indicate the distance you can expect to achieve from using that particular club.

One of the most important points you gain from this method is that, as soon as you know exactly what your minimum is, you know that for every pitch over a greater distance you will need more power.

By accelerating through the ball you will help effect back spin. That is how the confident tournament player gets his pitch shots to stop so quickly. So instead of a club golfer thinking that a 27m (30yd) pitch is a reduction of 55m (60yd) from his normal wedge shot, he can look at the 27m (30yd) shot as an 18m (20yd) increase on his minimum. It is amazing what a difference the positive increase through pitch shots makes to the quality of the shot and to the confidence of the player.

Another way of stopping the ball quickly on the green is to bring the ball down from a great height. To achieve this, accelerate the club head through the ball and it will carry higher into the air. You can get more height on any pitch shot, although there is a certain risk with very short shots.

To achieve still more height, hold the club nearer the top of the handle, reduce the width of the stance and increase the length of the arc, but not its pace. This will increase the height of the ball dramatically, but reduce its forward thrust.

The narrow stance will check the body turn and minimize the leg and foot movement, so the swing arc climbs upwards on a steep plane and the blade turns more 'open'. The swing weight of the longer club will play on the wrist joints which, because they are still travelling slowly, are likely to weaken and open the club face even more. Then, as the fuller arc cuts through under the ball, the club hits it up.

Ballesteros is one of the greatest masters of this shot ever seen. He is so good that he

The pitch shot is still part of a full shot and should always be regarded as such. All the muscles that are used in the normal swing must still be made to work, although to a lesser degree according to the distance to be covered. Many are tempted to use independent hand and wrist movements to play shorter pitch shots and so unbalance their swing for longer pitches.

demonstrates the shot with straight-faced irons, tossing the ball almost vertically.

Provided the lie is good, another and much safer way is to use the sand iron. Its extra loft and weight bring the ball up quickly with less risk. Because of its flanged sole, you must not use this club from tight lies. But it is ideal when pitching from the rough.

Compromise chipping

One of the fascinations of golf is the fact that there are never two shots exactly the same, particularly around the green where golf course architects tend to concentrate all their trickery. They design elevated plateau greens to make approach shots difficult to judge. They make sunken greens,

so the player either has to be bold enough to pitch all the way to the flag or calculate the bounce should he prefer to land on the down slope. Bunkers are cleverly placed to punish those who choose the wrong line.

You may sometimes get the ball very close to the green and need to play the shot with a good deal of height and at a very slow speed. These are the characteristics of a pitch shot, but the distance to be covered is less than the minimum you are capable of with this shot.

This is where you have to compromise between chipping and pitching and play the shot with the safety of the chip but with the flight characteristics of the pitch.

Provided the lie is good, set up for a chip shot, but make two adjustments. Stand with the ball far forward in the stance, even opposite the left toes, instead of opposite the centre of the stance. This brings the shaft of the club into a vertical line, directly under the left shoulder. Also hold the club a fraction longer, to allow you a bit of give in the wrist joints. You can then play the

143

stroke in a similar way to the normal chip shot, but a shade slower.

You should use a very lofted club, preferably a sand iron, for this type of shot. If you want to dilute the strength of the shot even more, address and strike the ball with the toe end of the blade.

Compromise pitching

The object of pitching a ball is to increase the elevation so that it soars and drops more steeply on to the green. There are occasions, however, when you want to play a stronger shot with a lower trajectory, one bearing many of the characteristics of a chip but over a much greater distance.

It is the sort of shot you might want to play into the wind or low out from under a tree, when bunkers prevent you from playing a normal running shot. You might want to use it when pitching into a split-level green with a step in the middle, where you would be wrong to attempt to pitch all the way to the top level, possibly down wind. In this case you should aim to pitch the ball on the lower tier, with sufficient forward momentum for it to climb the step.

To play these and similar shots, you have to introduce some of the chipping characteristics to the normal pitching method, most of which should be done at the setting-up stage.

Because of the driving nature of the shot, you may wish to choose a club with less loft than a wedge, possibly a No 8 or a No 9 iron, and aim the blade while holding the club farther down the grip than normal.

Take up a fairly wide stance and have the ball positioned well back behind centre. Then, as for the chip shot, take the club forward with the right hand to the left, so that the shaft is leaning firmly forward.

By setting up for the shot in this way, you will stabilize the wrists so they pro-

duce little activity during the shot, while increasing the shoulder and body turn. You drive the ball forward as in the chip shot, with none of the flick or turning forearm associated with pitching. Keep the left wrist in its forward position, although not so pronounced as in the chip shot, for as long as necessary into whatever follow-through you require for the length of shot.

Open stance for short shots

You will notice many top professionals and leading amateurs playing short chips and pitches with their feet and hips turned a considerable distance off to the left of the target. This is a throw-back to the days when the only 'square' stance you took up was when using the driver. Then you gradually opened the line of the feet down through the set-up until finally, using the most lofted club, you were turning almost face-on to the flag.

There is no doubt that this method helps you get a better view of the target. It is, in a way, like throwing a ball underarm – the most accurate method.

There is, however, considerable danger in lining up 'open'. Not only do the feet turn off to the left, but so does the upper part of the body. Since the direction of the club's swing path comes directly from that of the shoulders, you will be playing away from the shoulder line.

Those experts who choose to stand 'open' for their short shots know at exactly what distance from the hole they must bring the shoulders accurately to the target line. Some do so about 27m (30yd) out, others 36 or 46m (40 or 50yd). But whatever their preference, they can get the desired result. Novices and high-handicap players cannot, so they should play all chip and pitch shots from a square position.

There are as many experts playing their short game square-on as there are using the 'open' stance. and such is the value of a 'square' shoulder line that as many as 90 per cent of players are putting that way, with the other 10 per cent trying to.

Bob Charles, one of the finest exponents of the short game, plays a firm-wristed chip using a very lofted club, which provides sufficient elevation without involving the risk of a more wristy pitch shot.

Putting

It is often said that to be taught how to putt is unnecessary, an attitude that is probably responsible for many of the poor putting performances of those players with higher handicaps.

It is essential to learn a good putting action. Professionals call this a 'stroke', because with 18 holes to putt at, where the par for the course allows for two putts a hole, a few single putts can make a tremendous difference to your score. Taking three putts on a few holes destroys not only your total but also your morale, especially when you have played good shots to get the ball to the green.

Apart from developing a stroke, it is essential to be able to read the green. Bad putters do not give sufficient consideration to this skill. In many cases novices are warned that too much studying of the green prior to putting is the cause of slow play. While you do see the professional studying the green, he does a good deal of his putting preparation while the other player is taking his stroke, being careful not to interfere with the latter's concentration. The novice usually does little until it is his turn to play, hence the delay.

Another reason why poorer golfers do not develop a good putting technique is that few of the pressures of putting are placed upon them. Because their approach shot often misses the green, they play a lot of small chips and pitches and so are rarely faced with long putts.

Experts, who might hit the ball on to the green from 183m (200yd) or more, are likely to be putting regularly from the fringes, so it is necessary for them to get the ball very close to the hole with their approach putts. When they do miss a green and are forced to pitch up, their putt has to be holed, since

One of the finest putters in modern golf – American Raymond Floyd. Because of his physique, he always uses an extra long shafted putter.

they have no handicap allowance to deduct as others might.

Willie Park, the first winner of the British Open championship more than a century ago, said that a man who could putt was a match for anyone. This still applies today.

Reading a green

Three factors need to be taken into account before the actual putt: the texture of the grass, the slopes of the green and the weather conditions.

In Britain seaside links courses, built on sand and exposed to the elements, used to have the fastest greens. Many still have, particularly those on which the major championships are played. But watering is more frequently done now and even those greens notorious for fast pace have slowed considerably. With their very fine grass, however, they are still very slick, especially during the summer months.

Many inland courses boast fast-running surfaces and often those on which tournaments are played can be as fast as some seaside courses. When a course is prepared for a major event, the greens are often cut as much as twice a day for some time before the tournament. It is a test of the quality of the green that it can be maintained to play fast yet true.

The average golf course has a slightly thicker covering of coarse grass to withstand the wear and tear of players constantly walking over it. This thicker grass also acts as a protection in case of drought, when lack of water can cause the surface to burn off.

In certain countries, South Africa is one, the grain of the grass is sometimes so strong it can change the direction of a ball, even turning it uphill. Those who master such greens are obviously very good at reading the conditions correctly. By looking at the grass around the edge of a hole it is possible to see in which direction the

147

Putting

grass grows. To test the surface by rubbing it with the hand or club is illegal.

On certain American and Spanish courses, where there is no lack of water or sun, greens are cut extremely short and produce quite terrifying pace. This is a feature of the Augusta National Golf Course, where the US Masters is played annually. On such greens, approach shots stop and putts run fast.

Golfers who putt regularly on very fast greens quickly learn that a sense of feel is essential and the ability to roll the ball with a gentle stroke towards the hole is vital. On the slower-running greens, it is fairly safe to hit a putt of two feet or less directly at the hole, its firmness keeping it on course. On the faster surfaces, even the slightest slope must be catered for by aiming off centre.

Cross-green slopes

Allowing for a slope across the green by aiming off the target is referred to as 'taking a borrow' and it is exactly the amount borrowed from the top side of the hole that will allow gravity to bring the ball downhill into the hole.

A common expression used when a ball misses the hole on the top side is that it has 'passed on the professional's side'. If it passes on the lower side of the hole, this is known as the 'amateur's side'. Professionals tend to allow too much for swing, believing that with gravity a ball passing on the high side might just topple in. But it certainly cannot drop in if it passes below the hole.

Being able to read the borrow on a putt is a great gift and it is common for even the most expert player to ask the caddie to confirm his beliefs. Many caddies who work regularly over the same course have uncanny judgement, based on years of experience. Some of the touring caddies on the professional circuit, however, only have the memory of a few practice rounds, so they require a good eye.

There is, to a degree, a foolproof system called 'plumb bob lining-up', which en-

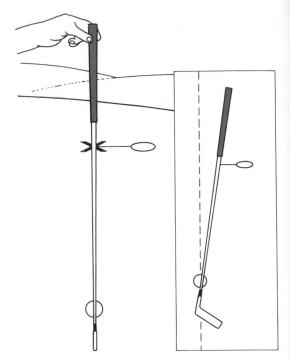

To work out the point on the green to aim at, using the 'plumb bob' method, hold the putter upright so the low part of the shaft passes visually through the centre of the ball. Look up the shaft until you reach that point on it that is opposite the hole. This is where you should aim the ball in order to use the slope correctly. The head of the putter must not lie across the line. If it does, the shaft will not hang vertically.

ables you to get a clear idea of how far the ball will turn.

This is normally carried out from a crouching position, with the ball lying directly between the line of your eye and the hole, although it can also be done from a standing position. This is ideal for older people or those who suffer from back trouble. When standing, the player needs to be farther away from the ball, whereas the normal crouch is done within just a few feet of it.

You should hold the putter lightly near the top of the handle, with the finger and thumb either side of the grip. Holding the side of the handle is essential, to ensure

Jan Stevenson, the Australian girl who plays the American circuit, lines up a putt using the 'plumb bob' method to work out the borrow required on the green.

that the toe of the putter is directly towards or away from the hole. Holding the top of the putter so the head hangs across the line will, because of the design of the putter, take the shaft off the vertical.

Once you have lined up the side of the shaft through the centre of the ball at a point just a few inches above the putter head, you should then sight up the shaft until you reach the point of the shaft that is opposite the hole.

Should the side of the shaft pass directly through the centre of the hole, then the putt is straight. Should it point several inches out to one side or the other, then that is the amount 'off' which is required to bring the ball back to the hole at the end of its roll.

Incidentally, this is good practice for when you tackle those chip-and-run shots from just off the edge of the putting green surface.

Up and down green slopes

The reason this 'plumb bob' technique only works to a limited degree is because it can be affected by the other slopes on the green, uphill and downhill, as well as the weather conditions. All these factors must be taken into consideration.

On a fast surface and going downhill, you should double the amount shown by the 'plumb bob' method or increase it even more if the green is exceptionally fast. On the other hand, for a putt up a steep slope you could require only half the amount, because the aggression of the strike together with a more sudden stop will cancel out much of the swing.

Weather

In heavy dew or rain, when you have to strike the ball more solidly, you need less borrow. Wind is probably the greatest problem, especially on exposed courses with fast greens. It is quite common for a cross wind to eliminate a fairly large borrow from the opposite side. When the wind is with the slope, together they so increase the curve that you have to make a

Putting

You will have to adjust the 'plumb bob' method when putting up or down a slope on the green. If you are putting up, where the ball must be hit firmly, you need only half the borrow. On the other hand, when playing down, you must increase the borrow because of the extra roll of the ball down the slope.

huge allowance because sometimes the ball cannot stop rolling.

You must never rush a putt in a strong wind. Professionals will mark the ball's position after a long approach putt, prior to holing out, just to make sure the ball is properly settled when replaced. There is nothing more distracting than the feeling that the ball might roll from its spot, blown by the wind, just as you are about to play the putt.

The putting stroke
Prior to a change in the rules some years ago, a putter was designed with a vertical shaft that entered the head at right angles. This enabled the player to swing his putter back between his legs then forwards in a direct line towards the hole. This was the croquet style, which permitted the only true pendulum movement in golf.

Even when croquet putters were legal, few players in fact used them.

With standard putters, the player must be to the side of the ball, and the shaft always enters the head at a slight angle. This makes stroking the ball less direct.

Putter shafts are still generally upright and short. With these it is not possible to have the hands directly above the centre of the ball, but you can lean the body forward, enabling the low, back-and-forth stroke of the putter to travel along the same line as the ball to the hole.

Despite allowing a direct view of the line of the shot, having your head and shoulders so far forward can cause one of putting's most common stroke problems. With longer shots, when your arms extend outwards, the shoulders take up a position where the left one is higher than the right. In this position the application of the right hand below the left becomes a fairly simple matter. When your head and shoulders come far out over a putt, the shoulders level out and it is difficult to apply the left hand

Modern computerized statistics show Nick Faldo to be a most consistent putter, often averaging as few as 27 putts per round.

Because of the upright lie of the putter, the handle must be allowed to pass through the palm of the left hand rather than across it, as with the grip on other clubs. To keep the left wrist forward, no knuckle joints should be seen from above. The thumbs of both hands must point directly down the handle.

to the grip without either breaking the wrist joint, buckling the elbow or turning the shoulder off line to the left.

One of the golden rules of putting is to keep everything square on: shoulders, arms, hips and feet. Certain adjustments have to be made to the set-up, but these only apply to this part of the game.

When you grip the putter, it should pass through the palm of the left hand just under the pad of the thumb, with the thumb itself placed directly on top of the handle. Unlike the standard grip, you can see the top of the handle – but none of your knuckle joints. When putting you do not rotate the forearms.

Standing so that the ball is opposite the toes of your left foot, take up the left-hand grip without any break in the wrist joint. Then add the right hand to the club, thumb on top, without the left coming back.

More players putt well in this position than in any other, although some individuals, like the Japanese player Isao Aoki, are also successful putting in an unorthodox position.

Having the left hand forward has long been recognized as a means of producing a smooth and accurate stroke, especially when under pressure. In the past, when the wrists were held farther back, many players engaged in what is called a 'forward press' where, just before starting the back stroke, the hands and wrists leaned to the left. Tom Watson, incidentally, still does this.

One who admits he would dearly love to be able to adopt this technique but

In order to keep his hands well forward, Jack Nicklaus engages a unique posture where his right side is very low and his stance 'open'.

seemingly cannot is the West German Bernhard Langer. He is so aware of the benefits, however, that he often applies his left hand below his right while putting.

Jack Nicklaus adopted an unusual posture with his whole body well behind his left arm. Although it meant having a very 'open' line of stance, it allowed the wrists to stay forward.

Apart from a slight rocking of the shoulders, mainly on the longer putts which require a fuller stroke, there should be very little body movement to enable the head to be kept very still. Turning to look at the hole a fraction too soon can affect the direction of the putter, taking it across the ball on the strike.

As far as the putting pace is concerned, this is a personal thing. Some prefer a stroke that is almost the same length, both back and through, with every putt, hitting the ball more firmly for the longer putt. Others prefer to keep the stroke slow, with a constant tempo, and lengthen the swing as the length of the shot increases.

Putting on tiered greens

Greens built on two or more levels are common on courses all over the world, as this provides an ideal way of constructing them on a natural hillside. Unfortunately, some designers have attempted to build them on courses where the ground around is as flat as a pancake, making the different levels with imported soil. The effect may well be the same when you are on the green, but the problem comes when you play too bold an approach shot and fall off the top deck. You are then often faced with an awkward shot back to the green.

You need plenty of skill to get down in two putts on these greens and very few

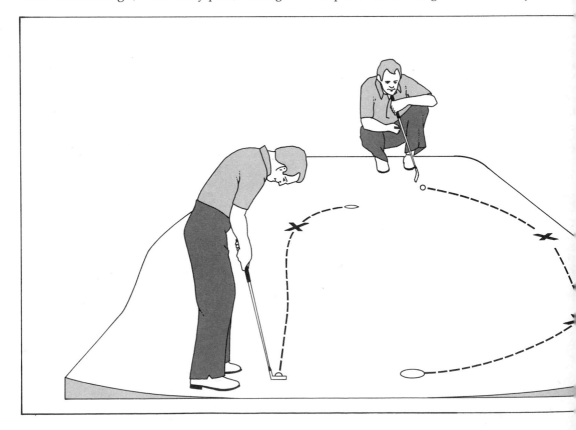

players can ever hope for a single putt, especially when it is long and the direction to the hole is diagonal. Much of the skill comes in reading the green correctly, but playing up or down a step requires a very different strategy.

Putting down a tiered green

The first thing you must check when playing downhill on a tiered green is the borrow on the bottom level so that you can fix the exact point over which the ball must pass to roll to the hole. The next point to establish is the one at the top of the slope from where the ball, running downhill, would travel over the first point on its way to the hole.

Finally, you have to work out what borrow, if any, you require to get the ball from where it lies to that point at the top of the slope. What you have is a route to the hole

When putting up a tiered green, because of the extra strength required in the shot, you only need one reference point for the borrow – at the top of the slope. Coming downhill, however, because of the extra pace generated on the ball as it runs down the slope you will need two reference points – one at the top of the slope and the other at the bottom.

via two checkpoints on the putting green.

The next problem is the pace, since the ball must get over the top of the slope and must not, under any circumstances, be left short. This might mean, if the slope is severe and the green fast, that the ball will roll beyond the hole. If you leave the putt short, you will still have to face the slope and may need as many as four putts.

With a more gentle slope, where there is some surface available at the bottom to allow the ball to run out, it is a case of judging how much additional roll the slope will give the ball and making the necessary allowance.

When striking the putt, your eyes must look at the point at the top of the slope and not be tempted towards the hole. All you can do is set the ball off towards that point, even though it may be very nearly at right angles if you are putting from the side of the green. Play the shot with conviction and let the hill do the rest.

Putting up a tiered green

Putting up from the bottom level to the top is not quite so difficult, for you will need to strike the ball more firmly to get it up the slope and this helps you to play positively. Also, when you are standing on the bottom, it is much easier to read the top part of the green since, being higher, it is nearer to your eye level.

You will need to make a greater allowance when coming up a slope from an angle and in this situation your reading of the top level will be crucial in determining whether you have to add to or subtract from this allowance.

If you are putting up and across a slope on a diagonal course, you may have to aim off a seemingly incredible amount. It is sound advice on a really tricky slope to over-borrow, since many players who have tried to be too exact have ended up back on the bottom level, on the opposite side.

There is really only one way to learn about putting up slopes from an angle and that is to practise.

Playing from bunkers

There are two types of bunker play – greenside and fairway. Greenside involves getting the ball up and out of the sand but without too much length in the shot. Fairway is when the bunker is a long way from the green and you require as much distance as possible for an effective recovery. In the latter case, it is possible that the ball is lying badly or close to a steep bank and therefore a greenside-type shot is your only way out.

Some top professionals are renowned for their skill at playing out of bunkers around the green; Gary Player is one. Skill, not strength, is the answer when the ball lies close to a steep bank, half buried in soft sand and with the pin not 6m (20ft) away.

In this case you are playing a trick shot where many of the adjustments you have to make would damage your normal swing if you over-practised them. You should only practise bunker play for short spells – never more than, say, 20 shots in any one practice session.

The splash shot
Just over a quarter of a century ago 'blasters' and 'exploders' were the names given to sand clubs. These very heavy clubs were, as their name suggests,

Left: One of the factors that contributes to Nick Faldo's low putting average is his ability to put the ball close to the hole – even from sand.
Below: When playing the splash shot, the very full swing required will send the ball upwards but only a short distance forward. The flight is weakened through the combination of the ball being far forward in the stance, with the feet, hips and shoulders aimed well to the left, and the club face lying 'open' from the resulting swing path. When playing this shot, the flange on the bottom of the sand wedge stops the club head penetrating too deeply into the sand. So you need only to aim the strike an inch or so before the ball (inset).

designed to get the ball out of sand. To achieve this, you had to aim at a point just short of the ball, ensuring that according to the rules you did not ground the club before the actual strike, then blast sand and ball the required distance out on to the green. If you had to send the ball just a very short distance, then you removed a greater amount of sand. The longer the shot, the less sand you took before the ball.

Gary Player has over the years gained the reputation of being one of the finest bunker players. Much of this is due to his 'never give up' type of determination as well as his skill in playing these types of shot.

The techniques of bringing the ball up and out of sand have changed considerably since then, with the introduction of lighter sand irons, although these do possess broad-flanged soles. The flange tends to make the club bounce rather than penetrate, so the heavier weight is no longer necessary since less sand has to be moved.

The latest technique does everything possible to reduce the power and swing required as you play through sand and ball. Unlike grass shots, where you need to keep the left side of your body firm to ensure good striking, here the left side almost crumbles completely.

Instead of swinging the club head directly into the ball to drive it forward, you deliberately lead it across the ball, totally defusing its power. The object is to get the ball to come up nearly vertical and travel forward as little as possible.

What causes a ball to rise steeply is the fullness of the swing arc. Poor bunker players, seeing the flag so close, tend to use a short swing and the ball does not lift. A lofted club and a very full arc will do the

job. The pace of the swing determines how far the ball will travel forward. With a full arc and extremely slow pace, you can get the ball to climb but travel only a short distance forward.

Another means of restraining the forward flight of the ball is to reduce the value of the impact by taking your left side out of the way to remove any resistance to the hit. You can do this by having the ball extremely far forward in the stance, at the same time allowing the line of the stance and the shoulders to turn off to the left. By adjusting the grip, you can set the leading edge of the blade of the club to face the flag.

Because of your body alignment, the entire swing arc is across what would be a ball-to-target line. The swing itself should be unhurried, fully back then fully through. If you accelerate at all through the swing, you could turn the blade of the club head and misdirect the ball to the left or even play it into the high face of the bunker.

Unlike with the old method of blasting, the point of contact should remain constant – about an inch before the ball. Only the pace of the swing should determine the length of the shot.

With the splash shot, the metal of the club does not come into direct contact with the ball, for there is always a thin layer of sand between. Nevertheless any abrasive sand will impart quite a back spin. As the swing arc across the ball causes a slight slicing effect, the ball will come to a halt very quickly when it lands on the green.

Plugged ball

If the ball is partly buried in the sand and the light splash shot proves unsuitable, then you will have to play the blasting type of shot. Here you need to play a strong, firm shot, so square up your body and stance. You will want a fairly long swing, but it must be firm, even accelerating into the sand behind the ball.

When you take up the stance, wriggle your feet well down into the sand, for two

You will need to play an aggressive shot when the ball is plugged in the sand, so square up the bodyline and stance and play the ball centrally. You will have to remove a fair amount of sand to get the ball out.

reasons. Firstly it is the only legal way of testing the sand's texture. Secondly it gets the potential base of the arc below the level of the ball, helping strengthen the shot.

Make sure the ball is opposite the centre of the stance and judge carefully how much sand you need to strike before the ball. The bottom of the club must get below the base point of the ball if this is to rise, so you may have to swing the club into the sand several inches short.

You will lose the advantage of the height gained from the splash shot. Another feature of this shot is that there can be no back spin. You must therefore make allowance for a considerable run-out across the green. If there is a bunker directly in line beyond the pin, you may even have to play away from the flag into space.

Ball on up-slope

This, according to the professionals, is one of the most difficult bunker shots. Yet to the average player it looks as though the up-slope is making it easier for the ball to travel up and out.

The problem is that there is no sand for the blade of the club to make contact with before it hits the ball. So the simple splash shot cannot be used. Nor can you take the risk of swinging into the ball with only the amount of strength required to get the ball to the flag, in case the leading edge of the blade touches the crumbling texture before hitting the ball.

The expert attempts to lean, but not into the hill, since this would result in driving the ball into the slope. He leans backwards, almost defying gravity, as though he was playing on a level surface.

This provides him with enough sand to splash through at the base of his swing, even if he overbalances afterwards.

Ball on down-slope

The difficulty here is that you are likely to hit the sand well before the club head gets anywhere near the ball. In this situation, the impact point is not just before the ball but also above it, so the club never gets to a level below the ball.

Make sure the ball is as far back in the

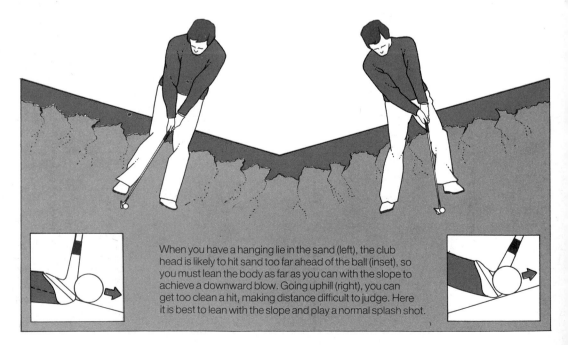

When you have a hanging lie in the sand (left), the club head is likely to hit sand too far ahead of the ball (inset), so you must lean the body as far as you can with the slope to achieve a downward blow. Going uphill (right), you can get too clean a hit, making distance difficult to judge. Here it is best to lean with the slope and play a normal splash shot.

stance as possible, even beyond the line of the right foot, if necessary. You must swing the club head upwards, almost vertical, then strike a firm downward blow behind the ball, aiming to continue on with whatever through swing you can achieve down the slope.

Unfortunately you cannot turn the blade of the club outwards when addressing the ball, since the flange would cause the blade to bounce right over it. With the face of the club head 'closed', the ball will fly forward on a low trajectory and without much back spin. But with this and many bunker shots, players are happy just to get out.

Wet sand

When the sand is wet and compacted and the ball sits on it with none of its circumference below the top level, you can play a form of splash shot known as a bounce.

If your sand iron has a low flange, you would be better off using the pitching wedge. Otherwise you follow most of the principles of the splash shot. Position yourself with the ball forward, the stance and body line off to the left and the club face laid fairly 'open' to the target. The difference here is that you must deliberately narrow the swing arc, bringing it almost up, down, then up again.

With skilful hand and wrist movement, you must bounce the bottom of the club on the compacted sand, at the exact point of contact with the ball, when the club head reaches the base of the 'U'.

This is a very difficult shot with a high chance of failure. But it was often attempted from the old compacted cinder road behind the famous 17th hole at St Andrews, as players competing in the Open championship tried to flick the ball over the steep bank to the green. Many succeeded, but just as many failed and wished they had not tried.

The alternative is to play a straightforward type of pitch shot, catching the sand just before the ball, but allowing the ball to travel to the far end of the green.

Fairway bunkers

Keeping a cool head and thinking constructively is essential when playing from a fairway bunker. You are bound to think that you are going to drop a stroke and therefore attempt a very risky shot in the hope of recovering it. You may try for too much distance by choosing a club with insufficient loft, so that the ball fails to gain enough height to clear the face of the bunker. By forcing the shot, you may catch the sand before the ball and lose distance rather than gain it. Or you may go for a distant green and land in another punishing hazard *en route*.

Provided the ball is not close up against the face of the bunker, in which case you should play one of the greenside bunker shots, then you are looking for a fairly normal shot. The club you choose should be at least one more lofted than the club that might get you out, because you must feel confident of the loft. Play towards the part of the fairway that affords the simplest next shot to the pin.

Position yourself with the ball opposite the centre of the stance. You only need to wriggle your feet slightly into the sand to gain a good footing. Do not go in too deep, for the bottom of this swing does not have to be low under the ball. It is worth gripping the club about an inch down the handle, for this stabilizes the wrist action and enables you to hit the ball off the sand more cleanly. You must not make contact with sand before the ball.

Provided you take these steps and the ball is sitting up well away from the face of a shallow bunker, it is worth a No 5 wood.

On the subject of 'steps', you should always tread carefully into a bunker and approach the stance position from the back of it and never down the face. Deep footprints can catch a ball that does not make it out on the first attempt and this will render it virtually unplayable. Footprints and the scuff mark from the club should be raked smooth before you leave the bunker; that is part of the etiquette of golf.

Getting out of trouble

In the 1983 season Nick Faldo won five major European events. At the time many believed he had equalled the record held by another Englishman – Bernard Hunt. The PGA, however, subsequently announced that Hunt's total included one event which was of only 36 holes and that major events had to be 72 holes.

Hunt announced at the close of the 1963 season, when the previous record was set, that at the start of that year he had decided on a policy for getting himself out of trouble. He would take absolutely no chances, but play safely back to the fairway. He stuck to it religiously through that year and it certainly paid off.

There are many players who, in hindsight, wish they had done the same. There is a long list of championships that have been lost at the very last hurdle by players taking a risk. It is always better to be wise before the event, for the expression 'out of the frying pan and into the fire' often applies when the over-ambitious player attempts a long shot from a poor situation.

Of course there are occasions, particularly in matchplay events, when there is no option other than to take a risk. If, for example, you are one down with only a hole to play and find yourself in the trees while your opponent is on the green, then you have to play a risky shot. Nevertheless it is sensible to seek the best point on the fairway and play to that. It is surprising how many times, when this has happened, the player has got down with a pitch and a putt to save his par.

Thick grass and heather

When the ball lies deep in thick grass, select a club with plenty of loft. This should be one more lofted than the club you feel you might just get out with. By playing the ball well back in the stance and striking it with a downward blow, you will still have sufficient loft on the club face to lift the ball out from the vegetation.

A good loft means a heavier head and a shorter shaft. These suit the upright swing arc required to produce the cleanest hit when the grass is thick just in front of the ball. However skilful a player you are, there is bound to be grass between the blade of the club and the ball. Whereas with a straight-faced club you would fail to lift the ball, by using one with more loft you can bring the leading edge well below the ball before the cushioning effect of the grass takes place.

You must grip the club quite tightly, particularly if the grass is heavy with rain. Sometimes you may even have to reduce the swing to a chop, keeping your back swing nearly vertical. If the situation is that serious, you should use a sand iron and

When playing out of thick rough, there will always be a cushion of grass between the blade of the club and the ball on impact; the less this cushion, the better. By using a lofted club and steepening the angle of the swing, you can still make powerful contact.

Left: Severiano Ballesteros prepares to play out of water in the 1979 Ryder Cup at The Greenbrier, West Virginia.

163

pick the most direct route to the fairway. If you find that a ball with this type of lie is within range of the green, remember you will not be able to impart any back spin to stop the ball. The cushion of grass prevents the club head from effecting any spin. Nevertheless it is better to have the ball running to the back of the green rather than to attempt a soft hit and leave the ball in the rough. If this happens, you have the same problem all over again – and this time your morale may be shattered.

The wiry texture of heather has a unique effect on the club, making it an ideal golfing hazard. It snarls up around the socket of the club and immediately turns the head inwards. Only the strongest player, using a vice-like grip, can keep the blade of the club going on towards the target. The average player must use plenty of loft and aim for the widest, nearest bit of fairway.

It is always surprising to see golfers tie a piece of heather on their bag to bring them good luck. It really is the most unlucky stuff in golf to tangle with.

Trees, bushes and gorse

There is an old saying that trees are 90 per cent air. But golfers who have attempted to play through the branches and leaves will tell you that they should be treated as if they are 100 per cent solid wood.

The same can be said of shrubbery and gorse. No one should ever play a shot directly at these in the hope that the ball will make its way through to the other side. They are objects which may be played under, over or around – but never through.

Up and over The choice of club depends on how high the obstacle is and how far away it is from the ball. Often, when a tree or bush is growing some way ahead, even though it lies in a direct line to the green, by playing a normal shot with the correct

Bernhard Langer found himself in this near-impossible situation at the side of the 17th green during the Benson & Hedges Tournament at Fulford, England, in August 1982 – and got the ball on to the green.

Getting out of trouble

length club you will hit the ball well over the obstacle anyway.

Problems arise when the ball is so close to the obstacle that you have to alter your normal swing to gain height early enough. Equally you may get an awkward length whereby the flight from a pitching wedge would take the ball high enough to get over the obstacle, but for the required distance you need to use, say, a No 7 iron. In this case, you must increase the lofting effect of the longer club.

Set the blade of the club to the ball with the face laid slightly 'open'. This does not, as you might think, send the ball more than fractionally off to the right. But it does add to the degree of loft on the face, while enabling you to use a longer iron to obtain a good length.

Bring the feet into an 'open' but fairly narrow stance, with the ball very well forward. Like the feet, your shoulder line

When playing up and over an obstacle, you will need to reduce the width of the stance and turn the body off line to the left. This will increase the amount of work in the hands and wrist during the swing and will cause the ball to climb very high.

When playing under and out from an obstacle, keep the ball well backward in the stance and the hands well forward, with the loft of the club turned down. Provided the hands stay forward through the strike, you will give the ball a low trajectory and it will shoot forward on landing.

should be slightly off to the left. Grip well up to the top of the handle.

Additional suppleness in the wrist action is the key and here the narrow stance will encourage the early wrist break you need during the back swing. It is good to overswing here otherwise, with the 'open' stance you have adopted, the chances are your shoulders may not turn enough. A full swing is an essential ingredient for extra height and you must continue this on into the follow-through, with the help of good footwork.

The swing plane will be fairly upright. Although this is mostly determined by the set-up, you should be aware of the steeper angle, which enables the hands to speed up the club head as it passes through under the ball at the base of the swing.

The closer the ball is to the obstacle, the more lofted the club you need and the lazier the swing. To gain height, go for full swing as the pace is not so important.

Under and out It is remarkable how quickly a ball flies up when you try to keep it low. Even the straighter-faced clubs seem to lift the ball high enough to collide with the one branch it looked sure to miss. To avoid this, use the chip-and-run technique, where the hands stay ahead of the blade. This you can do even with aggressive shots so the ball, once through and into the clear, can run on towards the green.

If there are low overhanging branches just ahead, use a fairly straight club. A No 4 or No 5 is the minimum, since if you set the hands forward, any straighter club will be delofted and the ball simply will not lift.

Aim the blade of the club at the chosen target and take up your stance fairly wide this time, with the ball well back almost in line with your right foot.

As for chipping, lean the club shaft forward, taking care that the blade's leading edge remains 'square', for it can easily be turned 'open' as you lean the shaft. Place the handle into the left hand at a point well forward of the ball.

By shortening the back swing, you get a better feeling of rigidity in the shot. Keep the back of the left wrist slightly hooded. It should stay that way during impact and on into what little through swing there is.

The satisfaction of playing this shot comes from the success gained rather than the quality of the strike, which is never that great because of the stunning effect of the blade on the ball.

Playing around trouble

Another way of avoiding trees is by playing around them – a fairly skilful exercise, especially when the ball has to turn from left to right. In comparison, hooking the ball is a much simpler method. The reason for this is that the hook spin can be put on the ball with any of the clubs – except,

Severiano Ballesteros looks anxiously after the ball to see how well he has recovered from this extraordinary and awkward position.

perhaps, the straightest-faced wood or iron. Only the straighter-faced clubs, however, can slice.

Slicing around This is best done when the ball is lying on firm ground. Even a spot that appears difficult because there is little grass is ideal for this shot. The last thing you want to do is strike the bottom of the ball since side spin of the slicing variety is created when hitting the ball almost halfway up.

When choosing your club, the straighter the face you use the better. Anything more lofted than a No 5 iron will make contact too low on the ball and cause back spin, the enemy of slice – and you cannot play this shot in thick grass. In this situation play the ball to a point on the fairway offering the best next shot.

As detailed in the chapter on spinning balls, you must swing the club head across the face of the ball. Keep the blade 'open' so that the ball, after setting off well to the left of the tree, turns back in towards the green. If the distance to the green is less than you would normally achieve with the straighter-faced iron, even from a weakened hit, hold the club lower down the handle and reduce the length and power of the swing. What you must not do is select a more lofted club.

Hooking around Hooking the ball around a tree is fairly simple. The easiest method, and one favoured by many experts including Greg Norman, is to set up to the ball for a straightforward swing, aiming to the right. Then, by simply turning the blade of the club in your hands so that it lies hooked, hit the ball forward as normal.

Even from a slightly turned-in club, the hook spin can be quite dramatic, so do not overdo it. Remember that this spin tends to cause the ball to shoot sharply forward on landing, so make allowance for this. It is no good pitching this type of shot directly on to the green.

There is another point to consider. A club turned in is a club delofted, so a No 8 iron will strike the ball with the loft of a No 7 or 6, depending on the amount of toe-in you apply. If you are not careful, you can easily smother the ball.

There is a more complicated method of hooking, used when the ball either has to turn sharply or when it has to come out from under trees on a low trajectory and then turn. It is extremely tricky and normally the reserve of the expert.

Apart from turning in the blade of the club, you have to direct the swing path very much from 'in' to 'out' (again detailed in the chapter on spinning balls) and use your hands to roll the club through the point of impact. Only attempt this when the lie is good, since the low angle of swing needed will cause the club to tie up with any leaves or long grass before it hits the ball.

Playing from a hazard

When the ball lies in a water hazard – lateral or ordinary (marked by red and yellow stakes respectively) – you can play it out rather than incur a penalty by dropping it clear. Only consider this, however, when the ball lies reasonably well. On occasions, when the water has receded, the ball may only lie in thickish grass, not mud or water, and may be playable.

At no time can you touch or remove anything near the ball that lies inside the line of the stakes. Nor can you ground your club while addressing the ball, just as in the rules relating to bunkers.

This type of shot requires great accuracy and the average player is advised to select a club with a short shaft and ample loft, so that he can stand well over the ball.

To even consider playing a ball out of the water, at least the top of it must be above the surface. To reach the base of a submerged ball means the club head has to enter the water 10cm (4in) or so short of it. The result of such an effort is usually a good soaking and very little else.

If the ball, although in water, still lies on grass, it could be persuaded to fly up because there is some resistance below. If it is in a pebble stream, where it cannot be driven farther down, there is a good chance of it bouncing.

The important thing to consider, before taking off your shoes and socks, is the advantage you might gain. Is it possible to get that shot on to the green? If so, then it is certainly worth a try. If, by gaining some yards down the fairway with this as the second shot you can then reach a par five hole with the third, then it could be worth the risk. If, however, by getting it out you are only reducing the next shot to the green by a few yards, then it is not worth it. In this case, the penalty drop will do almost the same thing – and without risk.

Other trouble shots

One of the greatest assets top professionals have is a pair of hands that can make a whole number of changes to the angle of attack on the ball. This allows them a far greater chance of recovering successfully.

When the water is this deep, all you get is wet!

When the problem is the lie of the ball, rather than something in the way, they can increase or reduce the angle of swing as required and contact the ball first, which is the key to playing successful trouble shots. **Divot holes.** Golfing etiquette insists that players replace any divots and tread them in. But it is fairly common to find, after playing a perfectly good shot down the fairway, that the ball is resting in a divot hole. Often the divots are removed by birds in search of food.

In a divot, the base of the ball is obviously below the surface so you have to bring the club head down steeply from the top of the back swing if you want to hit the ball cleanly. Use a more lofted club because much of the loft will be lost in the steep swing, and play with the ball backward in your stance. Using your hands and wrists, deliberately bring the club upwards, even slightly outwards, to a point that feels almost above your head, instead of around the shoulders as you would in a normal swing plane.

Your down swing will not be particularly elegant – more of a chop. This will drive the club head farther into the ground after contact with the ball. Even with fairly lofted irons, you will send the ball forward on a fairly low trajectory.

With such lofted clubs you will not normally get any slice spin. But in this case, because you are striking well up the ball, there is every chance of slice spin, which will cause the ball to veer to the right.
Raised ball On heathery courses, you will often find the ball raised some inches from the ground, held up by the plant. This can also happen with a clump of rough grass or gorse or a bramble bush.

Here your hands must show their skill by getting the back swing to flatten well below the normal swing plane. As with a sidehill lie when the ball is above the stance, they must control the wide swing arc to enable the club to hit the ball off its perch accurately. As with the sidehill shot, you should expect to hook the ball.

169

Coping with the weather

Golf at championship level used to be affected by weather much more than it is today. Competitors went out on the course in the order in which they were drawn from the hat, so it was possible to find one player finishing his round with a potential winning score while many of his rivals were yet to go out, often in changing weather conditions.

This was the case when Irishman Fred Daly won his British Open championship in 1947. It is said that as he holed his final putt of the round, having played in ideal weather, a sudden gust of wind blew the flags above the club house horizontal. They stayed there for the rest of the day and the remainder of the field was blown all over the course. So Daly's score, posted early on, eventually won the championship.

This should not happen today, since over the last two days of every strokeplay championship and tournament the players with the lowest scores are drawn together. It is anticipated that the winner will come from the last few groups of players, which means that the leaders play under the same conditions, whether they be good or bad, at the same time.

Golf almost produced one of the biggest ever upsets when, in the 1983 British Open championship at Royal Birkdale, the Australian Graham Marsh, having been sufficiently far down the field that he had commenced his round a good hour or more ahead of the leading group, recorded a phenomenal score.

When he birdied the long 17th, the breeze became much stronger and the flags surrounding the magnificent arena of the 18th hole stretched out. He admitted later

On some players the sun always shines, even when it's raining. On this occasion it is on Zimbabwe's Tony Johnstone, who holes a chip shot.

that, after getting his four at the last and recording a fantastic 64, he began to think he might steal the championship. Unfortunately for Marsh, as his final putt went in and the galleries roared, the flags went limp. The wind had gone – and with it his hopes of victory.

Strong wind

Strong wind is probably the greatest threat to the golfer as far as the elements are concerned, particularly when playing at a seaside links course. Apart from the fact that there is little shelter by way of trees, hillsides or buildings, there is often the question of changes in the tide.

Links normally have approximately half of their holes going in one direction along the coastline and the other half coming back – hence the golfing description of the nines as 'out' and 'in'. It is possible to play the first nine into a gale then find that, in conjunction with the turn of the tide, the wind is against you all the way back in as well.

Even on inland courses, with their sheltered fairways and high trees, the ball will soar above them. What appeared to be a straightforward shot to the player protected in the lee of a thick forest can turn out quite different, if the ball is blown off course once it climbs above the tree tops.

There is no such thing as a kindly wind, even though many golfers say they enjoy a drive with the wind behind for it minimizes the effect of side spin and helps the ball go down the fairway. Others claim to like a wind that blows from right to left across a fairway, pushing into the front of the body as they line up for the shot. Such a wind helps a player to turn his body more confidently than when it blows against the back or over the left shoulder.

While such winds may make for an easier swing on the tee shot, they will provide problems when the second shot is to be played. With the wind from behind, it is hard to stop the ball on the green and the wind from the player's right encourages a

hook spin which also makes stopping the ball difficult.

Over the years several players have gained a reputation for playing well in the wind – and most have been short in stature. This is because the shorter players are prone to have a shallow swing plane which, although it tends to cause a hook spin, keeps the ball on a lower trajectory. It was the continual playing on windy links-land courses that caused the development of what was known as a 'Scottish flat swing'.

One of the greatest players of all time in the wind was Australian Peter Thomson, whose Scottish name matched his style of swinging which won him no fewer than five British Open championships. Arnold Palmer, the great American who loved playing on British links courses, also had a shallow turn into the swing and his low boring drives made him a winner, too.

Apart from the shape of the swing, there is a great advantage in having a cool head and an ability to control the flight of the ball. There is a time to go with the wind and a time to fight it, a time to play a delicate shot and a time to punch. Knowing, for example, whether to slice-spin a ball against the wind or to aim off line and let the ball blow back with the wind can make even an average golfer do well in blustery conditions.

A cool head in a crisis and the ability to accept that the rest of the field is being affected in the same way, so that higher scores are bound to be recorded, is very necessary when things look bleak.

The following guidelines will prove helpful on a windy day and you should study them carefully and remember them when you have to play in such conditions. You must forget the old attitude that a well-struck ball will not be affected by the wind. Perhaps in the days of the 1.62in ball that might have been the case, but with today's larger ball always allow for the wind and presume that the flight will be affected by whatever kind of wind is blowing.

You only have to watch the tournament stars throwing bits of grass into the air, even on what appears to be the calmest of days, as they search for whatever breeze may be drifting about. If they are concerned by such breaths of air, then you should be, too.

Wind behind: tee shots

Players always tend to gain a feeling of confidence when the wind is directly behind them, since this helps the ball travel farther. If you force the drive and reduce the angle of the club face in the process, however, you will lose what advantage there might be from the wind. You must get the ball up so the wind can add to its flight – and the more loft you can put on the ball the better.

One way of doing this is by playing off a higher tee peg, and another is standing slightly backward of the ball. Some players prefer to use a No 3 wood rather than a driver and this is not a bad policy, because with the added back spin the ball will take on more of the tail wind and the accuracy and control of the shot will be increased.

Many of the course's hazards, such as ditches, streams and cross-fairway bunkers, can be brought into range of a driver when a very strong wind favours the shot and you must consider this problem before playing your shot. You should know the distance to the hazard, either through previous experience of the course or by using a distance chart. You must also know the distance you would carry the shot in normal conditions, so that you can make an accurate calculation using the wind.

With dog-leg holes, where the fairway turns either to the right or the left at just about the point where an average drive would land, it is possible with a very strong tail wind to overshoot the fairway and run into the rough or trees beyond the corner. In this situation you would be advised to hold back on your club selection, even to the extent of using an iron club from the tee.

Wind behind: tee shots at short holes

According to the strength of the wind, you would expect to choose a more lofted club to make allowance for the wind and still play a straightforward shot. Having the wind behind, however, can present other problems, particularly if, for example, the greenkeeper has positioned the flag directly behind a bunker guarding the front of the green. Here there are several options you should consider before rushing into the shot.

The first concerns the tee peg. Although the peg is not compulsory, no tee shot should be played without one if there is a tail wind. You can raise the peg so that the ball is perched almost half an inch above the turf, the normal height being about half that. This will allow you to have the ball farther forward in the stance, encouraging a lazier action in the swing.

The flight of the ball will then be higher and softer and this will enable you to drop the ball more gently on to the putting surface close to the bunker and pin. Since the stopping power you normally gain from more aggressive shots cannot be achieved down wind, the softer the ball lands the less distance it will run forward.

Another option you should consider is whether the risk of playing for that tricky pin position is sensible or not. A soft shot that plummets down into a deep guarding bunker will leave you a difficult next shot. Apart from the fact that the ball may plug into the sand, you will have very little room in which to land the ball on the green. The combination of blasting the ball free of the bunker and the down wind could carry the ball to the far side of the green or even beyond it.

It might be more sensible not to challenge the greenkeeper at all, but to play for the heart of the green and settle for a longer approach putt back to the hole. This is not a negative way of thinking. Bear in mind that the steady player will always do better in strong winds. The other advantage of this tactic is that the approach putt will be back into the wind and this will allow you a positive stroke.

Wind behind: second shots

Disaster always lurks when you come to play second shots, particularly those at par five holes where, with the benefit of the longer drive, you may be tempted to go for the green. A greedy selection of a very straight-faced wood really serves no purpose, since the advantage gained from the lifting spin of a No 3 or No 4 wood, together with the feeling of greater confidence in the actual hit, will make up for what might be achieved should you connect successfully with the more risky club.

When the ball is tight on the turf, the bottom of the club cannot make contact below the centre of the ball. It is almost certain that, while you will achieve some side spin on the ball, you cannot get any back spin on it. Using a No 4 wood, with its 20 degrees of loft and its heavy brass sole plate, you will be able to make contact well below the 'waistline' of the ball and effect a healthy back spin.

You can play second shots using an iron from a position just forward of normal with a slightly narrowed stance. This will cause the wrist to cock sooner going back and allow you more feel in the stroke. You will also achieve a softer, more soaring flight on the ball, which is ideal for getting it to land more gently on the green. Of course you should choose a more lofted club accordingly to suit the situation.

Wind behind: short shots

Once inside the range of a full-length shot, you will need a more delicate touch when playing to the greens, for even with the more lofted clubs very little stopping spin is available when hitting down wind. To get the ball to settle on the green, you will have to bring it down from the greatest height and at the slowest speed possible. This is not as difficult as it sounds and with the modern clubs and a knowledge of the

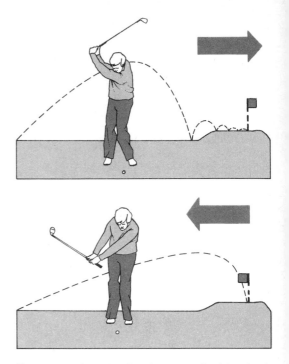

The way you play on to a tiered green may be determined by the strength and direction of the wind. When playing a high lob with the wind (top), you should aim to land the ball short and let it run since the following wind will counteract the back spin. When playing into a strong wind (bottom), you should hit a firm low pitch shot, since the ball will gain height and then come to a sudden standstill as the backspin, exaggerated by the head wind, takes effect.

techniques required these shots can be fun to play.

You will need plenty of loft in the shot and should not be afraid to use the sand iron from the grass, provided there is a reasonable amount of turf beneath the ball. One danger here is that with some sand irons the flange may make contact with the earth too soon if the lie is tight, with the result that you mishit the ball badly. In this situation, you can use a pitching wedge, with the face laid slightly 'open' to add more loft.

You should play the ball from a forward position, the effect of which will cause the shoulders to open and the swing to go slightly across the ball from 'out' to 'in', thus adding even more loft. You should narrow your stance considerably; this will result in a more than usual amount of wrist break in the back swing and a near flick of hands, wrists and club head through the ball. This will enable you to achieve the desired floating flight with the ball.

Wind against: tee shots

Hitting the ball into a strong wind is, without doubt, very difficult. There is always the temptation to hit the ball harder. If you narrow the swing, you will reduce the face angle of the club and smother the ball. One suggestion is to play with a more relaxed swing and hit the ball less hard.

Another option is to tee up with the ball farther back in the stance, yet keep the hands well forward. This way you can keep down the degree of loft on the club. But there is always the danger of contacting the ball too high on the face of the club, with the result that you balloon the ball up into the sky.

Many players claim that it was easier some years ago when drivers were made with as little as 6 degrees of loft and the smaller ball was in use. Perhaps it was, but in those days players used a more wristy swing. When playing into the wind, those who were prone to slicing – and a high percentage were – sliced enormous distances off line. Today's drivers may have as much as double the amount of loft and the ball may be bigger and more vulnerable to the wind, but together they have helped the swing technique to improve and slicing is not so prevalent.

The best method of taking on the drive into a strong head wind is as follows. First accept that you are going to sacrifice distance. If the wind makes a hole that is normally a long two-shotter into a three-shotter, then accept that on that particular day it will play as a par five. Probably the very next hole on the course will be a par five and, if it is in the opposite direction, it may well be reachable in two.

Cut down the length of the driver by gripping it 2.5cm (1in) down the handle. The effect is to reduce the club's swing weight, which in turn places less pressure on the wrist joints and dulls their activity. The less wrist movement there is in the swing, the less club head action there will be through the ball and therefore the less spin on it. It is this that keeps the ball from soaring upwards and losing its distance.

It is also perfectly acceptable to play the ball slightly backward in the stance. This has the effect of closing the shoulder line and causes the swing path of the club to be a touch from 'in-to-out'. This helps you to achieve a 'draw flight' on the ball and many top players prefer this when playing into the wind, since they gain the benefit of a bit of run.

You should never tee up with the ball too far forward, for this has the opposite effect. It turns the shoulder line 'open' to the left, encouraging an 'out-to-in' swing path and a sliced shot. If this happens, you will lose a lot of distance against the wind.

When driving into a wind, players are tempted to hit the ball harder and then any fault will be exaggerated. The best method is to position the ball slightly backward in a wider stance and reduce the length of the handle. Stability is essential when playing into a strong wind.

Coping with the weather

Wind against: tee shots at short holes

It is always sound policy to take a stronger club at the short holes when playing into a strong wind and to aim for the back of the green. Even from the best of iron shots, the ball will inevitably soar upwards to the peak of its flight and the subsequent descent will be vertical. This is all right if the ball falls on to the back of the green. But if you use an insufficient club and the ball drops into a bunker, it is almost certain to plug into the sand.

The use of a tee peg is largely a matter of choice, but for average players a low peg is recommended. You will find there are many experienced players who play the shot directly from the turf of the teeing area, since they prefer the feel of punching the ball from the tight turf and the control they gain from it a more positive strike.

When playing a short shot into the wind, use a straighter-faced iron, keep the swing down to threequarter-length and make sure your hands are ahead of the blade of the club at impact. Aim to land the ball beyond the flag, since you will impart a good deal of back spin on the ball even though the club loft is minimal.

This can be dangerous, for teeing areas are not like fairways. The turf becomes very compacted under players' feet. So even a good player, who is only a fraction out with his swing, may strike the turf before the ball and mishit badly.

Instead of teeing up, many tournament players knock the club head gently into the turf in the opposite direction to that in which they are playing, so that the turf bulges slightly. This gives the ball that comfortable bit of elevation, while still allowing the punchy type of impact the players prefer.

Depending on the strength of the wind, it is good advice to use as much as a three or four less lofted club than you would normally use over the required distance on a calm day. Grip the club down the handle to reduce the wrist action. This way you will drive the ball with a firm swing and a short, decisive finish, keeping the blade of the club true to the target.

This is often called a threequarter shot. It may sound simple, but it requires much practice, for it is very easy for the right shoulder to come into the strike when it senses a lack of hand and wrist movement.

Wind against: second shots

Using a driver from the ground can never be recommended. Many top professionals do so occasionally, but even they normally save that shot for a good lie on a calm day. Getting the few degrees of loft necessary on the face of a club requires great skill and accuracy for success and those attributes are not always readily available when the wind is playing havoc with your balance.

Using a good No 3 wood, with similar adjustments to the tee shot where the ball is drawn back and the hands are slightly down the grip, you will gain as much distance as is possible – and that is the amount you should settle for. If you try to force the ball into the wind, inaccuracies occur in the swing and any faults are exaggerated when the side spin on the ball is picked out by the strong wind.

You should play the second shot with an iron, exactly as described for the tee shot. In this case, it is good policy never to hit a full shot, whatever the iron. Always take an extra club and go down the handle to ensure the minimum of wrist and the minimum length of swing.

Wind against: short shots

Many of the second shots in these conditions will land up short of the green and you will need to play a lot of pitch shots directly into the wind. If you play them firmly, these shots can be very satisfying, since the ball should travel all the way to the flag. With the wind against you, by playing a firm, attacking stroke you should gain maximum back spin.

Whether the shot is 46m (50yd) and you use a No 8 or No 9, or even as short as 18 or 27m (20 or 30yd) and you use a wedge, you will get more positive results from a short swing. Hold the club down the handle with the ball fairly well backward in the stance, so the hands stay well forward through the strike.

Cross wind from the right

This is probably the easiest wind of all for a right-handed player, both for the driver from the tee and the fairway woods. By aiming off to the right according to the strength of the wind, you can gain a lot from a very full, free swing.

A healthy shoulder turn, which feels much easier and more natural in this kind of wind, will help produce a hook spin. After the ball has travelled a fair distance, this spin will turn it with the wind to achieve maximum length. You will also have the benefit of run on the ball when it lands on the ground.

The real problems with the right-to-left wind come when you are playing an iron shot to the green, whether from the tee or the fairway. For the hook spin, which suits the woods, is the last thing you want when your ball reaches the green, since there is little chance of it stopping. The problems

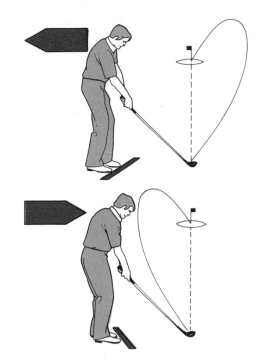

When driving, it is advisable not to argue with the wind, but deliberately aim out into it. This way you will gain the benefit of having the wind behind the ball later on in its flight towards the target.

are increased if the green is guarded on the front right-hand side by a bunker, since then you will not be able to bounce the ball short of the green.

Players of the calibre of Lee Trevino would play such a shot by aiming almost directly at the flag then, choosing an extra club, play a shot with a slight cut spin on it. This shot loses power, hence the choice of club, but the side spin will cancel out the effect of the cross wind gusting from the right of the green.

Under these circumstances the average golfer, who has not mastered spinning shots, may have to take one of three choices. He may select sufficient club to see him safely over the guarding bunker, aim out to allow for the wind and settle for finishing at the back left of the green. He can, if the shot is a longish one, play up short of the green, so avoiding the hazard, then chip from there to the pin. Or, by taking up a stance so the ball is farther back and using an extra club, he can push the ball towards the right into the wind. With this choice, he must not roll the wrists into the impact or he will put too much hook into the shot. The wrists must stay firm.

Unfortunately turning the club in the hands so that the blade lies 'open' a little does not, as many believe, have the effect of spinning the ball against the wind. With iron shots, it simply adds a bit more height to the shot and weakens it.

Cross wind from the left

Here the problem is reversed, for it is the wooden clubs that suffer more than the iron clubs.

A wind on the player's back tends to tilt his body weight forward and hampers a good shoulder turn. The result of this is a steeper swing arc and from this many shots are crushed by the heel of the club. Narrow swinging and slicing go together and a strong wind is waiting to exaggerate the slightest flaw.

Many very good players, among them professionals, prefer to use a more lofted wood such as a No 3, which has enough loft to survive a narrowed arc. They may also adjust their grip and turn the club face inwards a little. The degrees of loft on the club face permit this and, as a result, they apply a touch of hook spin to the ball to counteract the wind. The same technique is used for the wooden club shots from the fairway.

Those who prefer to stay with the driver from the tee must always aim off to the left and allow the wind to return the ball to the fairway. It is not good policy to attempt to hook a ball back against the wind with a club that has only a few degrees of loft.

Iron shots are more simple for, unlike the opposite wind where opening the blade merely makes the ball go higher, in this case if the blade is turned inwards the ball will definitely turn with a hook spin. Many good players therefore feel happier not aiming off to the left and allowing for the wind, but aiming straight at the pin and simply adjusting their grip so that the blade toes in the required amount. Only the slightest turn in provides many yards of argument between wind and ball and results in a straight flight.

Should you decide against this method, then aiming off the required amount to the left is the other solution. Unlike the hook spin coming in on the wind and gaining overspin, a ball turning from left to right will not run too far, even though it will be assisted by the wind when landing.

Wind around the greens

Whatever the direction of the wind, the lower you can keep the ball on short shots the better. You should avoid lofted pitch shots wherever possible and use more chip-and-run shots instead. On seaside links courses, the tight, sand-based turf lends itself to chipping, since the ball will usually bounce consistently from it. Admittedly, with the characteristic hummocks and hollows, you will have to anticipate the direction of some of the bounces. But if you read the conditions correctly, your skill will be rewarded.

On some of the softer parkland courses it is difficult to judge whether a chip shot, landing short of the putting green, will run forward as intended or come to a standstill too quickly. It is often necessary on such courses to play the low chip shot with a lofted club so that, although the ball will rise a little higher than desired, it will bounce first on the green where the effect of the loft will control its run forward. This is not easy and requires practice. Many top professionals play all of their low chip shots with a lofted club.

When putting, you must allow for the wind. A strong cross wind may cancel out a good deal of the borrow, or more than double it if the wind and the borrow are from the same side.

Whereas putting into a wind gives you the confidence to rap the ball directly at the hole, especially if the putt is also uphill, the opposite situation can be a nightmare. Going downhill on a fast surface, with the wind behind, is a very difficult stroke.

Rain

There is a popular joke that it never rains on a golf course. Unfortunately this is not true; rain can bring a golf tournament to a halt if it floods the putting greens. In major events, officials watch very closely and at the moment a green is sufficiently under water to make putting unfair, a siren is sounded and play on the course is stopped. When the rain has eased off, groundsmen use special rakes and rollers to remove the surface water so that play can continue.

While the rain is not flooding greens, play must continue and, with the exception of friendly matches, sheltering is not permitted – unless the rain also brings thunder and lightning, when players who wish to take shelter may do so.

When the rain persists, it is very easy to become depressed for, regardless of how good a player you are, you will drop strokes because of the conditions. So it is important to keep going in spite of the frustrations.

You should wear proper lightweight waterproof clothing in which you can swing freely. You should have more than one glove, so that you can change when the one you are wearing becomes too soggy. This will avoid the handle of the club slipping in the grip and ruining a shot. Wear a wide-brimmed cap if you have glasses, since bespectacled players are at a distinct disadvantage in the rain, especially if it is coming in on the wind. Make sure you have good length spikes on your shoes and handles on the clubs that are not old and liable to be slippery when wet.

Loft is the keyword for success in the rain. Apart from the tee shot, where the ball may be dried and the tee set a shade higher, you will have to play all the other shots with a wet ball, possibly covered in matted grass cuttings.

It is unwise to attempt to hit a wet ball with a straight-faced club, whether it is a wood or an iron, for it will skid unless the contact of the club can be made well below the centre of the ball.

At a distance from the green where you would expect to use a very long iron – say a No 2 or No 3 – you would do better to use a No 4 or No 5 wood, which will enable you to make contact nearer the bottom of the ball. Even if these woods contact the wet surface first, because of their flat sole plates they will slide their way through it.

From other parts of the fairway, where you are using middle or short irons, position the ball an inch or so backward in the stance, since it is essential that the club contacts the ball before the turf. If not, on heavy wet turf you will end up with a large divot and a fluffed shot.

Wet rough clings to the ball and to the club head approaching it, so it is unwise to risk attempting long shots in very damp conditions. It is far better to use a heavier headed, more lofted iron and select a safe route to a good position down the fairway.

If there is any advantage during heavy rain, then it is that the greens become more holding and from shots close to the green you can play boldly up to the pin. Even from just a few yards off the putting green, you will need to play fairly aggressive chips and pitches.

Those who prefer low-running chip shots using a No 5 or No 6 iron, which are good clubs on a dry day, should switch to a No 7 or No 8, still using the same technique but allowing for much less run.

You do not have to play from puddles and excessively wet areas which, if the body weight brings water to the surface, are ruled as 'casual water'. Wherever this condition appears on the course, according to the rules relief is permitted. On the green, you do not have to putt through a wet area even if the ball is not lying on one. You can place it at a point where the nearest dry route is available, although this must not be any nearer to the hole.

Playing the game

The great success of golf over many other sports is due partly to its handicapping system, which makes it possible to match the most modest club player against someone of the standard of Severiano Ballesteros or Jack Nicklaus. If a man can play round the course so that when his handicap is deducted he will equal or better par, then he is certainly a match for anyone.

Playing tennis against John McEnroe, no matter how many points start was given, would result in one-way traffic. And where could one raise a team of 50-year-old footballers to compete against Liverpool? Yet in golf there are successful Pro-Ams played prior to major tournaments, where the sponsors' guests – of all ages and standards – go out with the best players in the forthcoming event and play in competition, contributing in every way and gaining valuable experience.

A new golfer gains his handicap by submitting to the handicapping committee of his club three scorecards of rounds played over an official course. These have to be witnessed and signed by a full member of a club. Based on the average of the cards submitted, with certain allowances, a handicap is granted which when deducted would bring his score level with par for the course. The men have a handicap limit of 28 and the ladies 36.

For many years members' handicaps were reviewed by the club's handicapping committee and adjusted according to the player's performance. This could be done when an exceptionally good round was played, or on general play when it was clear that the player was doing much better than his existing handicap indicated. This

happened a lot because many players who grew nervous in a strokeplay competition would perform in other matches to a standard that really made nonsense of their handicap.

In today's age of computers, a system that originated in Australia has been introduced: it is now no longer possible to enter an event, play badly, make no return and forget it. Failure to return a score in an event means the addition of a decimal figure which, when added to those decimals gained from completed rounds over the allocated handicap, eventually causes the handicap allowance to be increased. Scores returned below the player's set handicap work on the same system, but in reverse. In Britain there is a winter period where, although handicaps can be reduced after a good return, they cannot be increased by a poor one.

Handicap categories The handicapping system divides the men into four categories as follows:

Category 1: 5 or less
Category 2: 6-12
Category 3: 13-20
Category 4: 21-28

When a player in a competition returns a score above his handicap, or if he fails to return one, he will have awarded to his records 0.1 of a stroke, regardless of his existing category. However, when his return is better than his handicap allowance, the reduction is made according to the category. For every stroke better, category 1 players are deducted 0.1 of a stroke, category 2 players 0.2, category 3 players 0.3 and category 4 players 0.4.

When the decimal points added to a player's handicap pass 0.5, the handicap is increased by one. Similarly when the decimal points deducted from a player's handicap pass 0.5, then the handicap is reduced by one.

Ladies' handicaps The ladies' handicap-

Two British professionals – Jim Farmer and Martin Gray – teamed up as a foursome partnership in a match against the United States for the PGA Cup at Muirfield in 1983, which the British team won.

ping system is that of the Ladies Golf Union. Although it may appear complex, it works very well.

A player must return four scores during any one year and these scores must be played at a club with a scratch score (SS) of not less than 60. Once a beginner has done this, she will obtain a 36 handicap which puts her into the Bronze Division. This is divided into two parts – 36*-30 and 29-19.

A player is assessed on her best score. If this is more than 36 strokes above SS, then her handicap will be 36*. If this score is between 30 and 36 strokes above SS, then her handicap is the difference between her gross score and SS. For example, if her best score is 107 and SS is 74, her handicap will be 33.

If a player should return a score that would bring her below 30, then the average of her two best scores is taken. If the average is more than 29, she will have a handicap of 30. Once a player has a handicap of between 29 and 19, she is handicapped on the average of her two best scores, whether from the same course or not.

The Silver Division is reached when a player has a handicap of 18*, 18-4, 3* or 3 and under. When a player from the Bronze Division returns two scores with an average of 18 or under, she will have a handicap of 18* until she has returned four scores that average 18 or less.

When a player reaches a handicap of between 18 and 4, she is now handicapped on the average of her four best scores returned on any course. As before, the SS is deducted from the scores then the totals are added together and divided by four. If a player of the Silver Division returns four scores that average 3¼ or less, she will obtain a handicap of 3*, until she has returned six scores, three of which must be on different courses.

If a player reaches a handicap of 3 and under, she must return six scores, only one of which may be on a home course. The two best scores from the away courses are combined with the player's four other best scores on courses with an SS of not less than 70. The average is then taken of the four worst scores of these six.

Forms of play and handicap allowances

There are two basic methods of scoring in golf – original matchplay and strokeplay.

Matchplay This is the favourite method at club level. It can be played as singles, where one player takes on another on a hole-by-hole basis, until one player is up by more holes than there are left to play. Matchplay can also be used with foursomes, with two players hitting one ball with alternate strokes matched against another pair. One from each team plays the tee shot at the odd holes and the other at the even holes.

Fourball is probably the most popular type of golf where two players, each playing his own ball, challenge two others doing the same. The score of the best result per hole is matched against the opponents' and the end result decided by the number of holes one team is ahead of the other.

The handicap allowance is as follows:

Singles matchplay: the low handicapper gives threequarters of the difference between his handicap and his opponent's.

Foursomes matchplay: three-eighths of the difference of the combined handicaps between the low pair and the opposition is given.

Fourball matchplay: all handicaps above that of the lowest player in the fourball receive threequarters of the difference of his and theirs.

Strokeplay Here the ball is played out on every hole and the total, whether it has had handicap deducted during the course of the round or at the completion of the round, is the nett result.

In singles strokeplay, the player completes the round with a partner, each marking the other's card. Here the handicaps are deducted at the end of the 18 holes, all of which have to be completed. Foursomes is recorded in the same way, two players playing alternate shots and marking the card of their playing partners. One from each team drives off at the odd holes, the other partner at the even holes.

The handicap allowance is as follows:

Singles strokeplay: the full allowance is taken from the total scored.

Foursomes strokeplay: half of the combined handicap.

Greensomes Another fairly popular form of golf, this is part-fourball and part-singles. Here all four players in a group, made up of two teams, drive off every tee. The best shot from the team is selected and

The card must be checked immediately after leaving the 18th green, as Sandy Lyle is doing here during the 1981 British Open at Royal St Georges.

played alternately from there to the hole. The second hit at each hole is made by the player whose ball has been picked up. This form is normally played as strokeplay.

The handicap allowance is as follows:

Greensome strokeplay: two-fifths of the higher handicap is added to three-fifths of the lower.

Greensome matchplay: threequarters of the difference between the low and high total is given.

Stableford Bogey This competition is very popular because it takes less time; the ball can be picked up when too many shots have been played on a hole. The scoring is done on a points system, where two points are awarded if the nett score at a hole equals par; handicaps are deducted hole by hole. A score one better than par would gain three points, and so on. Dropping a stroke to par would give the player one point and a score worse than that would get nothing.

It is possible to play Stableford either as singles, foursomes, fourball or even greensomes, although this is unusual. The handicap allowance is as follows:

Singles Stableford: seven-eighths of the handicap is given.

Foursomes Stableford: seven-sixteenths of the combined handicap is given.

Stableford Bogey has taken over from the older Bogey, a form of matchplay against the card. This was played in the days when bogey represented the number of strokes the hole was expected to be played in, based on its difficulty. Today the word has taken over the American meaning of the 'one over par' figure.

Bogey, which can still be played against the par of the hole, is a rather unfair form of golf. Even if a player drops only one stroke at, say, a very difficult par four, which measures well over 366m (400yd), he must record a loss on his Bogey scorecard. A fellow competitor might lose a couple of balls at the same hole and give up, yet his score is no worse. If a player scores a brilliant eagle, in the case of the Stableford he

would collect four points. In Bogey, it goes down just as a win, no better unfortunately than someone who made a birdie.

The allowance in Bogey competitions is threequarters of the handicap.

Texas Scramble This is becoming very popular, especially as the forerunner to a major event where professionals are playing. Four, or even five, players drive off at each hole. From the spot where the best shot lands, all the others play a second shot. The same happens for the third shot, and so on. This means that even the poorest player in the side might hole the crucial putt that produces the winning score.

There is no official handicapping here, although one-tenth of the total handicaps of the entire team is often deducted.

Par

Golf courses are either of 18 holes or 9, in which case the holes are played twice, often from different tees on the second round. Even on full-size courses, the 18 holes are divided into two halves – called outward and inward nines, or sometimes in the United States front and back sides.

The ideal golf course has a par of 72, made up of 10 par four holes, 4 par fives and 4 par threes, with the different par holes split evenly between the two nines.

Par threes are those up to 228m (250yd), a distance that can be covered in one shot by the good players. From there to a length of 434m (474yd) – or 430m (469yd) in the United States – the hole requires at least two hits to reach the green and is called a par four. Over that distance is deemed to be par five, although there are some par sixes scattered about the world. Two putts are always calculated into the par figures.

Standard Scratch Score

At one stage the degree of difficulty was allowed to determine that some longish par fours should be par fives. That is no longer the case, although the degree of difficulty was responsible for bringing about the Standard Scratch Score.

This is a means of showing how a course that has most of its par four holes around the 274m (300yd) mark cannot be compared with a course where the par fours are all well over 366m (400yd). This is the case with many of the championship courses, even though the holes have the same par.

The Standard Scratch Scoring system operates in the following way. An assessment is submitted to the appropriate golfing union, based entirely on the total measurement of the 18 holes or, in the case of a 9-hole course, double its distance. The assessment is based on the following chart:

Total course distance		SSS assessment
metres	yards	
6402-6584	7001-7200	74
6219-6401	6801-7000	73
6036-6218	6601-6800	72
5853-6035	6401-6600	71
5670-5852	6201-6400	70
5442-5669	5951-6200	69
5213-5441	5701-5950	68
4984-5212	5451-5700	67
4756-4983	5201-5450	66
4573-4755	5001-5200	65
4390-4572	4801-5000	64
4207-4389	4601-4800	63
4024-4206	4401-4600	62
3841-4023	4201-4400	61
3659-3840	4001-4200	60

Having received this assessment, the union sends officials to study the layout of the course. They take into account such things as the difficulty, or otherwise, of the terrain, whether for example the course is dry, so the ball will run, or soggy, which will reduce the length of tee shots. They check the difficulties offered by bunkers, water hazards and 'out of bounds' areas and whether the course is forest-lined or wide open. Normally allowance is made for seaside links, since these are exposed to strong winds much of the year – and the SSS is an all-year figure.

Having weighed up the facts, they may choose either to add to or subtract from the figure nominated by the measurement – or they may well feel it is appropriate.

The system has gone a long way to level out the handicapping of players all over the world, since handicaps are now based on the SSS and not the par of the course, which can be misleading.

Stroke Index

When the Stroke Index is set against the holes on the course – and, incidentally, printed on the scorecard – the ideal method is for the hardest par four to be known as stroke one. Stroke two would then be counted at the next most difficult hole, which is hopefully, although not necessarily, on the other half of the course. The distribution continues based on difficulty.

Strangely enough par fives, although the longest holes, are not normally considered to be the most difficult. In fact, they are probably among the easiest at which a par can be gained. Tournament professionals, who always play from scratch, enjoy the long holes for it is on these that they can often pick up a birdie.

In matches, once the handicap difference has been decided, bearing in mind that if in the calculation the fraction comes to a half or more another stroke is claimed, then any hole with an index of that figure or lower is one where a stroke is received.

Names for scores

The descriptive names given to the score recorded at a hole are as follows:

Par is when the figure set for the hole is matched.

Birdie is a score one better than par.

Eagle is two strokes better than par.

Albatross is three better than par. Normally this means holing the second shot at a par five, although it would also refer to a hole-in-one at a par four.

Bogey was originally used as a means of describing the difficulty of a hole, for example a par four as a bogey five. However the American use of the word has now taken over and means that one stroke over par has been scored. Two over is a double bogey, and so on.

185

Strategy on the course

Obviously there has to be a different strategy for matchplay and for strokeplay, since one is based on a hole-by-hole result and the other on the total result of all 18 holes. Many players say the best way to play is to pretend your opponent does not exist. Simply by playing against the par of the course, they believe this is the best way of stopping the other player from gaining a psychological advantage with a good shot.

This method may work for some players, but the majority believe that in matchplay you play the man, while in strokeplay you play the course. If your opponent plays 'out of bounds' on a particularly difficult driving hole, it is common sense for you to put away the driver and choose a club that ensures accuracy rather than distance.

When the opponent's ball thumps down into a deep bunker guarding a difficult pin position, it must make sense to play for the wider, safer part of the green, rather than follow him in. If faced with a tricky downhill putt and only needing two shots to win the hole, surely it is wise to lay the first putt up close to the hole to make sure of winning that hole with a short second putt. On the other hand, if that awkward putt is all that is left to gain a half and a miss would mean dropping a hole, then you must attack the hole. Of course, this should never be done in strokeplay.

There is no point in playing up short of a green with a second shot because there is some sort of hazard in front if your opponent is already on the green in two.

Matchplay

Sound strategy is often based on who plays first on each particular shot and on the state of the match at the time. The player going first should play the best and most sensible shot he can, then stand back and let his opponent do the worrying. Occasionally risks can be taken if a player is a number of holes in the lead, although these should never be unduly chancy.

When your opponent goes first and plays a good shot, you must try to match this. If he plays a poor shot, you should consider what his chances are of doing something with the shot he has left himself before deciding on your course of action. His disappointment will soon turn to delight if you also make a mistake.

There are many good golfers who play medal rounds consistently well, even though this is considered a more difficult form of golf. But even they find there are certain opponents they cannot beat in a head-to-head match, not because the opponent plays better but because they cannot find their usual form.

This is often due to the different mental approach needed to play against one opponent rather than against a complete field of players, some of whom may not even be on the course at the same part of the day.

It is extraordinary how often the old golfing expression 'two up and five to play never wins' proves to be the case. It is used as a form of gamesmanship by those players who find themselves two down at that stage. By winning the next hole, they can shatter the confidence of their opponent, who is convinced history is about to repeat itself yet again.

In matchplay you should never give up until the game is finally over. It is worth recalling the epic dual in the World Match Play championship at Wentworth in 1965 when, in the 36-hole match, Gary Player lost the opening hole of the second round to the late Tony Lema and found himself no less than seven down with 17 to play. He went on to win.

In 1983 Arnold Palmer was two up with two holes left against the much younger

One of the toughest competitors in the history of match play golf – Gary Player.

The famous chip shot that Severiano Ballesteros holed to square his match with Arnold Palmer in the 1983 World Match Play tournament. This 55m (60yd) piece of magic enabled him to take the match to extra holes, where he finally won.

Severiano Ballesteros in the same event. The Spaniard got down with a pitch and putt to birdie the 17th and so take the match to the 18th. Here Palmer, after only two shots, was just through the green at the par five hole and not 6m (20ft) from the pin. Ballesteros was 55m (60yd) short and in the rough grass. He is a player who never gives up and on this occasion hit a superb chip-and-run shot which swept into the hole for an eagle three. Palmer had his shot for the game, missed it and lost the match after extra holes.

Strokeplay

Unlike matchplay, where a wild shot or a poor decision can cost a hole, in strokeplay it is a very different matter, for that mistake is counted and added to the total score of the round. Depending on the seriousness of the error and the number of extra strokes incurred, the player's enthusiasm can easily be destroyed.

In strokeplay every shot carries a greater pressure of responsibility with it. Probably the greatest asset in strokeplay is understanding one's limitations and playing within them.

So many rounds are spoiled by a player attempting a shot that in his mind he knows he has little chance of getting. He may use a wood to get out from the thick rough and instead of hitting the ball out bury it further. Not only has he wasted a stroke, but he has given himself an even harder shot next time.

You only have to sit in a locker room after a competition and hear a dozen heartbreak stories that end in the words 'if only' to realize the value of clear thinking before, and not after, the shot.

Even at the top of the tournament game, players talk of their 'game plan', where they calculate in advance how they will play a particular course. There are certain holes at which they will be going for a birdie – par fives, for example, which with their power they can reach in two. Other holes are so difficult that they command respect from even the greatest players. Here they play the approach shot to the centre or wide part of the green and settle for a par. There are those dog-leg holes that are worth trying to carry and others where carrying the corner only means the difference of a couple of clubs for the second shot, which is not worth the risk of playing yourself into trouble.

Playing from tee to green
Imagine playing a hypothetical hole, one full of problems and hazards, and learn how to make the best of it.
On the tee The teeing area stretches in a direct line between two markers, then back from there a depth of two club lengths. You can tee up at any point within that area and your stance can be outside that oblong, provided the ball is inside.

This is important because if there is an 'out of bounds' area or other severe hazard such as bushes or a stream on the left, the closer you stand to the line of the hazard the more you can play away from it. So many inexperienced players move as far away from the side of the hazard as possible when they tee up the ball that they are committed to hit towards it.

When playing a short hole, you may feel the distance is too short to play a No 5, yet too far to play a No 6. You will be surprised that by standing at the back of the teeing area, which allows you only an extra couple of yards or so, you will feel confident enough to use the stronger club.

Another point worth considering, particularly if you go out late on a wet day after a large field has chewed up the teeing area, is to go back that couple of yards to find a less worn piece of turf. You can easily make up the sacrifice of these yards at the other end of the ball's flight.

Teeing off Do not make the driver the automatic choice for every hole other than the short ones. It can be more sensible to choose a fairway wood, or even an iron, as long as you remember to use a lower tee peg. The extra loft of the fairway woods offers more safety since the back spin helps the ball to stay on a more direct route. Equally the shorter handle boosts that feeling of confidence.

You will gain almost as much length by using a No 3 wood if there is a reasonable tail wind. As the ball climbs, it will pick up the wind advantage and stay up longer. You can often use this wood when a fierce wind is blowing from left to right across the fairway.

This is the worst wind for the right-handed player since it pushes at his back and undermines a confident shoulder turn. Many shots attempted with the slight loft of the driver, coupled with a minimum of body turn, will result in slice spin. So there is a good deal to be gained from having the loft of the No 3 wood here.

When course architects are restricted by the amount of land, they have a habit of designing some very short par fours and are inclined to create trouble spots around

Strategy on the course

The stimpmeter being used by officials at Augusta National Course to test the pace of the green prior to selecting the pin position for one of the holes.

the area where the tee shot will land, as well as hazards to guard the green.

From the point of view of distance, you should have no difficulty in getting up in two at such holes. But it is often an advantage to play a long iron shot from the tee. Because of its higher degree of accuracy and reduced carry as compared to the driver, it will keep the ball short of trouble.

Admittedly this will leave you extra ground to cover with your second shot. But, as many good players claim, you will get more control from a firm shot using a No 9 iron – and more back spin with which to stop the ball on the green – than from lobbing in a more delicate, shorter pitch shot. And you will be playing the shot from the fairway and not out of a hazard.

Second shots Assuming the shot is to a green that is out of range, although the ball is lying perfectly in the centre of the fairway you should consider from which point near the green it would be easiest to play a third shot. There is no point in blazing away in an attempt to gain extra distance from a forced swing and fail, when a well-hit No 3 or No 4 wood shot would have produced better results.

This may sound rather negative, but it is not. Take a situation where the ball is lying

within range of the target from a well-struck wood, even though the shot is a demanding 183m (200yd) hit across a lake to the green. Provided the distance is within your capabilities and the ball is lying right for the shot, then you should use that club. But when the shot required is probably beyond your capabilities, you should not play it.

It is just as positive to elect to play with a shorter club towards the front of the green or even to one side if there is a serious hazard or an 'out of bounds' fence close by. When the shot lands, all you will need is a chip and putt or possibly a long approach putt to secure a par.

When the hole is dog-legged, or after a miscued drive it plays like a dog-leg with the green out of sight, you may want to consider playing a trick shot. The choice is either to curve the ball around the obstacle or play safely back to the fairway.

You must establish how much of an escape route you have close to the green, particularly if the trick shot is to have hook spin. With slice spin the ball more or less stops where it drops, whereas hook spin can send the ball careering on.

If the green is fairly open, the shot is worth attempting. Where the green is surrounded by ditches, water or dense shrubbery, you should play the ball out safely and put the third shot on the green.

Playing short shots to the flag All championship courses have several pin positions on each green from which the tournament director may daily select a site for the hole. On the final day the toughest are normally chosen to sort out the best player in the event. They may be placed behind bunkers to ensure a premium in placing the tee shot on just the right part of the fairway to gain the best access to the flag with the next shot.

The player with the poorer tee shot is faced with problems. He must decide whether to attack the flag from the wrong direction, with the risk of landing in those hazards lying directly in his path, or to play away to the safe part of the green with the risk of three-putting.

The same problem applies to club golfers whose courses, although not as challenging as some of the major ones, still provide awkward shots to the flag. For example, playing a pitch shot to the green from rough grass, even light rough, provides little hope of putting any back spin on the ball. If a deep bunker lies in line to the flag, the ball cannot hope to stop on the green.

Miracles do not happen very often, so it is essential to look for the best way out, even though that may mean aiming not to the pin but to the heart of the green.

The scoring habit

Scoring at golf becomes a habit, regardless of your standard. A tournament professional scores within a shot or two each time he goes out on the course, although he will have the occasional flier where he scores better than normal. On another day the opposite will happen. Over the year, however, his average will come from a fairly steady pattern of scores.

A similar thing happens to club golfers. With the higher handicappers, however, out of each 18 holes played, one of the halves of nine holes reflects the way he would normally score while the other, be it the first or second nine, lets him down.

After a very good first nine, the pressure of sustaining the standard becomes too much and he blows up. Equally he may 'give up' after a poor opening nine, then play like an expert for the back nine when the pressure has been lifted.

The scoring habit is not easy to acquire and there are always those who will be frightened by their score. After a run of good holes, some players look for trouble instead of accepting their good fortune and carrying on. This type of negative attitude prevents many golfers, amateur and professional alike, from posting a score worthy of the way they can play.

It is important, particularly for young players, to mark a card at every opportunity, although care should be taken not to hold up others by putting out all the time when a matchplay game is in progress. Then it would be permissible, for personal records only, to accept the odd short putt that was conceded and record the score given. By continually using a card, players can overcome the shock they may get when engaged in a strokeplay event after months of matchplay.

You should look on a run of good holes confidently as the way you would expect to play, record the scores and then forget them. Dividing the course into two halves and adding up the figures of each nine played is not a good idea. By playing each hole as it comes, you will get rid of the attitude of defending what you have gained and keep the good play going.

Disastrous holes affect players differently. Some give up, while others fight back. Hardly a great round is compiled that does not have a turning point in it. So it is better to put that poor hole behind you and get on with the rest of the round. It could turn out to be the best one ever!

Etiquette in golf

Etiquette is possibly more important in golf than in any other game. One of the major reasons for this is the intense concentration required when playing a shot, and the obvious effects of being distracted – silence at such times is therefore of the utmost importance. In professional golf a competitor who ignores traditional golf etiquette is usually taken aside and reminded of the rules: the same goes for the amateur game, even at club level. Not surprisingly there is always a waiting list of would-be members at clubs where discipline is strong and the list is usually made up of members from clubs where it is weak.

Etiquette is closely linked with safety. If, for example, you stand behind someone who is playing and he is unaware of your exact position, you could be seriously injured by his swinging club. Also walking ahead before an opponent has played his shot can lead to tragedy. It is common sense therefore to stand well out of the way, and good manners to position yourself where you will not distract the player taking his shot.

On the tee the correct place to stand is at right angles to the teeing area and a few yards away. On the fairway, it is not always possible to be to the striking side of the person playing, but never be ahead of the striker and keep a reasonable distance.

If unlucky enough to land in a bunker, remember to leave it in the condition in which one would wish to find it. Footprints in the sand are a sure sign of ignorance and/or bad temper. Most courses provide rakes near the bunkers; but if none are available, use the back of the sand iron or even the sole of a shoe to smooth away any signs of disturbance.

On putting greens the grass is extremely fine and close-cut, so take great care even when just walking on them – spikes can do a great deal of damage when feet scuff the surface. When removing the pin from the hole, reach for it at arm's length. Equally, when collecting the ball from the hole, stand as far from it as possible. Too many footprints close to a hole can create a 'moat' effect and the turf immediately around the hole becomes crowned. Take care when replacing the pin, since it is quite easy to damage the rim of the hole – remember that there is a vulnerable layer of soil above the metal or plastic cup.

Putting probably taxes the golfer more than any other area of the game and has certainly prompted some of the most unlikely excuses for failure – players who have missed a tiny putt have complained of such things as the noise of a butterfly's wings and excessive traffic in the English Channel. Always stand out of your opponent's line of vision and keep as still and quiet as possible.

Respect for others

Golf is such an absorbing game that players in a group often tend to forget there are others playing behind them. Here, too, there is a code of conduct.

The first cause of irritation for those waiting is slow play and in the professional game this offence carries a fine. But at club level, where it is becoming more common, steps are being taken to stop it. When one player in a group loses his ball and his partners go to help him find it, they should call the next match through. When they find the missing ball, they must then wait until those behind play through and get out of range. Having been kept waiting hole after hole, a player is often so frustrated that eventually he plays before the slow players are out of range: two wrongs never make a right and such an action can cause serious injury.

All matches finish with a shake of hands, no matter what the form of golf. In this case it's Severiano Ballesteros and Bob Gilder during the 1983 Ryder Cup.

Etiquette in golf

Tradition has always given a two-ball match priority over a threesome or fourball game, while a player on his own has no standing whatsoever. With the heavy demand on many courses and the need to get as many as possible on to the course at one time, some clubs have waived that rule and given fourballs priority. Nevertheless, on a quiet day, no fourball should ever keep a twosome waiting if the course ahead is clear. It is also reasonable to expect players whose match is losing ground on the games ahead by more than a hole, to call through those waiting behind.

Pitchmarks

Before leaving a green, it is the duty of every player whose ball pitches heavily on to the putting green to locate the pitchmark and level it out. Apart from the fact that a player coming on to the green later, who has failed to notice the pitchmark, may have a good putt ruined, the putting surface can be spoiled if these marks are not levelled. The turf that is driven under by the ball rots and the exposed soil beneath dries out and after several careless golfers have passed through, the green looks very pock-marked.

Use a proper pitchfork to lift the buried turf carefully, then level off the damaged area by tapping lightly over it with the sole of your putter. Simply tapping down the area without recovering the original turf does more harm than good.

Marking the ball

When a ball has to be marked and lifted use a proper marker and place it directly behind the ball. Scratching the ground as a means of marking is not only bad etiquette but also contrary to the rules; it could be seen as a means of testing the surface, which is not allowed.

The marker used should be a small unobtrusive disc that will not distract other players. Should it interfere in any way with another player's shot, its repositioning in the desired direction can be requested. To

The markers (above) indicate the position of the two balls and clearly show why it was necessary for Severiano Ballesteros to mark his ball and lift it so that Ben Crenshaw could take up his stance (right). Ballesteros replaced his ball after Crenshaw had played his shot.

do this, place the toe of the putter against the disc and move the disc to behind the heel of the putter: the leading edge of the putter must be at right angles to the direction of the hole. The player can request that the disc is moved more than one putterhead's length away. To replace the ball after the shot has been played, simply reverse the procedure to bring the marker back to its original spot.

Gamesmanship

This is the term used when a somewhat unethical player wishes to stretch golfing etiquette without breaking the unwritten laws. Sometimes it is done intentionally to apply pressure on an opponent: 'Do you breathe in or out at the top of your back swing?' or 'I have never seen you swing the club so smoothly' are just a couple of the many ploys used by a player who is losing a match in the hope of putting his opponent off. Having driven straight down the middle of the fairway and then to suggest 'I was really quite worried about that out-of-bounds on the right' is a common form of gamesmanship through suggestion.

Fortunately, gamesmanship is more a part of the humour of the game and is generally given and accepted as such.

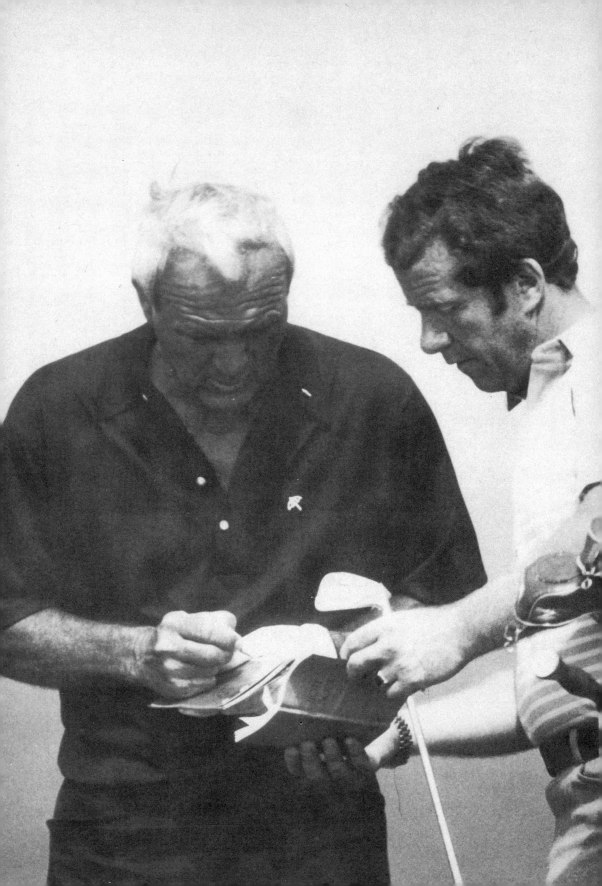

Practising your golf

One of the great points about golf is that even practising the game is enjoyable. Hitting a ball in the 'sweet spot' of the club is reward enough, let alone the pleasure of watching the ball soar towards the target. Indeed, in countries like Japan where there is a shortage of land on which to build courses, many people who cannot afford the enormous fees of the exclusive clubs spend their entire golfing life hitting balls on driving ranges.

Practising badly can be a mistake, as by trying to cure faults players may be building them even more into their game. Too often players arrive just a few minutes before their tee-off time, rush to the ground and unleash half a dozen balls with a driver. They jerk their muscles, which are cold from not having been flexed for some time, into full movement without any warm-up procedure. Others, who feel there must be some reward for hitting hundreds of balls in a session, are surprised and disappointed when they find the next day they have lost all feel for the game. One reason could be that this was their first session for six months.

At any major professional tournament a trip to the practice ground to watch the superstars at work is well worth the visit. They have a procedure for practice that varies very little from player to player. The one main difference will be in the time spent there, depending on what time of the day each player is due to tee off.

Normally, tournament competitors arrive one hour before the start time. At some major championship practice grounds, the balls are collected by a machine; otherwise it is the caddie who retrieves them. He will position himself about 36m (40yd) out, for that is as far as the opening shots are sent. Even though the

Nothing is left to chance as Arnold Palmer compares his personally compiled yardages with the official distances.

professional may be young and invariably fit, he warms up quietly and gradually.

As he hits the first dozen or so shots, he concentrates on blending the hands and wrists, arms and shoulders, feet and legs, to tune up the muscles needed in golf. The caddie then moves out another 23m (25yd) and the swing grows that bit more. A few more balls are hit, then the caddie moves again; now a bit more punch is put into the shots as the pitching wedge nears its full potential.

The professional will hit about 20 balls before he changes his club. Some like to go through the entire set, progressing from the wedge to the driver and hitting about four balls with each club. Others prefer to hit with selected clubs – a No 7, a No 5, a No 3, a fairway wood and then a driver to finish. Others, such as Severiano Ballesteros, wind their muscles back down by playing a few more tiny wedge shots as the caddie rejoins them.

From the hitting area, players proceed to the practice putting green, which is usually situated a short distance from the first tee and within hailing distance of the starter. Each player must report to him five minutes before the tee-off time. Some players prefer to hit one or two little chips from the fringe of the green to get the feel of the pace before they practise putting.

So much can be learned about all aspects of the game from watching the habits of the top players – not least their approach to practice. They never work on tired muscles, which is so often the case with those who go to driving ranges and feel that hitting one bucketful of balls is not enough. The momentum from hitting so many shots keeps the balls flying, however, and the player feels he is doing well. But after too many hits, the hands and wrists tire and the shoulders take over. Next morning the first half of the round is spoiled because his hands have no feel for the game and the shoulders, which take over, produce inaccuracies.

Practising with one club

It can be extremely harmful to indulge in long periods of practice using only one club. This has been proved with golfers whose courses have a practising area of limited length.

The swing plane, which should vary from shallow with the longer clubs to fairly upright with the shortest, can become fixed to suit that club being used. When the player goes out on the course again, he swings badly when using other clubs from his set.

If the facilities only allow you to use the short irons, it is better on a quiet day to play the course or part of it using a couple of balls. This stops your swing becoming grooved on one angle of plane.

Practising the short game

There is no limit to the amount you should work on the short game, apart from the fact that too much putting becomes painful on the back. You can have a lot of fun playing a chipping and putting competition against a rival.

Getting down in two from the edge of the green can be a great advantage and should win you many matches. So the more competitive you can make your practice here, the better.

Practising bunker shots

You should limit the amount of time you spend practising in bunkers, since by working excessively on the more independent hand and wrist action of sand shots you could harm your swing.

Having said that, no good player would go on to a strange course, particularly if playing in an important event, without trying a few shots from the practice bunker. There is such a variation in sand texture from course to course that it is essential to get a feel of it before playing, in case you find yourself in trouble on the course.

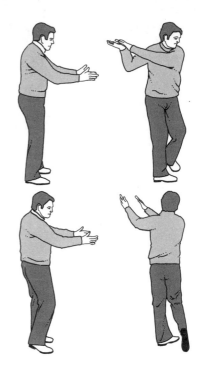

This is a useful swing exercise when you do not have a club handy. Place the palm of each hand parallel and swing them back and forth on a fairly horizontal plane around the body. By keeping your spine upright, you will encourage the feet to work as well.

Practising to a target

It is extremely important that you hit all practice shots towards a definite target, even if it is only a particular tree that stands out. Aiming the stance and body line becomes a habit – often a bad one. So it is very good policy to lay a spare club on the grass just beyond where the ball will be hit from and aimed at the target. Then you will find it quite easy to line up correctly.

If there is no green on the practice area, stick a rolled umbrella in the ground to act as the pin. After hitting, say, 10 balls to it from 23m (25yd), move back at 23m (25yd) intervals and play a similar amount of shots each time. You will find it more rewarding to land a number of balls in one area from different positions than to send the balls over a large area.

Spinning the ball in practice

To avoid getting bored during a long workout, many professionals will periodically play variation shots, where they deliberately fade some from left to right to the target, then the other way.

There are two good reasons why they try to maintain their feel for these trick shots. Firstly, they may be required to play this type of shot during the round. Secondly, like any other golfer, should they run into a spell of accidental hooking, for example, they have the perfect anti-hook device – the fade – to solve the problem.

Many professionals claim that if, during a tournament round, a hook or a slice does develop, they would not look for the cure on the course. They would make use of the particular shape being developed by their swing and only seek a cure when the round was over and they could get back to the practice area.

The first thing a player then does is to apply the opposite spin to the one he had gone along with during the round, rather than analyse what was causing the spin. With a good swing, it is only a slight imbalance that takes the swing path out of line and causes unintentional spin. So the player only needs to play a few shots deliberately creating the opposite spin to pull the balance point back into line. Similar action is taken by the teaching professionals when a well-established pupil gets caught up in a bout of side spin.

With the less-established golfer, however, it may be a serious fault that is causing the problem, in which case ironing it out may be more complicated.

Practising on windy days

You should avoid practising on days when the wind is strong, unless you can find a sheltered spot from which to strike the ball. Once the ball gets up in the sky, it does not matter that it will be blown about, since you can make allowances for that. But to stand out in a gale will only damage your swing technique.

Some players believe it is all right, provided you are hitting into the wind. But this is far from correct. If you do this, you will tend to lean on to your left leg to brace yourself against the wind, reduce your shoulder turn and steepen your swing. This will prove successful in a gale, with the ball flying low into the wind, just as a wind shot should. But if you go out the following day when the wind has dropped, you will find you have lost the tempo of your swing.

Working with a gale behind you can be very misleading, for any fault that creates side spin will not show up since the wind will carry the ball with it.

So how do you learn? After hitting most of the practice balls from a sheltered spot, go out into an exposed area and play just a few more shots, some with the wind and some against it.

Practising distance

Only a few years ago judging distance – and what club to use to cover that distance – was all a matter of guesswork. Today, neither professional nor caddie would venture out on the course without the most accurate distance chart. They do not even rely on the chart produced by the club, but will insist either on pacing out the course for themselves or going round it with a yardage wheel.

There would be little point in knowing the length of each hole if the distance hit by each club was an unknown quantity, so that too is measured. Every golfer should know how far he can hit with each club so that he can take advantage of the chart, if available, or at least at short holes where the distance is marked on the tee box.

It is very simple to find out your capabilities. You need to hit about 20 balls when your swing is in fairly good shape to ensure you hit solidly. Ignoring the poorest hit and the odd flyer that always arises from a bag of practice shots, pace out to where the best have landed from the striking point.

Practising your golf

Use a club that is fairly easy to play – say, a No 7 iron – which should cover somewhere between 115m (125yd) and 135m (150yd). If, when you measure the distance, it is close to 115m (125yd), then rather than test every club in the set add 9m (10yd) per club as the clubs get more powerful and subtract a similar amount for the more lofted ones. If you cover about 135m (150yd) with that iron – and that is a long way – you could probably add or subtract 14m (15yd). If your mathematics are not good enough to enable you to do your calculations during the round, then write down the distances achieved with each club in your set.

It is a good idea to do the same with the driver, because it does not send the ball as far as many claim. Then, if you are playing on a strange course with no distance chart, you can subtract the distance of the tee shot from the measure of the hole, which is on the scorecard, and get a good indication from this.

Positive thinking

Much is talked about the power of positive thought – and it is as important in golf as in any other sport. With the length of time between each shot, combined with the often frightening challenge of shots across ravines, over water hazards or through trees, it is very easy to lose confidence.

Often you arrive at the ball and immediately decide on the choice of club. But, because there are players on the green, you have to stand and wait. As the minutes pass by, the shot becomes longer and longer and you start to wonder whether the club you have chosen can possibly make the distance. This doubt in your mind causes you either to force the original choice of club or attempt a more gentle shot with your second selection, which you then mishit because of lack of conviction.

This is the reason why so many professionals insist on having an exact distance chart and a matching knowledge of how far they can hit with each club. Then they will go at the shot positively, even though their eyes may tempt them to change their mind.

Curing faults When you have to make an adjustment to your swing, do it positively. A very good example, and one that applies to beginners, is overswinging. This simply means that the back swing is not fully prepared in the correct amount of time and so the hands and wrists continue until it is.

The negative approach to rectifying this fault, which is often used, is 'I mustn't swing too far' and so the extra hand action at the top of the back swing is cut out. As a result, the swing is reduced and with it the power. The positive approach would be for the hands and wrists to get ready sooner, within the length and time allowed for the back swing.

Physical fitness

Probably the finest exercise for golf is playing it continually and following this with a balanced practice programme. A round of golf takes in a walk of some 7 or 8km (4 or 5 miles) and, with the amount of swinging involved, the needs of the average club player would easily be met if this was done two or three times a week.

This, however, may not always be possible, particularly in the winter when there are fewer daylight hours. So several exercises are recommended.

Henry Cotton was always a great advocate of the skipping rope. Not only can it be used in restricted areas, such as the garage, but its benefits are many: the leg muscles are strengthened; the hands and wrists are kept supple and co-ordinated as they work the rope, as are the feet and ankles which are so necessary for golf; good breathing is developed; and stamina is increased.

Another of Henry Cotton's specialities was the use of a car tyre, which he laid on the ground and struck with a club. Because the rubber absorbs the blow, no damage is done to the striker and the forearms and shoulders develop a strong, square-on sense of delivery. There are disadvantages with this exercise, since it can encourage

The ability to square the club face at impact can be practised by striking a rubber tyre. Here Henry Cotton, a great believer in this method, instructs a pupil.

the player to swing at the object – in this case the tyre but usually the ball – rather than swing through it. Also, the noise factor could upset the neighbours.

For the very young who are hoping to do well, press-ups and pull-ups are essential exercises. At his peak Gary Player would start and finish each day with no less then 75 press-ups – and on his fingertips! The up-and-coming Paul Way used to watch television through the steps of the open staircase in his home while pulling himself up and down by his fingertips.

Building up muscles using weights should be done carefully and with only the lightest of weights. Swinging Indian clubs is of more use than being able to lift heavy loads. Many of the best rugby players, who have such strong neck and shoulder muscles, cannot hit the golf ball with anything like the power their weight would suggest.

A lot of the great players suffer from back complaints which, I believe, are not caused by golf alone. It is the process of developing good muscles in the back from hours of playing and then damaging them by spending long hours sitting in aircraft or motor cars – Greg Norman, for example, flies more than 160,000km (100,000 miles) every year to a host of tournaments all round the world.

Famous back sufferers include Jack Nicklaus, Lee Trevino (who has had back surgery) and Severiano Ballesteros, who was at one time warned that he might have to give up golf altogether. Many players, including these three, use a back-exercise machine, which acts to pull the vertebrae apart as it suspends the body upside down, others use such devices as a means of prevention rather than cure.

Another useful piece of equipment is a heavy club; Gary Player always carries one which weighs as much as three times the normal club and he loosens up by swinging this. It is very easy to acquire such an implement from a club professional, since he will simply add lead weights to an old club. This work should be carried out by an expert, however – apart from the obvious dangers of melting lead, the weight must be placed in particular parts of the club head, otherwise it might fly out at high speed and cause severe injury.

The simple swinging back and through of the arms is an excellent exercise and can be done in the home or at the office. For the greatest benefit, the palms of the hands should face each other about 15cm (6in) apart, staying that way throughout, and the imaginary object swung through on an almost horizontal plane. By doing this exercise, the trunk of the body turns back, then through with the arms, in keeping with a good golfing movement.

This exercise works very well, too, when you hold a club. So often practice swings, done at the ground, place too much emphasis on the arms and wrists, with the body turn totally neglected. Horizontal swinging engages every movement – and even encourages good footwork.

The golf scene

There are many varied facilities where golf can be enjoyed in one form or another. It is possible to begin playing and remain through the whole of your playing career at the same establishment, but there are other alternatives which many members of golf clubs have tried. Anyone wishing to take up the game, particularly with no direct access to a private club, would be well advised to come through these channels.

Driving ranges

As a rule, no one would want to spend his golfing life simply hitting balls. But in countries like Japan, where land is in short supply and golf clubs are expensive, the game often involves hitting from driving range bays, hopefully with the occasional round on a public golf course.

Driving ranges can be found throughout the UK and most big cities have at least one. They make the ideal introduction for the beginner who might otherwise feel too embarrassed to go straight on to the course. These are usually rows of bays where, having purchased a bucket of balls, the player can hit away to his heart's content in private.

Most of the ranges employ teaching professionals, who offer tuition at a very reasonable cost; this is essential when starting to play. The professional also has a selection of equipment for hire, so it is possible to find out whether you have an aptitude for the game without incurring too much expense.

Normally these facilities sport a refreshment area and here the sensible player will take a break. It can do more harm than good to hit a lot of balls at one time without a

Left: Greenkeepers at The Greenbrier in the United States using a hole-cutting tool. Correctly, they are working with a special board, which has a hole in the middle. This is to prevent damaging the area around the hole. Unfortunately this precaution is not always taken. Below: Most major cities have a driving range, which provides an excellent means of practising, especially in poor weather.

rest, probably the one main problem of working out at a driving range. Socializing is encouraged at the ranges and an invitation to play on a course may arise from a casual meeting.

Golf centres

These are now springing up in reasonable numbers and they offer a course in addition to all of the range activities. The golf centre may have only nine holes, or even less, but that is not important. What matters is that it gives a beginner the chance of going out and trying the real thing, once he has got the feel of hitting the ball.

Some of these centres only have a course of par three holes, which means that the longest can be reached with just one hit and some of the very short holes only need a pitching club. Nevertheless, they are great fun and are part of learning the game. Most of the people playing on these courses are beginners, so there is no need to feel awkward.

Municipal courses

These are owned by local authorities and are provided for the benefit of residents, who pay a modest green fee to play on them. There was a time when these courses were subsidized by the authorities, but following the golf boom many have become self-supporting. Several of the great championship courses in Scotland are publicly owned, although a lot have clubs attached to them: St Andrews is the best-known example.

While no special privileges are awarded to members of a club at a municipal course, a club member does have the opportunity to obtain a handicap. The club will organize its own competitions and events, and handicaps are issued only to members of official clubs. It will have officers: a president, a captain, a handicapping committee and probably a social committee.

Once a player has reached handicap standard, he will often start looking for a private club to join, although this is by no means necessary. A handicap is a great asset, for at most clubs there is a long waiting list for membership and beginners are put at the bottom of it.

Artisan clubs

In Britain, when there were fewer clubs and the game was played by the more prosperous members of society, it became fairly common for artisan sections to be formed. The members, limited in number, were drawn from local tradesmen who were permitted to play, provided they started their games at certain restricted times that did not interfere with the demands of the main members.

In return they would pay either a very small fee to the club, or none at all, and would take on certain tasks such as tidying up the edges of bunkers and filling in the divot holes with soil and seed. Often they would be responsible for particular holes, in which they took great pride.

Today such sections are still very active at many clubs, although many have been absorbed into the main club or been done away with altogether as the need passed.

Those that are still active – and have been maintained out of tradition – provide tough competition among the members. Their events are always well-supported and matches are organized against other artisan sections – there is even an annual national championship.

Private clubs

The name 'private' is misleading since very few clubs are entirely so. Most are willing to accept visitors, visiting societies and members from other clubs. In some cases, however, it may be necessary to write or telephone to arrange a visit.

Private clubs are owned either by the membership or by a limited company. A member's club will be run by an elected committee, headed by the club captain, who is usually in office for one year. It is the responsibility of the committee to see that the fees charged to members, together with other incomes, are sufficient to support the running of the club.

A club that is owned privately or by a limited company will be operated by its owner or directors, who alone make the major decisions – hopefully to the benefit of the much-needed membership. Such a club will still require the structuring of a members' club so that handicaps, competitions, etc are properly organized.

The club secretary
The day-to-day running of the club is in the hands of the secretary who, at larger clubs, is a paid official. His is a most important job, since he carries out not only the decisions of the directors or committees, but also staff organization and administration.

He is responsible for recording handicaps, organizing matches and holding competitions. At many clubs he is also required to make a ruling in cases of dispute, and his decision is final.

The greenkeeper
Many clubs operate what is known as a 'greens committee', which is comprised of a few usually experienced members who take a keen interest in the course and its condition.

Apart from working with the club secretary, their most important man is the head greenkeeper, who, with his staff, carries out any course improvements that he agrees with, and maintains the course in the best possible condition.

Often clubs are content to leave the decisions to the secretary and the greenkeeper, rather than have committees that can be changed with each annual election.

The club professional
The club professional's primary role is as a coach and he is often at a disadvantage when it comes to coaching. With long waiting lists at clubs, beginners tend to start at driving ranges and municipal courses. The word 'private' at the entrance to a club also tends to frighten learners away when, in fact, they would be most welcome to visit the professional's shop and enjoy the services he offers.

The professional and his assistants are available to teach non-members. One advantage here is that the professional often has a large selection of second-hand clubs that are ideal for the beginner.

The recommendation of the club professional can weigh heavily in favour of a pupil when it comes to applying for membership to his club. Having spent most of his life in golf, he can prove a very good adviser – and friend.

The club steward
In many clubs known as the manager, the club steward is responsible for the smooth running of the club house. He performs a very important function at clubs with a large bar and restaurant trade. Unlike many businesses, which operate five days a week, the golf club is a seven-days-a-week, 365-days-a-year operation. Members expect their club house to open at dawn and not close until well after dark, so the steward must organize staff.

The club sections
The majority of a club's membership is male and consists of full members; country members, who are normally required to live at least 50 miles from the club; overseas members; and perhaps some honorary members, awarded this distinction for some special service to the club.

There is also a ladies' section, which operates with its own committees and has a lady captain in charge, who is voted for annually by the members. Such sections work in liaison with the Ladies Golf Union and the structuring of their handicaps is carefully scrutinized. Their competitions operate separately from the men's.

Many clubs support a junior section, which is an ideal way of encouraging youngsters to play, training them to fit into the club when they come of age. A junior captain is elected and he may be invited to sit in on certain senior committees.

The rules of golf

More than 200 years have passed since the original rules of the game were laid down. Many more were later added and these were often written in terminology that required a legal mind to interpret.

In 1980, the governing bodies of golf, the Royal and Ancient Golf Club of St Andrews and the United States Golf Association, decided it was time to produce a simpler book that incorporated all the rules. This version was launched early in 1984.

Basically the rules are unchanged, except for a few alterations. Two of the most significant changes relate to the marking of the ball on the putting green and to the way the ball is dropped when relief has been

Greg Norman, who is obviously confused about a rule, awaits the arrival of the rules official, who has been called out on to the course.

taken, either with or without a penalty.

Marking the ball In 1952 part of golfing history was changed when the 'stymie' was abolished. Before that time, when in matchplay an opponent's ball came to rest on the green directly between that of another player and the hole and provided there was a gap of more than 15cm (6in) between the two, the player farthest away had to play round, over or away from the obstruction. That was why course scorecards used to be 15cm (6in) long, so they could be used to measure the gap.

Although this was deemed to be unfair and was therefore removed, traces of the stymie still remained, this time to the advantage of the player farther away. He could, if he so wished, insist that his opponent left his ball where it was when it was to his advantage. He might, perhaps, want to use it as a backstop or as a marker to aim at in the case of a sloping green – or even to cannon off into the hole. Now Rule 22 permits a player to mark his ball and lift it, should he want to.

Dropping the ball When this was necessary, the correct method was to stand upright facing the hole and to drop the ball over the shoulder. The problem came if the ball hit the player as it dropped or rolled away either more than two club lengths from the point where it first hit the ground or closer to the hole. In these cases the ball had to be dropped again. If it did the same again, it had to be placed at exactly the point where it struck the ground. But because the player was facing in the opposite direction, he had no way of telling where this point was.

Now he can stand facing in any direction and drop the ball from shoulder height and at arm's length, although he must still not drop the ball any closer to the hole. By being able to see what happens to the ball, he will be in a position to judge the placing if a second attempt is unsuccessful.

For the first time, any ball that is lifted anywhere on the course must be marked. This used only to be the case on the green.

Famous players

Severiano Ballesteros

The meteoric rise of Severiano Ballesteros, the young Spaniard from Santander, seemed to start on the final hole at Royal Birkdale in the 1976 British Open. This handsome, yet then comparatively un-known lad, who had only just celebrated his 19th birthday, was playing with the eventual winner Johnny Miller – and was struggling to hold his score.

A four at the last would give him a tie for second place with Jack Nicklaus, but he had missed the green on the left and was faced with an awkward shot over the bunkers. Instead of hitting over them, cheekily he ran the ball along the ground between them to within inches of the hole. That shot announced Ballesteros' arrival and the same year he took the Dutch Open.

He won the 1979 British Open at Royal Lytham and St Annes in cavalier style and followed this up with the US Masters at Augusta in 1980 and again in 1983.

Famous players

Henry Cotton

When Henry Cotton won the British Open at Sandwich in 1934, he ended a 10-year domination by American players. In fact Sam Snead (in 1946) and Ben Hogan (in 1953) were the only other successful Americans until the Sixties. Cotton won the title again in 1937 at Carnoustie and in 1948 at Muirfield.

Not only was he a magnificent player and perfectionist in every sense, always being immaculately turned out, but he was also credited for raising the standard and conditions for his fellow professionals.

He was brought by Lord Roseberry to be professional at the Ashridge Golf Club, from where he won his 1937 Open title. Previously he had been attached to the Waterloo Club in Belgium.

At the end of his playing career, Cotton started designing courses, one of his favourites being Pennina in Portugal, where he now lives.

Nick Faldo

Nick Faldo is a player with a beautiful style of swing, which is not only graceful but also sends the ball a very long way; and he's an exceptionally good putter.

In the 1983 season he won in the region of £150,000 from the European circuit alone – a record. Of his five victories in that season, three of them were consecutive – the French Open, the Martini International and the Car Care Plan International.

Faldo also made a great bid to win the British Open at Royal Birkdale and was still in the lead well into the final round. His aggressive putting to make birdies, however, proved costly and caused him to take three putts at the crucial stage.

Although Faldo has suffered several defeats in matchplay, twice at the hands of Australia's Greg Norman, his record is excellent. He is the first British player to win in America since Tony Jacklin, taking the 1984 Heritage Classic.

Bernard Gallacher

In 1967 Bernard Gallacher, an 18-year-old from Bathgate in Scotland, ended the domination of Ronnie Shade as Scotland's leading amateur by winning the Scottish strokeplay championship and recording a final round of 66 over the Muirfield course.

His first assistant's post was to have been at Dyrham Park Golf Club, under professional Pat Keene. Instead of reporting to the club, however, he went to Berkhamsted to play in the Hertfordshire Assistants championship, which he won. When he reported for work the next day, he was told he was not required.

Fortunately for Gallacher, Tom Haliburton needed an assistant at Wentworth, so he started there and is now attached to that club as the senior professional.

Gallacher has played in every Ryder Cup match since 1969, one of his finest victories being against Jack Nicklaus at Royal Lytham and St Annes in 1977.

David Graham

Australian David Graham turned professional in 1962. Despite a few good performances, it was not until 1970 that his promise really showed. In that year he had victories in the Victoria, Tasmanian, Yomiuri, Thailand and French Open championships.

In 1979 he won his first 'major', the USPGA championship, but only after some nerve-racking moments. At the last hole, where it looked as though he had the event sewn up, he took four to get down from the very fringe of the green. He took three holes to beat Ben Crenshaw in the play-off.

It took some unlikely putting for him to achieve victory in the 1976 World Match Play championships at Wentworth, when he beat America's Hale Irwin. However it was not just putting that won Graham the US Open in 1981, for in the final round he performed the incredible feat of hitting all 18 greens to par.

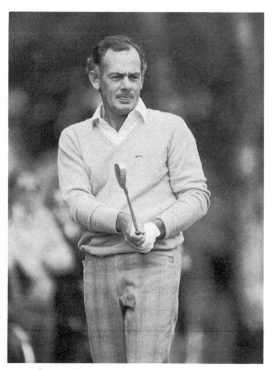

Ben Hogan

When Ben Hogan turned professional, he went through many lean seasons before gaining a tournament victory. He was just starting to make his mark when the Second World War intervened. Then, as he began to dominate the golf scene again – winning the 1948 US Open – his car was in head-on collision with a bus. His great courage saw him through, however, after the medical profession had said he would never play again.

That was in 1949. However he won the US Open title in 1950, 1951 and 1953. The last of those victories came prior to his only visit to the British Open – at Carnoustie – which he also won with a total of 282, a record at the time.

His theories on the golf swing have provided a major contribution to the sport. He was more or less responsible for drawing attention to the importance of the swing plane, which features strongly in this book.

Tony Jacklin

The story of Tony Jacklin is largely about winning and losing British Opens. As Jacklin stood by his ball in the centre of the 14th fairway at St Andrews in the 1970 British Open watching a threatening storm about to break, he held a massive lead. Not only was he defending the title he had won the previous year at Royal Lytham and St Annes, but he had also won the US Open only days before. He sliced the ball into a gorse bush and finished the round poorly the next morning.

The following year at Royal Birkdale, Jacklin came in third – two strokes behind Lee Trevino. But it was the 1972 Open that really took its toll. On the 71st hole he was short of the green in two, while his nearest rival Trevino was through the back in four. Jacklin pitched safely to the centre of the green, but what happened next is history. Trevino chipped into the hole and Jacklin three-putted.

Bobby Jones

Although Robert Tyre Jones retired from competitive golf at only 28 when still an amateur, he had created a record that is still unsurpassed. He won both the Amateur and Open championships of Britain and the United States all in the same year – 1930. On that note, he finished playing.

Bernhard Langer

Very few professionals have come from West Germany and none has had anything like the success of Bernhard Langer. Born in 1957, the son of a building worker, Langer turned professional very soon after leaving school and was, by 1976, already showing considerable form on the European Tour.

Despite problems with his putter, which virtually removed him from the scene in 1977, Langer has since put in some outstanding performances. He is one of the finest strikers of the ball in the world and his straight driving is the equal of anyone.

Langer has represented the Continental side in the Hennessy Cognac Cup since its inception and was captain in 1982. The previous year he had won the coveted Harry Vardon Trophy, given to the player who tops the PGA money-winner's list. He has since played in Ryder Cup matches against the United States.

Up until then he had represented the United States in every Walker Cup match. Apart from his grand slam year, he won the US Open in 1923, 1926 and 1929. He was runner up in 1922, 1924, 1925 and 1928, losing the last two in play-offs. He won the US Amateur championship in 1924, 1925, 1927 and 1928, while in Britain he also won the Open in 1926 and 1927.

Nancy Lopez

There has surely been no more meteoric a rise to the top of professional golf than that of Nancy Lopez, considering that at the time she came through – in 1978 – the competition was at its most fierce.

Players of the calibre of Hollis Stacy, Jo Anne Carner, Sandra Haynie and Judy Rankin were among the Americans to be beaten, from Australia there was Jan Stephenson and from South Africa Sally Little. However, in her opening season she was the leading money-winner.

Nancy Lopez has played in Britain on several occasions, winning the Colgate Womens' championship at Sunningdale. On one visit, to film a Men versus Women series, in partnership with Sally Little against Jerry Pate and Johnny Miller at the very long Duke's Course at Woburn, she proved just how long a hitter she was. On one hole Miller required a No 3 iron while Nancy Lopez used only a pitching wedge!

Johnny Miller

In 1973, at the age of 26, Johnny Miller looked the most likely player to take over Jack Nicklaus' crown. Even the promising young Tom Watson seemed certain to remain in Miller's shadow. An incredible round of 63 had helped the tall, slim Miller to win the US Open. He then came over to Britain and finished runner-up to Tom Weiskopf in the Open at Troon.

His seemingly inevitable victory in the British Open came at Royal Birkdale in 1976. But strangely enough, for he had just completed three of the most successful years any professional could have hoped for, it signalled one of the fastest declines in modern golf.

Despite the setbacks, Miller's courage kept him going. He claimed the Lancome Trophy in France in 1979, which he had previously won during his prime period in 1973, plus victory in the first Million Dollar Sun City Challenge in 1981.

Jack Nicklaus

It is hard to believe that when Jack Nicklaus first turned professional in 1961, he was not at all popular with American golf fans. He was only 21 and had already won the US Amateur championship twice and had been second in the US Open the previous year. The problem lay in the fact that it was very apparent Nicklaus would soon remove Arnold Palmer, 10 years his senior and America's favourite sportsman,

from his throne.

Nicklaus went on to prove that not only was he a winner of championships, having claimed more 'majors' than any other player, but that he was also a winner in the popularity stakes. You will find no finer example of good sportsmanship than the man from Columbus, Ohio.

His love for British golf has brought him to compete in no less than 22 consecutive Opens, resulting in three victories – in 1966, 1970 and 1978.

Arnold Palmer

It is generally claimed that Arnold Palmer was the cause of the great boom in modern-day golf which took place in the 1950s and 1960s. He caught the imagination of the television viewers as he clawed and carved his way out of the problems he created with his cavalier style of play.

Palmer certainly contributed a great deal to the success of the British Open when, after having been persuaded to come to St Andrews in 1960 as holder of the US Open title, he returned home and convinced his colleagues they could never consider themselves champions unless they had won the 'British'. Palmer has not missed the championship since.

The 1960 Open was the centenary championship and he so nearly brought off the double, finishing runner-up by just one stroke to Australia's Kel Nagle. The following year at Royal Birkdale Palmer went one better, winning the championship.

Greg Norman

In his first seven years as a professional golfer Greg Norman has won titles in no fewer than seven countries. His tremendous stamina and physical fitness enable this young Australian to endure the long hours of jet travel as he competes all over the world. Annually he covers over 100,000 miles in crossing oceans, on top of his internal flights.

Norman has won many important events and Open championships, including those of Hong Kong, France, Scandinavia and Australia. He has twice won the World Match Play championship – in 1980 and 1983, when he beat Nick Faldo in the final of the tournament.

Computerised statistics, which are now becoming part of the golfing scene, show him as not only one of the game's longest hitters but also in the top league of those who hit most greens in the regulation amount of shots.

Gary Player

When the young South African Gary Player was about to launch himself on the world of competitive golf, the British PGA Tour was the biggest outside the United States. His first season in the Tour proved to be a disaster. He hardly won a penny and also came in for a good deal of criticism about his technique.

Player took his first 'major' title, the British Open at Muirfield, in 1959.

But his success has not been just in tournaments and championships, of which he has won a total of 125, but also in the respect he has gained.

In matchplay golf he was a terrifying opponent, never knowing when to give up. In one particular game in the World Match Play championship, which he won no fewer than five times, he was no less than seven down to the late Tony Lema after 19 holes of the 36-hole match – but he still managed to win.

Dai Rees

Dai Rees's death in 1983 signalled the end of an era at the South Herts Golf Club for he had just overtaken the years spent at that club by his predecessor, the great Harry Vardon. Vardon was there from 1902 to 1937 and Dai, who came after the war, was club professional from 1946.

Rees, who was born in Barry, Glamorgan, in 1913, turned professional in 1929. Small in stature, but with the heart of a lion, he won many titles all over the world and in matchplay he was a particularly notorious opponent. He tried desperately to win the British Open championship, coming second no fewer than three times – in 1953, 1954 and 1961.

It was in Ryder Cup matches that Rees's greatest hour came. He played in nine and led the winning team at Lindrick Golf Club in Yorkshire in 1957, the first British victory since 1933, although his side trailed 3-1 after the foursomes.

Lee Trevino

The fact that Lee Trevino was voted Rookie of the Year on the USPGA Tour in 1967 yet won the US Open championship the following year proves how meteoric his rise was to the top of competitive golf.

At first his victory was seen by many as a fluke, for his swing was regarded as unique, appearing artificial and contrived. However, it was not long before he proved his critics wrong, especially in a glorious one-month spell in 1971 when he won no fewer than three national Open championships – those of the United States, Britain and Canada.

His personal preference for fading the ball in flight, curving it slightly from left to right, gave him tremendous control over the ball and proved that powering the ball over long distances was not the be-all and end-all of golf. The artistry he displayed by controlling the ball became a lesson to all professionals and many changed styles.

Peter Thomson

Known as the Melbourne Tiger, Peter Thomson was one of the finest ever players of links golf. He turned professional at the age of 20 in 1949 and came to Britain a couple of years later. At first he was criticised for being too greedy a player, for he fired every shot straight at the flag, giving no thought to playing safe. He finished in the top three in his first two British Open championships, then succeeded in winning three in a row – in 1954, 1955 and 1956 – a feat unequalled this century. He won the Open again in 1958 and 1965.

Thomson's skill on the links showed particularly in his control of the ball. This was when the links were much more bouncy, before heavy watering was introduced in the belief that this would encourage Americans to enter the championship. He played with a very low flight and used the contours of the ground in true Scottish style.

Tom Watson

It is said that the United States produces the world's best player every 10 years. This was based on the gap between Arnold Palmer, Jack Nicklaus and Tom Watson. So far the next American in line has not shown and, in the meantime, Watson is happy to soldier on.

After he had won the US Open in 1982, Watson went on to take the British Open at Royal Troon. It was his fourth win in that championship, all of which had been accomplished on Scottish courses. The first was at Carnoustie in 1975, after a dramatic play-off with Australia's Jack Newton. In 1977 he and Jack Nicklaus fought out what has come to be known as 'the duel in the sun' over the Turnberry links.

In 1980 he won at Muirfield. In his prize-giving speech, he announced that perhaps it was time he won in England. We only had to wait 12 months, when he triumphed at Royal Birkdale.

Paul Way

Paul Way is one of the game's most promising young players. At the age of 18 he gained his place in the Walker Cup team. Only two years later, by which time he had turned professional, he had made his way through to the Ryder Cup side that so nearly beat the Americans at Palm Beach Gardens. Way earned no less than 3½ points from a possible 5.

The team captain Tony Jacklin decided to play him in partnership with Severiano Ballesteros and they became a formidable duo. They do have something in common for when Way, in his first season as a professional, won the Dutch Open championship, there was a rush to the record books to check on ages. Ballesteros had also won that event in his first year – and also at the age of 19. Unfortunately for Way, the Spaniard had beaten him to it by three months, which kept him the youngest-ever winner on the European circuit.

Glossary

Arc The near-circular curve around the body made by the swinging club head.

Back spin The spin applied to the ball by the loft angle of the club face, which is exaggerated by the sharp descending blow from the lofted irons.

Back swing Those movements that take the club from the ball upwards and behind the body in preparation for the hit.

Balata The natural rubber material from which the skin of some balls is made, usually the balls preferred by professional players.

Ball position The point opposite the stance from where the ball is played. This varies according to the club being used and the type of shot being played.

Ball-to-target line The imaginary line from the ball directly to the target along which the player aims his club and parallel to which he takes up his stance.

Borrow The amount a player aims 'off' to make allowance for the slope of the ground over which the ball must roll.

Birdie A score that is one better than the par for the hole.

Blade The face of an iron club head.

Brassie The original name for the most powerful fairway wood, now the No 2 wood.

Chip Abbreviation for 'chip-and-run'. A shot normally played from close to the green using little wrist action and with no effort to gain any height other than that offered by the loft of the club face. Allowance must be made for the ball to run on landing.

Closed In the case of the stance, this means that the right foot and side of the body are drawn back from being parallel to the ball-to-target line. In the swing, it refers to the left wrist and/or club face being turned out of the line of the swing plane.

Cock The preparatory work of the left wrist joint in the back swing.

Draw A very mild form of hook spin,

mainly used by experts, often to increase the run on the ball when it lands.

Fade A very mild form of slice spin which is applied in order to control the flight of the ball and to encourage it to stop immediately on landing.

Feathery The name given to the oldest known ball, which consisted of a leather cover stuffed with feathers.

Flange The metal extension on the sole of an iron club which widens its base and adds extra weight at the low point of the club. The widest flange is normally on the sand iron.

Fluffing When the club head makes contact with the ground before hitting the ball.

Forward press A forward movement made by the hands, and often the right knee, prior to commencing the back swing.

Fourball A form of play involving four players, each using his own ball, either in matchplay or strokeplay.

Foursome A form of play involving four players made up of two teams, each sharing a ball, either in matchplay or strokeplay.

Handicap An allowance of strokes given to a player which, when subtracted from his score, should bring him to the par total of the course.

Hickory The type of wood from which club shafts were made prior to the introduction of steel shafts. Now it is only used occasionally for putters.

Hook spin A side spin applied to the ball from a club face that is turned 'in' from the direction of the swing path.

Interlock A form of grip on the club handle where the small finger of the lower (right) hand interlocks with the forefinger of the upper (left) hand.

Jigger A short hickory shaft club which was produced for the purpose of playing low-running shots, a requirement on links-type courses.

Laminate Layers of wood compressed together, from which club heads are made. Laminated heads appeared when persimmon supplies grew short.

Late hit When the preparatory movements of the swing fail to undo in time to meet the ball squarely.

Lie Either the situation of the stationary ball or the angle at which the shaft of the club enters the head.

Links The strips of land that lie between the beach and the mainland, on which the game of golf was originally played.

Loft Either the height of the ball's flight or the angle set by the manufacturer on the face of the club.

Majors Four events are recognized as the 'Majors'. These are, in chronological order, the US Masters championship, held at Augusta National; the US Open; the British Open; and the USPGA championship. The British, always referred to as 'The Championship', is only held on a links course.

Matchplay The form of golf where a side, made up of one or two players, takes on another on a hole-by-hole basis until one side is more holes 'up' than there are holes left to play. If after the nominated amount of holes are played the sides are level, the match is 'all-square'.

Open In the case of stance and body alignment, the left side is drawn back from being parallel to the ball-to-target line. During the swing it is when the left wrist and/or the club face turns away from the swing plane.

Overlap The original form of the Vardon Grip, where the small finger of the lower (right) hand is placed over the forefinger of the upper (left) hand.

Par The figure set for each hole, dependent on its length, representing the number of shots to be taken at that hole.

Persimmon The very hard wood from a species of 'ebony' from which wooden club heads are shaped. Because of its short supply and the time necessary for it to season, it is very expensive.

Pitch Any short shot that falls within the range of a full swing, in which all of the swing muscles are used.

Posture The attitude of the body taken up at the set-up stage of the swing.

Rolling 'open' Should the turning of the body in the back swing fail to keep time with the swing of the club and the movement of the hands and arms, the club face is likely to be turned outward from the plane of the swing. It is then 'open'.

Set A set of golf clubs consists of a maximum of 14 clubs. This may be made up from any preference of wood or iron clubs, but normally consists of three woods, 10 irons and a putter.

Set-up The aiming of the club to the ball, the taking-up of the stance and grip and the setting of the posture prior to swinging.

Shallow swing When the arc of the swing is made to work flatter around the body than the player's physique would normally determine.

Singles Two players playing together, either in matchplay or strokeplay.

Slice spin A side spin applied when the face of the club is turned 'out' from the direction of the swing path.

Smother When the club face meets the ball with insufficient loft showing to lift it.

Socket The part of the iron club into which the shaft is fitted at that point where it turns into the blade. Socket and shank are names given to the mis-hit when that part of the club makes contact with the ball.

Spoon The historical name given to what is now the No 3 wood.

Square In the case of the stance and body alignment, when they are parallel to the ball-to-target line. In the swing, when the working of the left wrist and/or the club face are true to the swing plane.

Stance The position taken up when the player has placed his feet, in alignment, at the correct width apart and opposite the ball for the shot to be played.

Steep swing A swing that brings the club towards the ball from an angle higher than the player's physique and the club being used would normally determine.

Strokeplay The form of golf where the score made at every hole is recorded and

from which the handicap, if applicable, is deducted. Most championships take this form and are played over a total of 72 holes.
Surlyn A man-made plastic type of material from which the covers of many balls are made. It is more scuff-resistant than natural rubber.
Sway Lateral movement of the head and upper part of the body during the swing.
Swing path The direction on which the club head is travelling as it passes through the hitting area, related to the ball-to-target line.
Swing plane The angle on which the club moves around the player during the swing.
Swing weight The balanced weight of any club in a matched set which makes all of the others, regardless of their varied lengths and total weight, feel the same when swung.
Tee The area at the start of each hole which extends between two tee markers, or back

from them as far as two club-lengths, from where the ball must be played.
Tilt A misguided form of shoulder movement, which takes the left shoulder down – rather than around – during the back swing.
Waggle A movement back and forth to the ball prior to swinging, which is used to keep the swing free from tension. It also helps in establishing the correct angle and direction of the swing.
Water hazard This can be one of two types. It is either a straightforward 'water hazard', which normally lies across the hole and is marked by yellow stakes, or a 'lateral water hazard', which is usually a stream running down the length of the hole and to the side and is marked by red stakes. A ball may be played from either or dropped clear under penalty, according to the rules.

Acknowledgments

All illustrations by Ken Lewis

Andrew Arthur/Golf Illustrated: 17
Peter Dazeley Photography: 6, 24, 29, 35, 42, 50, 53, 55, 59, 64, 71, 85(r), 88, 91, 118, 144, 158, 186, 201, 203, 210(br), 211(br), 217(tl).
Peter Dazeley Photography/Golf Illustrated: 47
Dunlop Golf: 48
Mary Evans Picture Library: 12, 13, 15, 23
Bernard Fallon: 214(br)
Hailey Sports Photographic: 32, 41, 45, 61, 64(tr), 64(br), 72, 84(l), 130, 132, 138, 146, 151, 156, 183, 188, 192, 194, 195, 196, 206, 207, 208(br), 209(tl), 209(br), 212(br), 214(tl), 216(tl), 216(br), 217(br)
Alex Hay: 10, 26, 52
Karsten (UK) Ltd: 40
Ken Lewis: 2, 9, 11, 22, 84/85(c), 98, 106, 110, 111(l), 124, 149, 153, 164, 213, 215(tl)
The Mansell Collection: 14
Bert Neale: 21, 112
Bert Neale/Golf Illustrated: 210(tl)
John Otway/Golf Illustrated: 169
S & G Press Agency: 62, 208(tl), 211(t), 212(tl), 215(br)
Ben Sayers Ltd: 33(t), 33(bl), 33(br)
Phil Sheldon: 4/5, 18/19, 27(lc), 27(rc), 27(b), 30, 34, 46, 126, 162, 170, 180, 202
Phil Sheldon/Golf Illustrated: 8

Index

222